CONSPIRACY

A Sanctuary Novel

COLLEEN COBLE

THOMAS NELSON
Since 1798

Conspiracy

Published in Nashville, Tennessee, by Thomas Nelson. Thomas Nelson is a registered trademark of HarperCollins Christian Publishing, Inc.

Thomas Nelson titles may be purchased in bulk for educational, business, fundraising, or sales promotional use. For information, please email SpecialMarkets@ThomasNelson.com.

HarperCollins Publishers, Macken House, 39/40 Mayor Street Upper, Dublin 1, D01 C9W8, Ireland (https://www.harpercollins.com)

Library of Congress Cataloging-in-Publication Data

Names: Coble, Colleen author
Title: Conspiracy / Colleen Coble.
Description: Nashville : Thomas Nelson, 2026. | Series: Sanctuary novels ; 3 |
Summary: "Conspiracy, the third book in USA TODAY bestselling author Colleen Coble's Sanctuary series (following Ambush and Prowl), delivers exactly what her fans want: the ideal blend of suspense that keeps you on the edge of your seat with just the right amount of romance"—Provided by publisher.
Identifiers: LCCN 2025054808 (print) | LCCN 2025054809 (ebook) | ISBN 9780840714671 paperback | ISBN 9780840714701 hardcover | ISBN 9780840714688 epub | ISBN 9780840714695
Subjects: LCGFT: Romance fiction | Detective and mystery fiction | Christian fiction | Novels
Classification: LCC PS3553.O2285 C66 2026 (print) | LCC PS3553.O2285 (ebook)
LC record available at https://lccn.loc.gov/2025054808
LC ebook record available at https://lccn.loc.gov/2025054809

Printed in the United States of America

26 27 28 29 30 LBC 5 4 3 2 1

ACCLAIM FOR COLLEEN COBLE

"Colleen Coble's sharp eye for detail and emotional depth brought her scenes and characters to life and kept me on the edge of my seat. A truly captivating read."

—Jenny Hale, *USA TODAY* bestselling author, on *Prowl*

"*Ambush* is electric—the perfect blend of romance, suspense, and characters you swear are real. With a deadly mystery, past trauma, and future hope, *Ambush* is just one more proof of Coble at the top of her game."

—Tosca Lee, *New York Times* bestselling author

"Coble's *Ambush* takes off at a roaring speed with razor-sharp writing. Expect the suspense to put claw marks on the pages as you hold on for the thrilling ride. This is an up-all-night must-read!"

—Jessica R. Patch, bestselling author of the critically acclaimed Strange Crimes Unit series

"Engaging characters, irresistible intrigue, and a slow-burning romance make *Fragile Designs* a captivating read."

—Mary Burton, *New York Times* bestselling author

"Excitement, evil antagonists, action, and romance are a few of the items that stand out in *Break of Day* by Colleen Coble . . . The world-building is excellent."

—*Mystery & Suspense Magazine*

"A law enforcement ranger investigates a cold case and searches for her kidnapped sister in this exciting series launch from Coble

(*A Stranger's Game*) . . . Coble expertly balances mounting tension from the murder investigation with the romantic tension between Annie and Jon. This fresh, addictive mystery delivers thrills, compassion, and hope."

—*Publishers Weekly* on *Edge of Dusk*

"This Christian romantic suspense novel packs a lot of plot into its pages, wrapping up only two of its biggest plot lines while leaving plenty of material for a sequel. Some of the plot twists were excellently paced surprises . . . Fans of Colleen Coble's works will welcome this brand new series set in the same world as her previous thrillers. Her love for the UP is palpable, and I really liked learning about the Finnish influences on the area. Ms. Coble is a great ambassador for the UP's natural beauty and cuisine, and speaks knowledgeably and at length on celiac disease, including recommendations at the end of the book that are super helpful for anyone wanting a list of gluten-free brands."

—Criminal Element on *Edge of Dusk*

"Coble's clear-cut prose makes it easy for the reader to follow the numerous scenarios and characters. This is just the ticket for readers of romantic suspense."

—*Publishers Weekly* on *Three Missing Days*

"Colleen Coble is my go-to author for the best romantic suspense today. *Three Missing Days* is now my favorite in the series, and I adored the other two. A stay-up-all-night page-turning story!"

—Carrie Stuart Parks, bestselling and award-winning author of *Relative Silence*

"You can't go wrong with a Colleen Coble novel. She always brings readers great characters and edgy, intense storylines."

—BestInSuspense.com on *Two Reasons to Run*

"Colleen Coble's latest has it all: characters to root for, a sinister villain, and a story that just won't stop."

—Siri Mitchell, author of *State of Lies*, on *Two Reasons to Run*

"Colleen Coble's superpower is transporting her readers into beautiful settings in vivid detail. *Two Reasons to Run* is no exception. Add to that the suspense that keeps you wanting to know more and characters that pull at your heart. These are the ingredients of a fun read!"

—Terri Blackstock, bestselling author of *If I Run*, *If I'm Found*, and *If I Live*

"This is a romantic suspense novel that will be a surprise when the last page reveals all of the secrets."

—*Parkersburg News and Sentinel* on *One Little Lie*

"There are just enough threads left dangling at the end of this well-crafted romantic suspense to leave fans hungrily awaiting the next installment."

—*Publishers Weekly* on *One Little Lie*

"Colleen Coble once again proves she is at the pinnacle of Christian romantic suspense. Filled with characters you'll come to love, faith lost and found, and scenes that will have you holding your breath, Jane Hardy's story deftly follows the complex and tangled web that can be woven by one little lie."

—Lisa Wingate, #1 *New York Times* bestselling author of *Before We Were Yours*, on *One Little Lie*

"Colleen Coble always raises the notch on romantic suspense, and *One Little Lie* is my favorite yet! The story took me on a wild and wonderful ride."

—DiAnn Mills, bestselling author

"Coble's latest, *One Little Lie*, is a powerful read . . . one of her absolute best. I stayed up way too late finishing this book because I literally couldn't go to sleep without knowing what happened. This is a must read! Highly recommend!"

—Robin Caroll, bestselling author
of the Darkwater Inn series

"I always look forward to Colleen Coble's new releases. *One Little Lie* is One Phenomenal Read. I don't know how she does it, but she just keeps getting better. Be sure to have plenty of time to flip the pages in this one because you won't want to put it down. I devoured it! Thank you, Colleen, for more hours of edge-of-the-seat entertainment. I'm already looking forward to the next one!"

—Lynette Eason, award-winning and
bestselling author of the Blue Justice series

"In *One Little Lie* the repercussions of one lie skid through the town of Pelican Harbor, creating ripples of chaos and suspense. Who will survive the questions? *One Little Lie* is the latest page-turner from Colleen Coble. Set on the Gulf Coast of Alabama, Jane Hardy is the new police chief who is fighting to clear her father. Reid Dixon has secrets of his own as he follows Jane around town for a documentary. Together they must face their secrets and decide when a secret becomes a lie. And when does it become too much to forgive?"

—Cara Putman, bestselling and award-winning author

"Coble wows with this suspense-filled inspirational . . . With startling twists and endearing characters, Coble's engrossing story explores the tragedy, betrayal, and redemption of faithful people all searching to reclaim their sense of identity."

—*Publishers Weekly* on *Strands of Truth*

"Just when I think Colleen Coble's stories can't get any better, she proves me wrong. In *Strands of Truth*, I couldn't turn the pages fast enough. The characterization of Ridge and Harper and their relationship pulled me immediately into the story. Fast-paced, with so many unexpected twists and turns, I read this book in one sitting. Coble has pushed the bar higher than I'd imagined. This book is one not to be missed. Highly recommend!"

—Robin Caroll, bestselling author
of the Darkwater Inn series

"Free-dive into a romantic suspense that will leave you breathless and craving for more."

—DiAnn Mills, bestselling author, on *Strands of Truth*

"Colleen Coble's latest book, *Strands of Truth*, grips you on page one with a heart-pounding opening and doesn't let go until the last satisfying word. I love her skill in pulling the reader in with believable, likable characters, interesting locations, and a mystery just waiting to be untangled. Highly recommended."

—Carrie Stuart Parks, bestselling and
award-winning author of *Relative Silence*

"It's in her blood! Colleen Coble once again shows her suspense prowess with a thriller as intricate and beautiful as a strand of DNA. *Strands of Truth* dives into an unusual profession involving mollusks and shell beds that weaves a unique, silky thread throughout the story. So fascinating I couldn't stop reading!"

—Ronie Kendig, bestselling author of the Tox Files series

"Once again, Colleen Coble delivers an intriguing, suspenseful tale in *Strands of Truth*. The mystery and tension mount toward an explosive and satisfying finish. Well done."

—Creston Mapes, bestselling author

"*Secrets at Cedar Cabin* is filled with twists and turns that will keep readers turning the pages as they plunge into the horrific world of sex trafficking where they come face-to-face with evil. Colleen Coble delivers a fast-paced story with a strong, lovable ensemble cast and a sweet, heaping helping of romance."

—Kelly Irvin, author of *Tell Her No Lies*

"Coble . . . weaves a suspense-filled romance set during the Revolutionary War. Coble's fine historical novel introduces a strong heroine—both in faith and character—that will appeal deeply to readers."

—*Publishers Weekly* on *Freedom's Light*

"This follow-up to *The View from Rainshadow Bay* features delightful characters and an evocative, atmospheric setting. Ideal for fans of romantic suspense and authors Dani Pettrey, Dee Henderson, and Brandilyn Collins."

—*Library Journal* on *The House at Saltwater Point*

"Set on Washington State's Olympic Peninsula, this first volume of Coble's new suspense series is a tensely plotted and harrowing tale of murder, corporate greed, and family secrets. Devotees of

Dani Pettrey, Brenda Novak, and Allison Brennan will find a new favorite here."

—*Library Journal* on *The View from Rainshadow Bay*

"Coble (*Twilight at Blueberry Barrens*) keeps the tension tight and the action moving in this gripping tale, the first in her Lavender Tides series set in the Pacific Northwest."

—*Publishers Weekly* on *The View from Rainshadow Bay*

"Filled with the suspense for which Coble is known, the novel is rich in detail with a healthy dose of romance, allowing readers to bask in the beauty of Washington State's lavender fields, lush forests, and jagged coastline."

—*BookPage* on *The View from Rainshadow Bay*

"Prepare to stay up all night with Colleen Coble. Coble's beautiful, emotional prose coupled with her keen sense of pacing, escalating danger, and very real characters place her firmly at the top of the suspense genre. I could not put this book down."

—Allison Brennan, *New York Times* bestselling author of *Shattered*, on *The View from Rainshadow Bay*

"Colleen is a master storyteller."

—Karen Kingsbury, #1 *New York Times* bestselling author

CONSPIRACY

ALSO BY COLLEEN COBLE

Sanctuary Novels

Ambush

Prowl

Conspiracy

Tupelo Grove Novels

(coauthored with Rick Acker)

What We Hide

Where Secrets Lie

When Justice Comes

Annie Pederson Novels

Edge of Dusk

Dark of Night

Break of Day

Pelican Harbor Novels

One Little Lie

Two Reasons to Run

Three Missing Days

Lavender Tides Novels

The View from Rainshadow Bay

Leaving Lavender Tides (novella)

The House at Saltwater Point

Secrets at Cedar Cabin

Rock Harbor Novels

Without a Trace

Beyond a Doubt

Into the Deep

Cry in the Night

Haven of Swans (formerly titled *Abomination*)

Silent Night: A Rock Harbor Christmas Novella (e-book only)

Beneath Copper Falls

Sunset Cove Novels

The Inn at Ocean's Edge

Mermaid Moon

Twilight at Blueberry Barrens

Hope Beach Novels

Tidewater Inn

Rosemary Cottage

Seagrass Pier

All Is Bright: A Hope Beach Christmas Novella (e-book only)

Under Texas Stars Novels

Blue Moon Promise

Safe in His Arms

Bluebonnet Bride (novella, e-book only)

The Aloha Reef Novels

Distant Echoes

Black Sands

Dangerous Depths

Midnight Sea

Holy Night: An Aloha Reef Christmas Novella (e-book only)

The Mercy Falls Series

The Lightkeeper's Daughter

The Lightkeeper's Bride

The Lightkeeper's Ball

Journey of the Heart Series

A Heart's Disguise

A Heart's Obsession

A Heart's Danger

A Heart's Betrayal

A Heart's Promise

A Heart's Home

Lonestar Novels

Lonestar Sanctuary

Lonestar Secrets

Lonestar Homecoming

Lonestar Angel

All Is Calm: A Lonestar Christmas Novella (e-book only)

Stand-Alone Novels

I Think I Was Murdered (coauthored with Rick Acker)

Fragile Designs

A Stranger's Game

Strands of Truth

Freedom's Light

Alaska Twilight

Fire Dancer

Where Shadows Meet (formerly titled *Anathema*)

Butterfly Palace

Because You're Mine

For my grandsons, Elijah and Silas,
who provided such great inspiration for Levi and Isaac.

Love you both so much!

CHAPTER 1

WILDLIFE VETERINARIAN PARADISE ALDEN smiled at the two tiny lemurs as they nudged closer to their mother, Fiona. Paradise backed away from the indoor nest to give the new family unit some privacy. "I think that's the last one." She tugged Blake's little half brother, Levi, away too.

Lemurs had a special place in her heart, especially these blue-eyed black lemurs. The females had burnt-orange fur, and only the males had the distinctive black color. She didn't know the gender of these two babies, but right now they were the same color as their mama and blended into her chest fur. If either of them were male, their coats would turn black in about six weeks.

She stripped off her gloves before lathering her arms under the sink to remove the musky lemur scent.

"Can I hold one?" Levi begged. The seven-year-old was obsessed with lemurs, and his mother, Jenna Anderson, principal owner of The Sanctuary Wildlife Preserve, had allowed him to witness the birth of the pups.

Paradise couldn't resist his dimples when he smiled like that. She dried her hands and went back to watch the new family with him. "They're much too small and fragile. Right now they need milk. Being born is a hard job for them and their mama. Fiona needs to sleep, and it's way past your bedtime."

Levi yawned. "Mama said I could sleep in."

The door to her treatment room opened behind her and Blake Lawson, the man she'd loved since she was fifteen, entered. His lazy smile in her direction made her pulse race when his gaze dropped to her lips. The front of his thick dark brown hair stood up in a plume that needed to be trimmed to lie flat. At twenty-nine he was at the peak of good shape.

Exhaustion tugged at her muscles, and she wanted nothing more than to curl up next to him on the sofa with her head on his broad chest and his strong arm around her. That would have to wait for a while.

Blake scooped up Levi. "Let's get you home, big guy."

Paradise peered at the warmer temperature on the gauge. "I'll be along shortly once I'm sure the little ones are happy and toasty."

Blake nodded and carried Levi out of the animal medical building while Paradise knelt beside the nest she'd created with straw and old blankets for Fiona. The pups were nursing well, and the heat from the lamp was perfect. She set out fresh water and food for the exhausted mama, then switched off the lights and locked the door behind her.

The June moon glimmered a silvery outline on the barns and buildings scattered around the animal refuge, and the familiar scent of lion scat mingled with the aroma of freshly mown hay from the nearby field. The wind rustled in the leaves and in the moss hanging from the oak trees along the path to the house. It was a perfect night, and the tension in her shoulders eased.

Her phone sounded with "Brother" by NEEDTOBREATHE,

and she smiled before answering it. "Hey, Drew." She hadn't known an older brother existed until a few weeks ago, and she still felt shy and uncertain around Andrew Bartley, the child her mother had given up for adoption when she was a teenager.

"You don't sound sleepy." Drew's deep voice rumbled in her ear. "I was afraid I was waking you."

Oyster shells crunched under her sandals as she headed for the house. "I just delivered two blue-eyed black lemurs. Well, let me amend that. I stood by in case the mama needed me, but she was a pro and didn't require my help."

"You'll have to show me when I get there. What's a group of lemurs called?"

"A conspiracy."

He went silent a moment. "Seems appropriate since we're about to find out what happened to our parents. I plan to arrive on Saturday if that's okay. I'm going to drive down."

"That's wonderful! How long can you stay?"

"I took a month's leave of absence. If I need more time, I can take it. It's important to me to get to the bottom of who killed our mom and your dad."

"And yours," she said. Drew had been last here a month ago, and she was ready to see him again.

The web of lies and murder ran deep and dark, but having Drew in on the investigation meant the world to Paradise. As an Atlanta detective, he had resources beyond what she could imagine, but her joy went deeper than having help. She'd get to *know* him, to build a relationship with him. After growing up in foster care and having no one, she'd discovered a brother. It was like finding buried treasure.

"I'll text you my itinerary. See you Saturday."

"See you," she echoed.

A cloud covered the moon and plunged the yard into darkness. She walked on toward the house, then paused when something rustled in the tree line to her left. The wind? No, the wind didn't sound like that.

The hair stood up on the back of her neck at the coughing noise that was almost like a well-running lawn mower.

It was the sound a leopard made when warning off an enemy.

She froze and studied the trees for the gleam of a big cat's eyes. She'd helped Blake feed their leopards hours ago, and they were secure in their enclosure. Her mouth went dry when the sound came again, and this time she caught the distinct glow of two eyes.

The shoulder injury caused by a black panther throbbed with the memory, and she wanted to bolt. That would be the wrong move—it would trigger the leopard to chase her and attack. She didn't move except to cautiously call Blake on her phone.

He answered on the first ring and she didn't wait for him to speak. "There's a leopard in one of the trees beside the house."

"That's impossible." His voice rose with alarm.

"I can see its eyes. It's there, Blake."

"I'll grab a tranq gun and be right there. Don't move."

The moon came out from behind the clouds, and she spotted the leopard on a large branch ten feet from her. She flicked off her phone and watched the leopard as it watched her. Her chest squeezed. This was how prey felt.

The leopard stood on the big limb as if it couldn't decide whether to leap or rest. Its tail lashed back and forth, and she caught the stench of its urine as it sprayed the area. And was that a *collar* around its neck? The cat couldn't be one of theirs. The size told her it was a male.

Leopards were solitary hunters and took down their prey

quickly due to their massive size and lightning-fast strikes. Leopards suffocated their prey with a bite to the back of the neck. Her hand crept to the back of her neck and stayed there in case the big cat pounced. The slight movement made the cat crawl closer along the tree branch. It bared its teeth at her, and its tail began to swish.

She wanted to run, but her legs were jelly, and she knew trying to flee would bring certain death.

Blake had better hurry. The back door opened, and she spotted him exiting onto the deck. She drew in a relieved gulp of air. He wore night-vision goggles and carried a tranq rifle. She didn't dare move her arm to point so she angled her gaze back at the big cat, which had moved into pouncing position. Even if Blake shot it right now with the dart, it wouldn't take the cat down for several minutes.

Would she have time to reach the safety of the house before its teeth sank into her neck?

The rifle spat out a dart and she flinched. The leopard snarled when the point sank into its skin. It reached around and bit at its flank before disappearing into the leaves. Instead of running, she moved slowly toward Blake while staying alert to an impending attack. There was a thump as the big cat leaped from the tree and loped toward the tree line.

She'd barely reached Blake when her phone sounded with a text. *Drew might not handle a big cat so well. His death will be on your hands.*

Someone had sent this animal to attack on purpose? Who would want so badly to prevent Drew from helping her?

Blake studied the surrounding field through the night-vision goggles and didn't spot the big cat. "You're sure it wore a collar?" He caught the stench of big cat urine where it had marked its territory. A pile of scat soiled the path as well.

Paradise edged close enough for him to catch her plumeria scent. "Positive. The collar was white and the moon clearly glimmered on it. And besides, this text message shows someone was behind the leopard's appearance." She held out her phone.

He read the text about Drew, and his senses, already on high alert, went into overdrive. "That leopard must be trained to kill, babe. We have to find it."

Would problems at the park ever stop? This one was clearly aimed at Paradise and not him, which was even more concerning than the past incidents. No one had released a big cat from an enclosure this time—they'd brought their own. Whoever was behind it knew about Paradise's fear of big cats—and the reason for Drew's planned visit. Blake fisted his hands. Whoever it was would have to go through him to get to her.

She hugged herself and followed close behind him as he moved toward the brush. "You gave the cat a large dose? I saw the dart go in."

"It should be unconscious by now, but where is it?" The night goggles cast everything in a monochromatic green, and he slowly turned his head to examine every bit of the landscape he could see. He spotted discarded pop tabs, a crumpled hamburger wrapper, and a couple of hair ties but no big cat.

The sound of an engine and tires popping on gravel came from across the field by the road. He turned that way and ran with Paradise on his heels. They reached the road as red taillights faded into the night at the park exit. He squatted to examine the marks in the red dirt. The night goggles brought everything into sharp relief, and he pointed out flattened grass. "It looks like something was dragged through here. The cat's owner might have loaded it into a truck or vehicle here."

She moved under the security light and took out her phone. "We'd better call Jane."

"Snap some pictures of the tire tracks and drag marks so you can send them to her. Make sure you tell her the cat had a collar."

"I will." Paradise took snapshots and tapped out a text message. Moments later a return message came. "She'll be here with Augusta and Nora shortly."

A wave of protective emotion drew him closer to her, and he slipped his arm around her waist. Things could have gone terribly wrong tonight.

Sometimes Blake wanted to pinch himself to make sure Paradise was really here with him. Her lioness mane of light brown hair was like none other he'd ever seen, and he could look into her amber eyes for hours at a time. She was beautiful inside and out. His family loved her almost as much as he did.

She shivered, and Blake kissed the top of her head. "Are you cold? You're shaking." It was probably seventy-five but there was a breeze.

She leaned against him. "It's reaction. I expected the leopard to attack."

He pressed a kiss on her forehead, and her trembling began to slow. "You didn't run though."

"I wanted to, but I knew better than to run from a leopard. Besides, I was confident you'd be there shortly. I was about to turn my flashlight on to try to scare it away when you arrived."

"Someone doesn't want you and Drew investigating your parents' murders. The question is why."

"And the only reason I can think of is that someone is afraid the truth will come out."

"Drew won't be frightened away, but I don't like having you at the center of the danger." He settled on a concrete ledge and pulled her onto his lap to warm her.

Her trembling stilled even more. "I'll face whatever I have to if it leads to the truth."

He loved how brave she was. Fear didn't paralyze her. "Want some chocolate-covered peanuts? I had grabbed a baggie full when I got your text and stuck them in my pocket." He retrieved the treat and opened the top.

She took a handful. "You know me too well."

"Not nearly well enough, but I'm working on it."

The headlamps from two vehicles swept the parking lot. Jane Dixon, Pelican Harbor police chief, got out of the first SUV and hurried toward them. "Did you call the sheriff?" Her petite stature masked a powerhouse of dedication to upholding law and order. Her looks had always put Blake in mind of a young Reese Witherspoon.

Blake released Paradise and shook his head. "I couldn't tolerate the thought of Creed Greene's smirking face tonight." Technically the preserve was the sheriff department's jurisdiction, but Greene tended to assume everything that had happened here was Blake's fault, and the deputy had yet to investigate any of the incidents here over the past few months without bias. The Pelican Harbor PD oversaw Nova Cambridge law enforcement, and Jane was quick to take jurisdiction when she could since The Sanctuary was so close to Nova Cambridge. Greene and the police chief had clashed several times, but Jane had managed to keep him in line so far.

Detective Augusta Richards and forensic tech Nora Craft exited the second SUV. Nora snapped pictures and took measurements of the drag marks and tire tracks while Augusta and Jane listened to Paradise recount the terrifying event.

"I wish you'd managed to get a picture of the big cat," Jane said.

"The leopard showed signs of an imminent attack, and I didn't want to make any movements that might trigger it before Blake got outside with the tranq gun." A thread of distress ran through Paradise's voice.

Blake took her hand. "You did the right thing."

"Of course," Jane agreed quickly. "Someone has an attack leopard? Seems crazy. How would anyone control a cat like that?"

"It would have to be highly trained from the time it was a cub," Paradise said. "And even then it wouldn't be easy. There are plenty of instances of owners being mauled by big cats they trusted. Our predator keepers here interact with our tigers and lions but always carefully and not without risk."

Paradise's fingers inched to the healed injury on her left shoulder from a black jaguar mauling she'd endured, and Blake squeezed her other hand. She'd made inroads in getting over her fear of big cats, but this incident might set her back.

He folded his arms across his chest. "The bigger question is, what did the trainer hope to gain by letting it loose? It was a deliberate attempt to intimidate Paradise. Show Augusta and Jane the text, babe."

She swiped on her phone before she handed it to Jane. "There's a subtle threat there you'll recognize."

Jane studied the phone before she gave it to Augusta. "Have you had any leopards go missing over the years? Or heard of anyone with one for a pet?"

"Nope," Blake said. "The Big Cat Public Safety Act was signed in 2022 and made it illegal to own big cats. But I'm sure plenty of people have kept their ownership quiet. We're near the coast and someone could have brought a cub in illegally by water."

"You're certain it was a leopard and not a jaguar?" Augusta said. "Jaguars are in the Americas and might be easier to smuggle."

"Good question, Detective." Blake turned to Paradise. "You're sure?"

"Positive. Jaguars are stockier with a broad head and shorter legs. It was a leopard."

That didn't get them any closer to figuring out who owned an illegal big cat. Blake made a mental note to have a tranq gun and a regular one on his person at all times and to make sure his mother knew to keep his little brothers safe. He'd make sure Paradise was well armed too. This wouldn't be over soon.

CHAPTER 2

LEVI'S FINGERS TIGHTENED AROUND Paradise's hand as he eyed the Ferris wheel at The Wharf, a popular mall and marina near Orange Beach. The Gulf breeze lifted his dark brown hair. "I don't think I want to ride that."

The boy had developed a fear of heights, and Paradise remembered when she'd felt the same. Even now her spine tingled at the thought of getting stuck in one of the cars at the top. "You don't have to ride it." She shifted the bag of boy clothes from one hand to the other. "We have what we came for."

"I'll go!" Isaac, Levi's five-year-old brother, kicked off his shoes.

Jenna nudged his flip-flop closer to his left foot. "Get your shoes back on. Developing a bit of fear might be good for you. I don't like Ferris wheels either, so I'll let Blake take you."

"Gee, thanks, Mom." Blake released Paradise's other hand and reached for Isaac's. "I can handle it though. Sure you don't want to come, Levi? I'll hang on to you the whole time."

Fear vied with interest in Levi's brown eyes, and he cautiously edged closer to his older half brother. "The whole time?"

"Yep." Blake took him by the hand and led both boys toward the ticket booth.

Though they could probably squeeze all four of them in the car, Paradise stayed put with Jenna. She and Blake's mother were more than wildlife veterinarian and employer—they'd quickly developed a solid friendship. Paradise pointed out a Build-A-Bear Workshop. "We might want to steer them down another street when they get off the ride."

"We'll take them for Kilwins. Ice cream will win out over stuffies. There's an empty bench over there."

The June sun warmed Paradise's arms and face, and she inhaled the aroma of sugared nuts roasting from a nearby sweet shop. She waved at the boys. Blake held Levi tight against his side while Isaac waved with enthusiasm and shouted something the wind snatched away. "Those boys make me laugh every time. You're so lucky."

Jenna tucked a strand of her dark brown bob behind her ear. "Don't I know it. I wish their dad were here to see what great sons they are. Blake has been a wonderful father figure for them. I don't know what I would have done without his help. He'll be a great dad someday."

Paradise knew where Jenna was going, but Blake's mom didn't have to point out Blake's many positive attributes. He had always been the man of her dreams, and she looked forward to someday holding a baby boy with his blue eyes and shock of dark hair.

Would it ever happen? She'd been gobsmacked when Blake turned down her marriage proposal. He'd claimed it was because she was only doing it so his mother and brothers would have a place to stay if the worst happened with the animal park, but she wasn't so sure anymore. Maybe neither of them were quite ready.

The incident two days ago with the leopard had shown her

she wasn't over her fear of big cats. She was better, but they still reduced her to a quivering ball of terror.

She took a tie from her purse and caught her flying hair in a ponytail. "I can't wait for Saturday to get here. A whole month with my brother will be heaven."

"I'm excited to get to know him. Do you have a good starting point for the investigation?"

"He has a list of leads he wants to check out. I'll let him take point."

"Did you tell him about the leopard?"

Paradise caught the worry in Jenna's blue eyes. "No, he called just before I spotted it, but I'll tell him when he gets here. You've been keeping the boys with you?"

"When they head to the backyard, I go along with a weapon." The frown between Jenna's eyes deepened. "Nothing from Jane about any rumors of big cats held by private owners?"

"Nothing. But the threat against my brother makes me even more determined to find out who killed our parents. Whoever has that leopard knows something and wants to keep it secret. Drew will bring a lot of expertise to the investigation."

The ride ended, and the boys sprinted in front of Blake toward their mother. Jenna and Paradise stood as the children reached them, and Isaac clambered up Paradise. "Did you see me? I wasn't scared at all."

She kissed his cheek. "I saw how brave you were! And your brother too." She set his feet back on the ground. "I have something sticky on my hand, so I'm going to pop into the restroom. I'll meet you at the ice cream shop. I'll have two scoops of chocolate peanut butter in a cup."

She watched the group troop across the street toward Kilwins before heading to the restroom, which was down a quiet side path and up on the second floor. The escalator wasn't working so she took the stairs. The hair on the back of her neck tingled, and she resisted turning around to see if anyone was watching her. The episode two nights ago had her jumpy, that's all.

The bathroom was empty, and she washed her hands. When she exited into the enclosed foyer, she glanced around but saw no one. That feeling of danger intensified, though she couldn't spot any reason for it.

Trust yourself. The past few months had taught her to listen to that inner voice of reason to determine danger. *Better safe than sorry.* She slipped her hand into her purse and curled her fingers around the butt of the little pistol Blake had bought her, then opened the door to the outside and went down the steps.

A blur of movement from the fence surrounding the dumpster hurled her heart to her throat, and she started to pull the gun out.

Hard fingers whirled her around, then grabbed her purse and yanked it. The gun flipped out of her hand.

She went flying through the air and landed in the grass. Her head slammed against the fence, and the world went black.

Blake checked his watch. Where was Paradise? The sweet scents of ice cream and waffle cones blended with those of caramel corn and fudge. The boys had already finished their ice cream and were getting antsy. The double scoop of chocolate peanut butter he'd gotten Paradise puddled in the cup on the table.

He exchanged a worried glance with his mother. "I'm going to go check."

She regarded the boys squirming on their seats. "I'll take these two over to the marina to watch the boats. Text me when you're ready to go to the van."

He left Kilwins and checked the sidewalks first but didn't see Paradise. The mall wasn't busy today, and he darted across the street and upstairs to the enclosed area outside the restroom entries. He stopped a woman exiting the ladies' room. "Excuse me, but is there anyone else in there? I'm worried about my girlfriend."

She shook her head. "It's empty."

He thanked her and walked back down and headed toward the parking lot. Maybe she wasn't feeling well and had gone to the van. He kept a sharp eye out for any sign of Paradise.

A black-and-white tiger-striped flip-flop lay upside down on the sidewalk along the way, and the first inkling of terror struck him when he saw a blue dot of ink on the top band. Isaac had taken a marker to it a couple of weeks ago. There was no doubt the shoe belonged to Paradise.

He spun wildly in a circle looking for her. "Paradise!"

Her SIG P365 lay nearly hidden in a section of taller grass and her purse was a few feet away. He tucked her small pistol into her purse and slung her bag over one shoulder while he continued to search.

There. Drag marks flattened the grass.

He followed the impression toward the fence-enclosed dumpster area. The partner to the flip-flop lay at the base of the trash bin.

"Paradise!" he yelled again. Two gulls stared at him with beady black eyes and approached in hopes of a handout.

He yanked out his phone and started to call Jane, but a soft sound stilled his fingers. Was that a moan? He leaped toward the dumpster where the lid on one side was open. When he peered in he found Paradise curled in a ball, her light brown hair matted with blood.

Blake muttered a "please, God" before he vaulted over the top. He ignored the stench of garbage, then touched her carotid artery, which thumped erratically under his fingers. Her normally tanned skin was pale and clammy.

At least she was alive.

Blood still flowed from a cut on her head, and his paramedic training in the Marines kicked in. He yanked off his tee to press it to the wound, then tucked his phone under his chin and ordered it to call 911. When the dispatcher answered, he said, "I need an ambulance out at The Wharf near the enclosed dumpsters in the back parking lot. Send the police too. Tell Chief Dixon someone attacked Paradise Alden and she's bleeding with a head wound."

"We have help on the way, sir."

He checked her pulse. Way too fast at nearly two hundred beats per minute. "I'm a paramedic so I'm going to sign off and tend to her until help arrives." He gave his name before he ended the call and dropped the phone into her purse still over his shoulder.

He didn't dare move her in case she had a spinal injury. He checked the wound, and the flow of blood was slowing. He renewed the pressure on the cut. "Paradise, can you hear me? Open your eyes, babe."

She had to be all right. Head wounds bled a lot. He reached for her hand and squeezed it, praying for answering pressure from her fingers, but they lay slack in his grip. She was still out cold. Not good. A lump formed in his throat, and he checked her pulse again. Steadier now and slower at just over a hundred beats per minute.

He allowed a ray of hope to blossom. "Paradise, I'm here. You're all right."

Her fingers moved slightly in his, and he leaned closer to her face. Her eyelids fluttered, and she coughed. He checked the wound and found it starting to clot. *Thank you, God.* She moved her head, which was an even better sign.

A siren wailed and grew louder, and she frowned as if the noise bothered her. "They're coming to help you, babe. Hang on. You're going to be all right. Can you open your eyes?"

Her lids fluttered before opening to slits. "The light," she muttered.

He shielded her with his hand from the glare streaming in the top of the dumpster. The siren cut off nearby and doors slammed. There wasn't much room in the dumpster with bags heaped all around them, so he'd have to climb out for the paramedics to have room to check her out with proper equipment.

Her hand moved to her neck. "My locket."

He'd given her his great-grandmother's locket for her thirtieth birthday a few months ago, and she never took it off. He'd often caught her opening it and smiling at the picture of the two of them on one side and her with his brothers on the other. It meant the world to her.

He ran his fingers around her neck and found it. "It's right here, babe." He guided her fingers to touch the filigree and the stress on her face relaxed.

Someone banged on the outside of the dumpster, and he reluctantly let go of her hand to struggle to his feet. "She's in here. I'll get out." He clambered over the side to join two men with a backboard. "I got the bleeding stopped."

"We'll take it from here. You related?"

"I'm her boyfriend. When she didn't show up to get her ice cream, I went looking for her."

A police car came to a stop in the lot by the ambulance, and two officers got out. Neither of them were familiar, and he was relieved that Detective Greene was not with them.

Blake intercepted the officers. "Someone attacked my girlfriend." He told them about finding the flip-flop and following the drag marks to the dumpster. "My mom is here somewhere with my little brothers. I need to let her know what's happened."

"Any idea who might want to harm her?" the younger officer asked.

"She's been investigating the murders of her parents, and there have been some other threats."

The officer jotted down the other incidents, and Blake took the opportunity to text his mother. Paradise attacked. EMS is here. She's got a head wound but is starting to wake up. Better not let the boys see this.

His mother's answer came back immediately. Oh no! Praying. I'll take the boys to get pizza. Keep me posted.

Will do.

The paramedics motioned to them. "We could use some help getting her out of here. To be on the safe side, we'll transport her on the board until we get tests done."

Blake jogged over to help. Paradise's beautiful amber eyes were open, and she looked alert as she emerged from the dumpster. He picked a piece of wilted lettuce from her hair and thanked God she was alive.

CHAPTER 3

PARADISE TRIED TO FOCUS her gaze, but her eyes drifted shut despite the noise of beeping machines and the flurry of nurses tending to her. Some kind of antiseptic odor stung her nose, and she reached up to touch her aching head. "Blake?" She wanted him here, holding her.

"Right here, babe," he murmured to her left.

She forced her eyes open again and blinked to try to focus on his square-jawed face. "What happened?"

His lips brushed her cheek. "You're going to be okay. No need to remember anything now. Rest and you'll feel better."

She frowned. "My head hurts."

"You have a mild concussion. The doctor is keeping you overnight for observation."

She closed her eyes, and the next thing she heard were voices whispering around her. The words *sedative* and *pain med*. She opened her eyes and blinked. Morning light streamed through the open blinds of a quiet room. Blake sprawled in a chair beside her with his head back at an awkward angle, and a slight snore escaped his mouth. She must have slept for hours.

An IV dripped fluid into her arm, but her mouth was dry. She raised the head of her bed and pulled the table over her lap, then reached for the water glass and gulped the tepid water. The moisture slaked her dry mouth and throat.

"You're awake."

She turned to Blake and smiled into his tired blue eyes. "You should have gone home and gotten some rest."

"I wanted to be here. You don't remember, but I rode in the ambulance with you yesterday."

She had chaotic memories of a dark figure rushing toward her and the stench of trash. She sniffed the skin on her arm. "I think I was in a dumpster. I still smell garbage."

He grimaced and pointed out stains on his shirt. "It's probably me. I was in there with you, but I didn't get a fresh gown like you."

"Did the police find who attacked me?"

"You remember the attack?"

"Just impressions. I didn't see his face."

"He?"

She couldn't bring the figure in her brain into focus. "It would have to have been a man to lift me up over the side of the dumpster."

He bent down to give her a lingering kiss. Her pulse jumped and she palmed his scruffy cheeks before wrapping her arms around his neck and bringing his head down for a proper kiss. When he straightened, she smiled. "You're whiskery and you smell like rotten meat, but I love you anyway. And I'm glad you're here."

"I'll remedy both of those as soon as I can. Is your head feeling better? You kissed me like you meant it."

"I did mean it. The pain is better, and my vision isn't blurry. I want to go home."

The door opened and a male voice boomed into her room. “Did someone say they were ready to go home?” A balding doctor in his sixties with a congenial smile stepped into view.

She struggled to sit up. “That would be me. Can you bust me out of this joint?”

“What, you don’t enjoy the hospital food and the constant fussing?”

“If I could remember it all, I’m sure you took very good care of me.”

The doctor listened to her heart and lungs, checked her eyes, then stepped back. “I think we can let you go home, if only to let Blake here get a shower. I could tell I was nearly to your room when I was twenty feet from the door. I’ll start the paperwork.”

Blake raised a brow. “I can tell when I’m not wanted. I’ll take an Uber home and grab my truck, then come back to get her. Once I’ve had a shave and shower, of course.”

“It will take about an hour to process her out. Plenty of time to get rid of that stench.” The doctor winked and turned toward the door. “We’ll take good care of her until you get back.”

Blake followed the doctor to the door. “I’ll be right back with clean clothes for you, too, babe.”

The door closed behind them, and Paradise threw back the sheet and swung her legs over the side of the bed. She’d use the restroom and get a shower herself. Her hair reeked of garbage, but it was sweet of the men to blame the stench on Blake. She found a clean gown and towel on the bedside table and headed for the bathroom. The hot water and shampoo washed the horrible odor out of her hair and off her skin, and she felt nearly human by the time she donned the clean gown.

The sound of the door shutting came from in her room and she called out, “Did you forget something?”

When Blake didn't answer, she tied the gown as modestly as possible, which wasn't saying much, then poked her head out the bathroom door. The room was empty. Maybe a nurse had come in to check on her. Paradise started for the bed, then realized the sheets would smell and veered in the direction of a chair instead. A yellow sticky note on her pillow caught her attention.

She reversed direction again and reached for the note.

> You know what you have to do if you want to live to get to know your brother. FINAL WARNING.

Chills shuddered down her back, and she let the note fall from her fingers. She could handle threats against herself, but it was different when someone targeted her brother. Should she cancel his visit?

She reached for the phone, then drew back her hand. Drew wouldn't change his plans for this. If anything, he'd be more determined than ever to find the man who murdered her parents and his father. There had to be a connection, and this threat proved it.

Blake stood beside Jane and studied the video on the screen in the small security office of the hospital. He tugged the neck of his tee. The space was claustrophobic and too hot. "Can you slow down the video?"

The tech nodded and the frame-by-frame rollout made it easier to see the figure draped in a blue surgical gown in the hallway of the hospital. A disposable blue cap covered his hair and was pulled down low to conceal his eyebrows as well. A mask hid his mouth and nose so that only his eyes were visible. The angle of the video made it impossible to make out his eye color. The figure slipped into room 211, and the closing door hid him from view until he emerged a few seconds later, still masked and gowned.

"That didn't tell us much," Jane said. "I'd guess he's six-one or so. Nora is swabbing for prints and DNA, but he wore gloves so I doubt we'll get any hits."

"I was afraid of that." Blake turned toward the door. "I'd better get Paradise home so she can rest." He'd left her in a different room under the care of a guard at the door.

"Stay with her," Jane called after him. "I don't like this, not any of it. Two attacks in three days."

At least Jane was taking the leopard sighting seriously too. He waved his hand and headed to the elevator to go back to the second floor. He nodded to the guard, then stepped quietly into the room where Paradise rested in a recliner with her eyes closed. Even bruised and traumatized, she was the most beautiful sight he'd ever seen.

He had to keep her safe, but she wouldn't thank him for the call he'd made on the way back from his shower.

Her eyes opened. "Hey, you're back. What did the video show?"

"Not much. A guy covered from head to toe in surgical garb. We couldn't even tell his eye color. He was clever. No one would have questioned him."

She rose. "Let's get out of here. I want to see the boys. They're probably scared."

She always thought about how his little brothers would react instead of herself. "I'll bring the truck around while they take you out in a wheelchair."

"I can walk."

"You know the drill."

She rolled her eyes. "Fine." She pressed the button to call the nurse.

He left her and hurried down the elevator and out the building to the parking lot. By the time he drove his truck to the hospital exit, his phone was ringing. Right on time. "Hey, Drew, you on your way?"

"I'm on my way. How is she?"

"Getting released right now. I struggled with calling you, but I realized that while I tend to be overprotective, there's such a thing as doing the reasonable thing when it's needed. She might kill me anyway."

"You did the right thing. I was coming anyway—I just moved the trip up by a few days. I thought about flying so I could get there right away, but you can handle protection for a few hours, right?"

"I'm taking her to my cousin's house. Hez and Savannah have plenty of room, and I don't think whoever is after her will think to look there. Her apartment isn't safe and neither is the refuge. I want her tucked away where no one knows to look. At least until you get here and we can plan a strategy."

"I'll be there in three hours. Are you staying at your cousin's too?"

"Yeah. Mom has some friends who will fill in for me at the park. See you soon."

He spotted Paradise in the wheelchair with the nurse and guard and drove toward them. He parked and went around to help her into the truck.

It was a big step up, but her jaw was tight when she waved away his help. "I can do it."

He ignored her comment and took her arm to steady her. She

climbed into the truck and flashed a triumphant smile. "Let's get home. I want to see the boys."

He thanked the nurse and climbed under the wheel. "We're not going home. Hez and Savannah have a room all ready for you. I'll stay too until Drew gets here and we figure out how to keep you safe."

The smile fell off her face, and he saw the wheels turning. He braced for the argument.

"I can't say I'm happy about it since I wanted to go home. The boys need to see me, and I need to see them."

That was a much milder reaction than he'd expected. "I asked Abby to bring them over. No one would likely follow her." Her best friend since childhood could keep a secret too. Abby was Roger Dillard's daughter and had helped them every step of the way the last few months.

Paradise sighed. "I've been figuring out that allowing other people to help me isn't being weak—it's being prudent when the situation warrants it."

He brushed her lips with his. "I'm proud of you for realizing that."

"And it's only for two days. Then we can get back to work."

"It's actually about three hours."

"You called Drew?" she asked, her voice incredulous.

"Wouldn't you want to know if something like this happened to him? He offered to come immediately. He's your family."

She absorbed the news and gave a reluctant nod. "You're right. I don't have to like it, but I would have immediately called your mom if you were injured and she was out of town."

He saw the way she absently rubbed her forehead. "You have a concussion, Paradise. If I hadn't found you, you likely would have died when the truck picked up the dumpster. This was no casual attack. I'm glad you're taking this seriously."

"I'd thought about telling Drew not to come at all. I don't want him in danger. But our brief relationship so far has shown me he wouldn't listen. He wants the truth as much as I do, and no threat will make me stop digging." She closed her eyes for a moment and pressed her fingers to her head. "Would you get the boys right away? I want them to see I'm all right."

"Abby's on her way to pick them up. Little-boy hugs will make you feel much better. They're going to bring your kittens too."

But those comforts wouldn't ease his worry at all. At least he'd have Hez to help out until Drew arrived.

CHAPTER 4

THIS WAS THE FIRST time Paradise had been inside the Websters' home. She wandered the inlaid wood floors and admired the stained-glass windows before following Blake and his cousin out to the back deck overlooking Mobile Bay. Waves lapped at the pier, and she smiled at ten-year-old Simon shooing away gulls trying to get his bait as he walked toward the water to fish from the shore. Hez and Savannah had recently adopted him after the death of his mother.

The salty breeze lifted Paradise's hair and she batted strands out of her eyes. She and Blake dropped into Adirondack chairs. The sun made her head pound, and she dug sunglasses out of her purse.

Blake noticed. "You want to go back inside? Is your head hurting more?"

"I'm all right. I'd rather be out here smelling the bay and listening to the gulls." She smiled at Hez. "Thanks for letting us barge in like this. Blake is a worrywart."

The smile in Hez's blue eyes vanished. "He's not, you know.

Things could have turned out much worse, and he can't be everywhere at once. A little help was all he needed, and it's what family is all about."

Her chest warmed at how accepting he was that she was family. "Well, thank you. There's something about the sound of the waves that sapped the tension right out of me."

"It's a special place." Hez nodded.

Blake checked his phone. "Drew is about two hours away."

"I really should be at my apartment getting things ready for him." She winced at the thought of old leftovers in her fridge and the sheets that needed changing in the guest room. The boys had likely left crumbs in the bed from their last sleepover.

"Mom is taking care of it. She's doing it right now while Abby has the boys."

A car door slammed, and Isaac's and Levi's voices rang out from the front yard. Blake rose. "I'll let them know we're back here." He bounded down the steps to the yard and waved to attract their attention.

Abby waved back and came toward them with his brothers. Her auburn hair was up in a ponytail, and her brown eyes were narrowed with concern.

The boys threw themselves at Blake's legs in a boisterous hug before they spotted Simon at the water's edge. "Can we fish too?" Levi asked.

"Sure," Hez said. "Simon has extra fishing poles there for you. Stay with Simon and don't go on the pier. The water is just right for fishing from the shore."

"We aren't babies," Isaac scoffed. "Mommy says we swim like fishes."

"That's true, but we don't want you in the water today," Blake said. "It's a fishing spot, not a swimming spot."

Isaac spotted Paradise, and his eyes widened. "You've got some scratches, Paradise." He came up the steps to her side and examined her face. "Does it hurt?"

"Not so much." She embraced him and pressed her lips against his soft cheek. "I missed you and your brother." She pulled him onto her lap and inhaled his little boy scent.

Levi ran up to hug her, too, then jabbed his brother. "Let's go fishing."

"Go ahead." Seeing them had assured Paradise that they weren't traumatized by what had happened to her. Jenna had probably downplayed it so they weren't frightened.

Blake walked toward them. "I'll help you bait your hooks."

Paradise watched his little brothers run ahead of Blake's tall, stalwart figure and marveled at his patience with them. They loved him so much, and so did she. She might have wanted to be consulted before he'd called Drew, but Blake was all heart and a fierce protector of those he loved. She was a blessed woman.

Abby reached her and studied her face. "Your poor face. Does it hurt?"

"My head aches." Paradise gestured to the chair beside her, and Abby settled in it.

Abby had been through so much too. Her father, Roger Dillard, had died in the swamp while in the process of trying to cover up his part in a plot to force Blake and Jenna to sell The Sanctuary to investors who wanted the rare-earth elements under it. Together they'd all figured it out and stopped the plan, but Abby's eyes still radiated hurt.

The boys reached Simon, who welcomed them with fishing poles. The three children knelt around the bait pail, and Blake put worms on his brothers' hooks. If her head didn't hurt so badly, she would have gone down to join in on the excitement.

She dug out the meds the doctor had given her. "I'm going to get some water," she told Hez and Abby.

Hez started to rise. "There are cold bottles in the fridge. I'll get you one."

She put her hand on his arm and shook her head. "I'll get it. I'd like to get out of the sun for a few minutes." She went inside and found the kitchen. It had been recently renovated and gleamed with stainless steel and clean white counters contrasting the gray cabinets. She instantly loved it.

After plucking a bottle of water from the fridge, she walked into the dim coolness of the living room and settled on the sofa while she waited for the med to calm the pounding in her head. The clock on the mantel ticked, and the distant sound of tires on the road outside filtered into the room.

Someone didn't want Drew here, yet yesterday's action was bringing him to town sooner rather than later. Was it because Drew was a police detective and the perp feared he'd have more luck finding the killer than Paradise by herself? They already suspected the murders of her parents were somehow connected with the death of Drew's father. If Drew discovered who his father was, would that lead to the killer?

There was enough worm goo on Blake's jeans to choke a swamp gator and make it spit up its lunch. But his little brothers were all smiles, which made the mess worth it. They'd each caught two fish, and he promised to clean them and fry them up for dinner. They moved from the bay to Simon's tree house in a tupelo tree on the east side of the property. The cool shadows held the scent of old leaves and moss.

Isaac clambered up the makeshift ladder without a qualm, but Levi eyed the slabs of wood dubiously. Blake touched the boy's shoulder. "I'll be right here to catch you if you slip. You can do it."

Levi placed his right foot on the first rung. "Stay right there."

"I will." Blake didn't help his brother because he wanted him to gain confidence by doing it himself. And sure enough, the seven-year-old managed to reach the platform with Simon and Isaac on his own.

Smiling, Blake started toward the house. A rustle of dead leaves and the crack of a footfall on twigs caught his attention. He could see Hez still on the deck, but there was no sign of Paradise. "Paradise?" he called.

A flurry of movement and the sound of someone running through the woods followed. Blake took off in pursuit. Paradise wouldn't have run. He caught a glimpse of a green shirt that nearly faded into the canopy of leaves. Blake spotted a blue ball cap on the man's head before the guy reached a rusty brown pickup parked along the ditch by the neighbor's house. A billow of black smoke belched from the truck muffler before it rattled out of sight around the curve in the road.

Panting, Blake stopped to catch his breath. Who had been watching them? Had Paradise's attacker already found her? He retraced his steps and reached the driveway in time to see a muscular man slide out of a blue truck. Drew had arrived, and his biceps indicated he'd intensified his workouts.

Drew spotted him and waited for Blake to reach him. Blake shook his hand. "You made good time."

Drew gestured to the removable light on his truck. "I decided the attack warranted the siren. Where's Paradise?"

"I think she's inside. Someone was skulking around though."

Blake told him about the trespasser. "It could have been innocent, but my gut says it wasn't."

"My gut is speaking the same language. I don't like it."

"She's a little miffed I called you." Blake beckoned for Drew to follow him to the house. They went up the steps to the door, and he let Drew go ahead of him into the house. Paradise would be thrilled to see her brother.

They found her curled up on the sofa sleeping. Dark circles shadowed her eyes, and her color hadn't improved much. Her head probably hurt. Blake put his finger to his lips and gestured for Drew to leave the living room, but Paradise opened her eyes and spotted them.

She sat up. "Drew, you're here."

Drew went to her and settled beside her. He put his arm around her, and she tipped her head to rest it on his shoulder. "I didn't let any grass grow under my feet. How are you feeling?"

"Fine. My headache finally let up. I'm just a little groggy from the pain med." She lifted her head. "You didn't have to change your plans, but I'm glad you came."

"I only moved them up a few days. We need to figure out what's going on. I'm glad Blake called me."

Her gaze locked with Blake's. "I am too. Someone doesn't want you here, which means that's exactly where you should be. I think you know more than you think you do, and all the deaths are going to tie together."

"Maybe. One thing I've learned is never assume anything. We'll take it one step at a time and figure this out."

She sent an appealing glance Blake's way. "Can we go home now? I just want my own bed. I'm hoping I'll wake up tomorrow and feel totally fine."

"That's a little too optimistic with a concussion," Blake said.

"But you might be at 50 percent." The plan had been for her to stay here for a few days, but after the discovery of an intruder, he'd made the instant decision to get her out of here. Maybe there was no place she'd be truly safe, but at the park at least a lot of people would be around.

He left them and went out the back door to thank Hez and gather the boys. Once the fish were cleaned, he'd help his mom with dinner and maybe they could have a normal evening. He'd almost forgotten what one of those felt like.

CHAPTER 5

PARADISE GRIMACED AT THE smear of fish guts on Blake's arm. "I'll ride with my brother." She'd gone most of her life without a sibling, and yet it felt so natural to refer to Drew as her brother. There was so much she didn't know about him, but the relationship had settled more firmly into place when she woke and saw him. A little more red shot through his tawny hair than hers, but their amber eyes were alike. Others would be able to guess at their relationship.

Blake corralled his brothers. "I'll meet you at the park. Abby, you want to join us for dinner?"

"Maybe next time. I need to get Quinn."

Quinn was her ten-years-old-going-on-twenty daughter.

Abby smiled at Drew. "Nice to finally meet you, Drew. Take good care of my bestie." She hugged Paradise before heading for her car.

Blake and Paradise thanked Hez again for his hospitality and told him to pass their gratitude along to Savannah. Paradise walked with Drew toward his pickup while Blake steered his brothers toward his truck. Drew kept glancing around with a laser focus. The breeze stirred his short light brown hair.

"Are you watching for someone?" she asked when they reached his truck.

"There was an intruder in the woods. I want to get you out of here before something happens." He opened the door and helped her up into the four-wheel drive.

She shivered and glanced toward the woods around the Webster property. The heavy foliage blocked the view, and she didn't see much. "That's why Blake agreed when I wanted to go home," she said when he climbed under the wheel.

"Except we're not going home. We both agreed the park is safer. There's room for all of us, and I'll be able to help protect you."

The reality that they were all putting themselves at risk for her made her shift in her seat, but she held her tongue. Wouldn't she do the same if he or Blake were the target? Of course she would.

He fastened his seat belt and started the truck. "I see your expression, Sis, and I know how hard this is for you."

She bit her lower lip. "I want you to consider you might be the target now that you're here, Drew. The warnings have been that you'd be in danger if you came here. You might be in more danger than me."

"I agree he doesn't want me here, but I think he doesn't want either of us to uncover anything about your parents' murders, and he knows our joint efforts will be more powerful."

"How will we go about figuring out who your father is? When we first met, you said you thought your dad's murder was connected to my parents' murders. I didn't believe it then, but I do now."

"We're on the cusp of some big discovery, Sis. This guy will likely get more dangerous. I want you to close the veterinary clinic for now and always have me or Blake with you."

His use of the fond term *Sis* warmed her. "My patients need me. I'm the only vet in Nova Cambridge, Drew. I don't want to cut and run."

"I know you don't, but you could go on vacation for a week or two and put your focus on helping me figure this out."

His plea made sense. Working didn't allow much time to investigate. Drew would be here for a month, and they could put all their effort into getting to the bottom of the murders. "All right, you've convinced me. I'll have emergency calls redirected to Honey. There's a vet in Foley who might help out."

Honey Hopkins had been a great hire for the vet clinic. She understood the demands that could arise at the park since her husband, Evan, was one of the predator keepers. They lived in Paradise's childhood home.

Drew turned the truck into the drive back to the park. "I always knew any sister of mine would have a lot of sense."

She smiled. "I hate that we didn't get to grow up together."

"Me too. I always wanted a sibling. But it will make getting to know each other better all the more fun." Keeping his eyes on the road, he pulled a paper from his pocket. "I have a list of where to start."

She unfolded the paper and stared at his blocky, printed note.

- Examine autopsy and murder files
- Find early friends
- Talk to coworkers
- Talk to neighbors
- Find detectives on the original case

She refolded it. "These are all very good. I have some avenues I started to trace before I tabled it to figure out who was trying to shut down the park. Now that The Sanctuary is on solid footing, I can concentrate on the murders. No one seems to know who your real father was. I think maybe my cousin Lily knows, but if she does, she's denied it."

"Maybe I can get her to talk. We'll hit the ground running tomorrow by talking to your family first. You have several cousins in the area, right?"

"Yes, and they're your cousins, too, since they're all on Mom's side. One works for the sheriff's department, so maybe Rod'll tell you more than he has me. His mom is the one I think might know who your father is."

"Perfect place to start."

She stared at his ringless left hand. "You've never been married?" He was thirty-five, five years older than her, and a handsome guy like him normally would have been married by now.

"I was once for about a year when I was in my early twenties. She cheated on me with my partner. I nearly left the police force when that happened, but my partner left instead and I stayed. It's been hard to trust anyone since then."

Betrayed by the two people he wouldn't have suspected of it. "I'm sorry. I'll always be here for you, Drew. I don't say that lightly. Loyalty is the most important thing to me."

He shot her a smile. "I believe you, Paradise. And I'll be here for you. Finding you is the best thing that's ever happened to me. And I like your guy. Blake is one in a million."

"He is. And he'll help in whatever way we need him to." She slid a sideways glance Drew's way. If they were ever to claim their birthright as siblings, she needed to open up to him. Taking a deep breath, she plunged in. "I grew up in foster care after my parents were killed. I-it wasn't good. Blake tried to protect me from Lloyd during my first placement. It backfired and I got shipped farther away from everyone I knew and loved. The second foster home was worse than the first, a-and the son living there raped me."

He tensed and his expression flashed hot with outrage. "I'm sorry, Paradise." He reached over and took her hand. "I assumed someone in the family took you in. That had to have been so hard. Yet here you are—a strong and accomplished wildlife vet. You overcame all of it. I'm in awe."

"My parents taught me about pushing through hard things, and I'm glad I had those first nine years with them." Her eyes filled with tears, but she held his gaze. "I'm glad you're my brother."

"Me too, Sis. Me too."

The future looked bright if they could all manage to stay alive.

Dinner was over, and they'd gotten out the set of dominoes to play with the boys, though Paradise wasn't sure she'd be able to stay awake for very long. A dull ache circled her head, but she felt better than she did when she awakened in the hospital. The kittens curled beside her as if they knew she needed extra comfort.

Her phone blipped with a text. A lemur has me trapped in my bedroom!

Paradise stared at the text message from an unknown number. "Wow."

"What's wrong?" Blake asked.

"I'm not sure who sent this." She showed him the text.

"I'd better go. Is it okay if I text the sender and ask for the address?"

She nodded and handed him her phone. He tapped out a response. "It's an owner over in Magnolia Springs. He wants to turn the animal over to us. It's already bitten him, and he's bleeding. He doesn't want to call animal control because he doesn't want it injured."

This was something she needed to help with. "I'll go with you."

The boys' faces fell, and Isaac's brown eyes filled with tears. "You said you'd play dominoes with us."

"I know, buddy, but there's a lemur that needs us." She reached down to slip on her sandals.

"I'll play," Drew said. "You two go rescue the lemur, and I'll whip these boys into shape."

"Yay!" Levi threw his arms around Drew's neck. "Can you be our brother too? Paradise is going to be our sister."

"I'd be honored."

When Drew grinned at her with such joy, Paradise wanted to hug him. He'd grown up without siblings too. Blake's family was quick to welcome people searching for a place to belong, and she mouthed a *thank you* to Jenna. Having Drew so quickly assimilated into the family warmed Paradise's heart.

She grabbed a banana and a container of blueberries from the kitchen before they left the house. Bribing the lemur would help them calm it.

Blake interlocked his fingers with hers, and they walked out to his truck together in the fading sunshine. "You sure you're up to this? I can go tranq the little guy and bring him back."

"It helps to have two of us, and I need to walk some of the soreness off. My legs and arms ache." She clung to his hand and relished his proprietary grip. He'd been there for her through every minute of this ordeal. If not for Blake, she might be dead in that dumpster.

"Getting thrown out like trash isn't for the faint of heart." He opened the passenger door and helped her into the truck.

Magnolia Springs was only ten minutes away. "Did the guy tell you anything about the situation?"

"No, just what you saw. He or she texted me the location."

She fell silent as they drove the short distance to the house. It was in one of her favorite neighborhoods. She stared at the address. "You know what—I think this is Elowen and Wade's house." Wade Greene, a firefighter, was Detective Creed Greene's brother, though they were estranged.

The address on Bay Street wasn't far from Jesse's Restaurant. Live oaks draped with Spanish moss stretched their branches in a green arch over the roads, and the sun's dying rays bathed the neighborhood with a welcoming glow that wouldn't last long.

The shotgun-style home was just as she remembered it with white shutters and a charming porch. No one was outside tonight. She climbed out of the truck while Blake grabbed the tranquilizer gun, a medical kit, and a net from the back of the pickup and followed her.

She rang the bell, then remembered Elowen was likely still trapped in the bedroom. "It has to be Elowen who texted. Wade wouldn't be frightened of a lemur even if it was biting and scratching."

"Unless he had Tessa with him. She's only two, so the lemur could hurt her."

"I'm going in." Paradise twisted the doorknob, and it opened into the living room cluttered with toys and stuffed animals. She spotted one of the pandas from the gift shop at The Sanctuary.

She picked it up and carried it with her down the dark hall she guessed led to the bedrooms.

There was no mistaking the lemur shriek ahead of her. The animal grunted and barked, vocal signals of agitation. She held the banana out. "Let me try calming it first. Maybe you won't have to use the tranquilizer. I'd rather use the net."

"Me too, but this guy sounds mad."

Enraged was more like it. What had set it off? She ran her fingers over the wall of the windowless hallway and found the switch. She flipped it on and light flooded the snug space. The lemur stood on its back legs at the bedroom door and shook the doorknob. The animal turned when the lights came on and barked at her. It was a male and would be more docile than a female. Females ruled the pack.

She extended the banana. "Hey there, buddy. It's okay. We're not going to hurt you."

"Paradise, thank the Lord you're here." Elowen's tearful voice came from the other side of the door. "I've got Tessa with me, but I haven't been able to reach Wade. He's at a fire and probably doesn't have his phone with him."

"We'll take care of it, Elowen." She took a step nearer the lemur. "You hungry?" she asked in a coaxing voice. The lemur's tail quit lashing so hard, and it reached out agile fingers to pluck the banana from her hand. It didn't bother to peel the banana but bit off a chunk and chewed.

"Is that good? I have blueberries too." She planned to scatter them on the floor so the lemur would have to pick them up. That should distract it long enough for Blake to toss the net over it.

She waited until the animal finished the banana, then opened the container lid and rolled a handful of blueberries toward the lemur. It dropped onto all fours and began plucking up the berries and throwing them in its mouth. The agitation leached out of its face.

"Now," she whispered to Blake.

He unfurled the net and tossed it over the lemur, but the animal didn't seem to mind. She handed Blake the blueberry container. "I think it was just hungry."

CHAPTER 6

BLAKE GOT THE LEMUR, grunting and shrieking, into the truck where it settled down when he draped a tarp over it so it didn't see him and Paradise. The lemur's scent glands had gone into overdrive, and the stench hung in the air.

Elowen, holding her toddler Tessa, followed them outside. The woman's long blonde hair was mussed, and her blue eyes were shadowed. Dried blood caked the side of her hand.

"Let me tend to that scratch." Blake opened his medical pack and took her hand to clean the wound. "Have a seat. This might sting a little."

"He was mad." Tessa hid her face in her mother's shoulder.

Blake studied the wound. "I don't think you'll need stitches. Just antibiotic cream and a bandage. But have your doctor take a look." He smiled at Tessa. "He's just a little upset, but he'll be fine. I didn't know you had a lemur."

"He's not ours," Elowen said. "He belongs to Creed."

Creed Greene had been a thorn in Blake's side ever since Paradise arrived. She'd rebuffed an advance from the detective, and he'd never forgiven her. Greene had focused on Blake for months, trying to pin a crime on him at every turn. The detective wouldn't be happy they'd taken control of his lemur. And what was he doing with a lemur anyway?

"Did you try calling him?" Blake asked.

Elowen shook her head. "He and his family are out of town for another week, so there wouldn't have been anything he could have done. He told us to keep him caged, but that felt so mean. He played nicely with Tessa a couple of days ago, so I thought we could let him loose to run around and get some exercise."

"He's still a wild animal, Elowen, and an unknown one," Paradise said. "Once they reach sexual maturity, their behavior can change rapidly." She peeked into the truck bed. "He's calm now. Lemurs need their social structure, and they don't make good pets. They don't do well without other lemurs, and this often results in aggressive behavior like this guy just showed. I would guess he was taken from his mother too early as well, and he doesn't know how to act. Do we have your permission to take him to the park and assimilate him into the lemur conspiracy?"

Elowen bit her lip. "Creed won't be happy, but I can't take care of him. King Julien bared his teeth at Tessa, and I had to wrestle him off. I threw him across the room, grabbed Tessa, and locked us in the bedroom when he came at us again." Elowen squared her shoulders. "Creed shouldn't have even had this animal, should he?"

"No," Paradise said. "While it's not illegal in Alabama to own wild animals, it's not humane, especially for primates, and it's bad for both the lemur and the owner. Lemurs can transmit diseases to humans and vice versa. They're expensive to feed properly, and they need enrichment programs to keep them from getting depressed. And Julien shouldn't have been caged like that."

Paradise braced her hands on her hips. "Why on earth would Creed have a lemur? Do you know where he got it?"

"I think he won it in a poker game a couple of weeks ago. I don't know why he didn't just take it to you guys in the first place. He thought Julien was cute, and his son was crazy about him."

Creed wouldn't do anything that might benefit the park. Blake kept his opinion to himself. "We'll deal with Creed when he returns."

Paradise put her hand on the truck door handle. "I'll need to check Julien out. We have to be careful not to transmit any diseases among the lemurs. An illness could have triggered his aggression. Maybe he just doesn't feel well."

Elowen shifted Tessa to her other arm. "Thanks for coming so quickly. I was a little scared. He'd been acting fine and suddenly started growling and making noises. He scratched me as well as the bite." She extended her arm to show a long, oozing scratch.

"Make sure you clean that well with peroxide," Paradise said. "I'm glad it bled well. Blake can clean it for you."

"I can do it," Elowen said. "You've helped enough."

"Can we come see King Julien?" Tessa asked.

Paradise opened the truck door. "You sure can, but give him a few days. You'll want to see him after he's gotten used to us a bit and is able to be with his new family. We'll see you soon."

Blake said his goodbyes as well and got behind the wheel. He started the truck and pulled away from the Greene house. "Creed is going to be a problem."

"I know. Is there anything we can do to keep him from taking the lemur? Maybe turn him in to the humane society or something?"

"I'll check our options with Hez. It'll be complicated because in normal circumstances, we'd report animal abuse to the sheriff's department."

"I could talk to Rod while Creed is gone."

Her cousin Rod McShea was the sergeant over the Bon Secour sheriff's substation. "That might be the best idea. We could get it accomplished before Creed gets back in town."

"I'll call him after I examine Julien. If there's any evidence of mistreatment or disease, it will help our cause. If we get the lemur acclimated to our conspiracy, Creed probably wouldn't be able to tell which one was which. King Julien looks like most every other ring-tailed lemur, and he hasn't had the animal long enough to identify him. At least I doubt it. So he couldn't just walk in and take him."

Blake inwardly groaned at the upcoming confrontation. Things had settled down for a while, and he hated to see the vendetta continued. Creed wouldn't let this affront go.

It wasn't too late to call Rod. Paradise washed and dried her hands after examining the lemur, then dug the phone out of her purse.

Rod answered on the first ring. "Hey, Paradise, how are you feeling?"

"The headache is improving. I think I'll live. Hey, Rod, my brother is here. He's eager to meet you and the rest of the family."

"That's great! How long will he be around?"

"About a month. We're going to look into my parents' murders."

"If there's anything I can do to help, let me know."

"I will, thanks. Listen, there's another reason for my call. I have a sticky situation." She told him about the call from Elowen. "We have the lemur here, and he shows clear signs of neglect. His paws are abraded from trying to escape the cage he's been kept in.

Primates shouldn't be caged like that. He's obese and has diabetes and heart disease, probably caused by an improper diet. I want to get him well and assimilate him into the group here. The problem is, his owner is Creed Greene, who is out of town. Creed left the lemur in the care of his brother and his wife, and the lemur attacked their little girl."

"Wow, I was not expecting that. I didn't know he had a lemur."

"Elowen thinks he won it in a card game a few weeks ago, so the lemur's health problems started a long time ago."

"Do what you have to do, and I'll handle it on my end when Creed gets back. He should have known better than to keep a primate caged. Even I know that's not okay."

What a relief Rod was being agreeable. "I appreciate that more than you know, Rod. Lemurs need socialization. They don't do well in isolation, and this one is very sick. Even if Creed knew how to care for King Julien properly, he couldn't fix the community issue."

"I know you'll take good care of him. I'll talk to Mom about when we can get the family together to meet Drew."

Paradise thanked him and ended the call. She checked one final time on King Julien in his solitary enclosure. She would let him get used to roaming around it before she integrated him with the other lemurs. He'd be able to see them, smell them, and hear them in the next enclosure over, which would help. She locked the door of the medical building and went to find Blake and Drew. Isaac and Levi would be in bed by now.

The murmur of male voices from the back patio mingled with the low hum of the bug zapper that also gave off a soft glow. Blake and Drew seemed relaxed with each other, and happiness zinged through her. *Family.* That's what it was all about. Something she'd never really had before. This place and these people had crept into her soul and become as necessary to her as breathing.

Blake spotted her when she moved again, and his expression went soft. "How's the king?"

"Not great. Diabetes and heart disease. Hopefully a better diet will change things, along with more exercise." She climbed the steps to the deck. "I talked to Rod. He says to do what we need to and he'll deal with Creed."

Blake kissed the top of her head. "That's my girl. I wasn't sure Rod would go up against Creed like that, but if anyone could make him see the truth, it's you. How's Julien acting?"

"He's roaming the enclosure and marking his scent, of course. I think he likes it."

Blake laced his fingers with hers. "Hungry? We've got popcorn." He gestured at a bowl on the table by the chairs.

"Don't mind if I do." She scooped up a handful, then dropped into the chair by her brother. "You should be in bed, Drew. You had a long drive."

His amber eyes, so like her own, were bright and alert. "I was reviewing the contents of the tub Evan gave you." Drew gestured to the tub by his chair.

Evan Hopkins now owned the house where she'd grown up. He'd found a tub of her mother's belongings in the attic, which was how Paradise discovered she had a brother she didn't know about. She and Drew had gone through the things together, but there hadn't been any surprises. "And?"

He held up a black onyx cuff link. "This was caught in the baby blanket. Did you see it when you first examined the contents?"

She took it and rolled it around in her fingers. "No." She studied the cuff link. "It's beautiful and very distinctive with that fancy *C* on it. Maybe your dad's last name begins with a *C*, though that doesn't help much."

"It's a start."

"Why would only one be in the baby blanket?"

"Maybe my father lost it, and our mom found it and kept it? Or maybe it came from the man she was having the affair with before she died."

"Could have belonged to my father. Let's examine this together." He lifted out the old jewelry box, a packet of letters tied with pink ribbon, a baby book, and infant clothing, as well as several pieces of maternity clothing.

She touched the iconic *LV* monogram top in green canvas on the jewelry box. The gleaming brass latches and lock added beautiful bling, and it had a leather handle at the front. "Blake checked the current price of this Louis Vuitton, and it was six thousand dollars. We didn't discover its original price."

She didn't have to remove the expensive jewelry because she'd held every piece. A gorgeous set of sapphire earrings, a ring with a huge topaz stone, a diamond tennis bracelet with matching earrings, and a diamond engagement ring in a velvet box.

Drew picked up the ring. "I was struck by this too. My father must have given it to her, so what happened? Why didn't they marry?"

So many questions and no answers.

CHAPTER 7

IT WAS AFTER MIDNIGHT, but Drew showed no signs of needing to hit the mattress. Blake swatted a mosquito on his arm and listened to the night sounds of the park through the open window. The intermittent roaring of the big cats and the cacophony of crickets and katydids were a familiar backdrop that relaxed him.

He knew he should go to bed because the governor's aide was coming tomorrow, but he wasn't sleepy. Drew reminded him so much of Paradise—same amber eyes and tawny lion's mane, though Drew's was cropped short in a military-style cut. Blake had hit it off with him immediately, and he knew Drew felt the connection too.

The rap on the back door startled Blake, and he jumped to his feet. "Maybe Evan found the leopard."

He opened the door to find Evan standing on the deck. "Come on in."

Evan stepped inside. "I wanted to check in and let you know I've followed every pad print I could find, but I think whoever let that leopard loose on you took it away. At least for now." His worried expression spoke volumes.

Blake caught what he was saying. "You can't track him, and you also can't guarantee it won't happen again."

"Unfortunately." Evan opened the door. "I'd better get going. I'll keep my eyes peeled."

Blake shut the door and rejoined Drew. He told him what Evan had found. "So the big cat is gone for now. I hope it stays gone, but I'm not counting on it."

"It's wise to stay on guard." Drew leaned over and repacked the tub Evan had given Paradise. "I should let you get to bed. I'm always wired after a road trip, but there's no reason you have to join me in my insanity."

"I don't mind keeping you company a little longer. It's not every day something like this happens. It's been great to see Paradise so excited."

"Tell me about my new sister. She's not the most open book."

"She's been hurt a lot, so she hides her softness. She was shuffled from one foster home to another and experienced some horrific abuse. In spite of everything she turned out to be an amazing person."

"She told me about the rape."

Blake paused. "She doesn't talk about it, so if she told you, she must trust you. Most of that stuff she buries down deep. Coming here has healed a lot of her trauma. The boys have helped."

Drew replaced the lid on the tub. "Why didn't her family take her in? She's got cousins, right? Any aunts or uncles who could have helped out?"

"Her cousins live here. What I've picked up on is that the cousin who could have saved her from all that, Lily, was jealous of Becky. They were first cousins, and Lily had her own kids to raise and refused to take Paradise. They're still a little reserved with each other. I think Lily regrets it now, and Paradise doesn't hold a grudge, but that rift might never really heal."

"Rod is Lily's son?"

"Yes, and he's been helpful as Paradise has tried to sort things out. She doesn't feel like an integral part of their family though, and it's great to see her open her arms to a relationship with you."

"You've loved her a long time."

Blake's face burned at Drew's thoughtful stare. "Since we were teenagers. She asked me to marry her a few weeks back, and I stupidly put her off. I thought she was doing it because we were about to lose the park and she wanted to make sure we had a place to go. And while I think that was true, she was hurt and has gone back into her shell a bit. Things often haven't worked out in her life, and I think she's trying to protect herself."

"I don't know her well yet, but I know human nature. I've seen it on full display in my career. Maybe it's time you prove to her how much you love her."

"I'm not sure how to do that. I had a ring made for her, and it's ready, but—" He shrugged. "She wants to find her parents' killer before we start a new life together. Are you optimistic that you'll get to the bottom of all this?"

Drew reached for his soda and took a sip. "I wouldn't say I'm optimistic. Maybe *hopeful* would be a better word. It's been over twenty years, and cold cases are hard to crack."

Blake's chest tightened. "I'm not sure she'll ever give up."

"She's tenacious," Drew agreed. "I'm the last person to give relationship advice, but it might take a special push to get things moving between you two again."

A special push? Paradise didn't like being pushed. She was a woman who thought things through, and she didn't take kindly to feeling like she was being manipulated or coddled. He'd never push her. Either she wanted a life together with him or she didn't.

And he wasn't yet sure if she was ready to put the past behind them and grab the future with both hands.

King Julien appeared much happier this morning when Paradise checked on him. He'd eaten all his food and stared at Paradise with contented red eyes from his perch on the rocks. The enclosure reeked of his scent markings, and she smiled at how ready he was to assert his dominance over the space.

He scampered toward her when he saw the banana in her hand. "You like it here, don't you?" She poked the banana through the fencing, and he snatched it from her fingers.

There was no barking or aggressive behavior, and his eyes were brighter. It would take some time on the proper diet with exercise to get his diabetes and excess weight under control, but he was on the mend. She left him and walked into the wildlife clinic where she found Warren Gibson, her vet tech, with a red fox. It wasn't an animal Paradise had seen in the park.

She approached the sedated animal. "What do we have here, Warren?"

"Someone dropped her off. She's blind."

Paradise winced. "Not being properly fed?"

"She's very malnourished. I think it's too late to save her sight."

"But she'll find a home here with our skulk."

Warren smiled at the term. "I'm still learning all the names for groups of animals. You want to examine her?"

"I sure do." She washed her hands and pulled on gloves before probing the fox's mouth and extremities. She palpated the animal's belly. "Does she have a name?"

"Ember."

"I like it." Paradise finished her exam. "I think her electrolytes are off. Let's give her an IV to pump up her nutrition and fluids." She prepped a balanced solution of electrolytes, glucose, amino acids, and lipids. "I'll let you administer it. Any other patients today?"

"Nope. You probably noticed King Julien's improvement on the way in."

"I did. Let's have him on his own for a few more days before introducing him to the conspiracy."

"I thought you'd say that. The other lemurs have caught wind of his scent and are very curious, but it's wise to take our time."

"Good. I hope they welcome him." She stripped off her gloves and tossed them in the trash. "I'm going to grab my brother and head out for a while. Call me if anything comes up."

With a light schedule here at the park, she and Drew could begin their investigation. Blake had hired a college student to help with tours so he'd be free to go with them too. Paradise walked toward Jenna's cottage and paused where she'd seen the leopard the other night. The park had taken in two animals since then. Was there any connection among the animals? A red fox, a lemur, and a leopard all in the area seemed suspicious. She reversed direction to see what she could find out about Ember.

She nearly ran into Warren on his way out. "Evan found Ember. She was left in a crate in the parking lot, and Evan found her when he got to work. He brought her straight to the clinic."

"How weird. I'm going to ask Blake to check the cameras and see if he can tell who dropped her off." If it was Creed Greene, he had some explaining to do.

She found the men on the back deck and stopped by Blake's

chair. "Before we go, could you check the cameras? Someone dropped off a red fox in a crate in our parking lot. It seems odd we've acquired two animals back-to-back, plus we saw that stray leopard."

"That *is* strange." He grabbed his phone and studied the camera recording. "Which area of the parking lot?"

"Warren didn't say."

"I'll check all the cameras." He fell silent as he flipped through his phone. "Here it is. It's not under a light so I can't tell who it is, and they left the crate clear out in the far lot. Maybe a guy and he's in a pickup. That's all the detail I can make out."

"I guess it doesn't matter, but it seemed odd."

He rose and slipped his arm around her waist. "How's your head?"

"Totally fine. I haven't had a headache in a couple of days now."

Drew, dressed in khaki shorts and a tee with a Blue Line emblem, stood. "Could I see the house you grew up in today? You already cleared it, right?"

She nodded. "Evan said Honey left it unlocked and we could go on in. She was taking the kids to an arcade in Foley this afternoon."

"I want to walk the house and yard and see if I can tell how the killer likely got in."

"I think I let him in, or at least left the door unlocked. The cable guy came and gave me a monkey music box like in *The Phantom of the Opera* that had been left on our porch before going into the living room. The police found no sign of forced entry."

"I noticed there was no mention of forced entry in the police report. I want to look at things like shrubbery, trees, other ways someone might hide and get into the home."

"Those things might have changed over the years," Blake said.

"I'll take that into account."

They walked around the house to Blake's truck. She got in the back seat while the men claimed the front. It would give her time to steel herself for the upcoming trip down memory lane.

CHAPTER 8

BLAKE STEPPED BACK AND let Paradise and Drew wander the home and yard where Paradise had spent most of her childhood. He tried seeing it through their eyes—the new paint and floors, the freshly updated kitchen, rich with the sweet scent of maple syrup on the morning's pancakes. He'd hoped the differences would keep the pain at bay for the woman he loved, but the shadows in her amber eyes told the true story.

While Paradise showed Drew where the box of belongings had been found, Blake wandered to her old bedroom and stared at the closet where she'd hidden while a killer bludgeoned her mother to death. It was still decorated for a little girl since Evan and Honey's daughter had claimed the room. The fairy princess room was an explosion of bubblegum-pink walls with a matching comforter. He stepped closer to the closet.

What had happened here was something no child should have had to go through. Had anyone examined the closet for anything left from those old days? Honey had said to poke through anything they wanted, and he made the quick decision to do just that.

He opened the closet door and pushed all the hanging clothes to one side, then removed the mishmash of shoes and toys on the floor. He turned on his phone's flashlight app and shone it around the floor and walls. There didn't appear to be any cuts in the drywall that would indicate a hidden panel. He moved the desk chair to the closet and stood on it to peer around the walls above the closet shelf before training the light on the ceiling.

It was a bust.

He sighed and put everything back the way he'd found it and started for the door. Then he swung back and stared at the closet. What about the floorboards? He went back to the closet and moved aside toys and doll clothes again. He checked each wooden plank one by one until his fingers brushed ridged edges. The board didn't feel tight. He used his pocketknife to pry at the board, praying he didn't do any damage. Evan might not appreciate the defacement of his daughter's room.

Blake was about to give up when the edge of the board popped loose, and he lifted it up, revealing a small storage pocket underneath.

His fingers grazed something, and he shone his light inside. A pink diary held closed by a discolored brass clasp lay covered in dust in the cramped space under the floor. His pulse shot through the roof. It had to be Paradise's. Almost reverently he lifted it out and put the floorboard back into place and stared at the diary.

Though he wanted to open it and read it, he stopped himself. This was Paradise's privilege. Maybe he should check to make sure there weren't any surprises that would ambush her emotions. His fingers moved toward the clasp, but he drew back his hand. She wouldn't thank him for interfering in her quest. These were her secrets to discover and unwrap. Hers to confront, no matter how difficult they might be.

He rose and stepped to the hall. Their footsteps were above his head, moving toward the ladder they'd climbed to the attic. He waited for them with the diary clutched against his body. Paradise descended first, smiling up the pull-down ladder at her brother. The sight of her joy swelled Blake's heart. Discovering her brother had been good for her.

Drew's big shoes came next, and he landed next to her, then slung his arm around her shoulders. Their camaraderie was so natural it could have been lifelong. Blake smiled to think how their relationship would grow over the years. Drew would be a good uncle. He was a natural with the boys.

Blake cleared his throat and Paradise's smile veered his way. "We didn't find anything but dust and spiders that I had to kill for Drew. Who knew a big, strong detective would scream like a girl when a spider scurried his way."

"I did *not* scream."

Her gaze returned to her brother, and she poked him in the ribs. "Sounded like a scream to me. And you backpedaled so fast you nearly fell."

"It startled me."

"We were in an *attic*, Drew. You should always expect creepy-crawlies."

He removed his hand from around her and gave her a little shove. "You're a vet. You have to like all the animals."

Her expression sparkled with mirth that faded when she approached Blake and spotted what he held in his hands. "Is that a diary?"

He held it out. "I found it under a loose floorboard."

Her eyes widened, and she reached out to touch it. "I—I think I recognize it." She took it and fiddled with the lock. "I probably don't have the key any longer."

Blake took out his pocketknife and bent over the diary in her hands. "I think they're easy to pop open." One little twist of the blade and the clasp released. "There you go."

She stared at it. "I'm not sure I want to read it. What if the truth about their deaths is in here, and it's my fault?"

"Babe, it's not your fault. No matter what happened, you have to remember you were nine years old. You've never had a mean bone in your body." He lifted the diary's cover. "Maybe go straight to the back and see when you last wrote in it."

She glanced at Drew, who gave her an encouraging nod. "Let's get coffee. I think I need fortification for this. Pray for me," she whispered for Blake's ears alone.

"Always," he said.

The hiss of the coffee steamers mingled with the conversation flowing in University Grounds. In spite of joking around about spiders, Paradise still reeled from the ordeal of watching her brother walk the backyard where her father had died. She'd stood in the backyard where she'd once hung her legs over the edge of the tree house. Her mind's eye saw what the autopsy had revealed—her father sprawled out here dead, and even with the hiss of the steamers and the strong scent of brewing coffee, she couldn't erase the images. Her father had been bludgeoned with the same bat the killer had used on her mother while Paradise hid in the closet.

Why couldn't she remember all of it? Only bits and pieces had filtered back to her consciousness. Her feelings of guilt increased with every small memory that resurrected itself.

Drew placed an iced peppermint mocha in front of her on the

outside table. Tupelo Grove University students usually thronged the sidewalks and the porch with their notebooks and computers spread out on the iron-and-glass tables, but it was summer break. They had the porch to themselves today.

Blake exited University Grounds with his drink in one hand and a plate of beignets in the other. "Sustenance." He slid the plate of treats in front of her.

Paradise stared at the diary on the table. "I need a pot of coffee before I tackle this." The pink cover with its old clasp was so familiar yet so alien. The gilding on the paper edges was even still there.

Her biggest question was, why had she hidden it?

She took a sip of her drink before she reached for the book. It felt terrifying in her hands, though she knew she'd once loved writing on its pages. It felt all wrong to have this now, to feel the smooth faux-leather cover. The pen was missing. Maybe it was still in that hiding place.

"Want me to read it first?" Drew asked. "Or Blake?"

She shook her head. "I think I'll start at the beginning. Maybe some of the events will jog my memory." She lifted the cover and stared at the first entry: March 15, 2004.

> I've never had a diary before! My birthday was so fun. Mommy curled my hair, and I wore my new pink dress. Abby got me this diary along with a bright pink pen, and I'm going to write down everything that happens this year.

Her eight-year-old self sounded so joyous and excited. Had she ever been that happy since the year before she lost her parents? She gazed at Blake sitting across the table from her and at Drew beside her. Maybe now was even happier. She knew loss and heartbreak yet had weathered them both to find a new life. She appreciated those contented days more than she had as a child. When you never knew pain, you couldn't fully be grateful for the blessings.

She flipped each page slowly, reading about school and tests, then came to one with a different tone in October.

> Mommy told me I had to stay in my tree house until she called. She had a visitor, and she didn't want me in the house. I had my binoculars with me in my backpack and my snacks. My tin of Cheez Balls was gone first, then I used my binoculars and looked in the kitchen window. I didn't know the man there. She was crying, and she kissed him! Right on the mouth like she does Daddy. I didn't want to see so I put my binoculars in my backpack.

Paradise caught her breath. "Drew, look here." She slid the diary to him. "Could your father have come to see her?"

Drew's frown deepened as he read the entry. "You'd never seen your mother with another man?"

"The sheriff used to come by sometimes, but I never saw her kiss him. I'd heard that a neighbor reported they'd kissed, but it wasn't in the file. I don't think it was true. His wife said they were having an affair, but I've never found confirmation of that."

"This was four months before she died. It might mean something." He snapped a picture of the page with his phone. "Are there a lot more entries?"

She fanned through the pages. The diary was nearly full. "There are a lot more."

He glanced at his phone. "I don't want you to miss anything, but I need to call my partner. He has a question about a case we're working on."

"And I need to get back to the park," Blake said. "Let's table the diary until after dinner, unless you want to read it by yourself while I take care of the night meal for the predators."

She pushed back her chair and rose. "I'll help you. We can reconvene after dinner and see if there are any other clues. This feels like it could be important though. Why would Mom not want me around? It had to be a discussion she thought would get back to Dad."

Drew took his phone and put it to his ear, then went down the steps to the sidewalk. His words were soft and muffled from the distance.

"Maybe she thought you wouldn't understand," Blake said.

"I didn't understand the kiss."

"Do you remember the incident at all?"

She closed her eyes and tried to remember how she felt sitting in the tree house with the leaves fluttering around her. The view to the house was decent, but most days she'd lain on the hard pine floor and stared at the foliage over her head. She'd watched ants crawl on the tree's bark and listened to the neighbors argue. They were always arguing, and she'd been glad her parents never fought.

A memory slammed into her brain. Her dad yelling, her mom crying. The sound of a door slamming. Her eyes flew open. "I just remembered something that happened a few days before they were murdered. I'll tell you on the drive."

CHAPTER 9

PARADISE FASTENED HER SEAT belt but waited until her brother got in the back seat of the truck and Blake started the engine. She gave a last, lingering look at the house where her life had changed forever. Coming back here wasn't something she wanted to do ever again. It was too painful.

Blake turned the truck toward the Kate Norris Bridge. His window was down, and the salty scent of the Gulf wafted in as they passed the houses on stilts along County Road 1. "What did you remember?"

"I was thinking about the tree house and how I would lie back on the boards and listen to the neighbors arguing. I heard that a lot and was always thankful that my parents never fought. But they argued a few days before they were killed. Mom had given me a muffin and told me to go outside, so I took my book and climbed to the platform. It was *Harry Potter and the Order of the Phoenix*. I'd already hugged my dad goodbye because he had a business trip. Mom seemed tense that morning and kept glancing out the window."

Blake reached over and took her hand. "You're shaking."

She hadn't realized it. When she laced her fingers with his, the trembling stopped. "The screen door was open, and I heard Dad yelling at her. He said, 'Becky, you had a *child* with another man and never told me. Who is he? And how could you keep something like this from me? And don't try to lie. I heard the message from the private investigator on the answering machine.'"

Behind her in the back seat, Drew gasped. "Granger knew about me? What did you think when you heard about it?"

"I sat up and wished I had my binoculars. I was mad. I'd asked and asked for a baby brother or sister, and Mom never said a word about me already having an older brother. I was ready to go down and join Dad in yelling at her."

"What happened next?" Blake asked.

"Mom started crying and apologizing. She said she wanted to tell him but was afraid he'd be angry. Mom said she'd been contacted by a private investigator who was looking for information about you, Drew. Someone was trying to find you."

"I'm here now." His voice was grim. "And this time I'm looking too."

"Do you know if your mom told the PI anything?" Blake asked.

Paradise closed her eyes and tried to sort the memories flooding back. "She told him she didn't know anything. She said the PI started stalking the house and threatened to tell Dad if she didn't reveal Drew's real name and whereabouts."

Drew leaned back. "Who would hire a PI to track me down? It seems very odd."

Paradise released Blake's hand and reached for a water bottle to soothe her dry mouth. "And about the time my parents were killed. Was the PI's client the person who killed your dad, Drew? It would make sense."

"And maybe he killed all three of them," Drew said. "This is even more connected than I thought it would be. What if the man she kissed was my dad?"

Paradise sipped her water. "That's what I wondered."

"Was there any clue to who the PI might be?" Drew asked.

She stared out the window toward the bridge. "I didn't hear a name. But what if we could find that old answering machine? My cousin Lily had a few of their things in a box. She was going to get it for me when I was there a few weeks ago, but it didn't happen. We could get it and see if the answering machine is in there."

"We could try, but it's not likely she kept something like that," Drew said. "Could you arrange for us to go see her? I want to meet her anyway."

"You could invite everyone over for a cookout," Blake said. "The whole family would likely want to meet Drew—especially Rod since they're both in law enforcement."

"That's a great idea," Paradise said. "When?"

"How about Sunday? Drew can find out what a Gulf Shores shrimp boil is like. I'll grab shrimp from Billy's Seafood and corn on the cob from the farmer's market. We've got sausage and potatoes."

"I'm already drooling," Drew said.

Paradise pulled out her phone and began to tap out a message. "I'll ask Lily to bring the box of stuff with her." Paradise sent off the message, then started another to the rest of the family. "I'll tell them to come at six."

"That gives us two days to do some other digging," Drew said. "What about their best friends?"

"Trisha and Wes Miller. They were good friends with my parents ever since high school. They played cards together almost every weekend."

"They have to know something."

"Trisha admitted she knew about you, but she wouldn't tell me anything more."

"Maybe she'll talk to me when she sees Becky's son in the flesh. The shock might loosen her tongue."

Paradise glanced at the clock on the dashboard. "It's almost time for her pottery shop to close. We could try to catch her before she leaves."

"I guess that means we're turning around." Blake braked and swerved into the parking lot of the Mary Ann Nelson Park.

Closed. Blake took a step back from The Red Firepot. The pottery shop's hours clearly read it closed at five, but it was only four thirty. "She must have gone home a little early tonight. She and Wes live down the road from Hez and Savannah's house. I saw them in the yard the first time Hez showed me the property."

He held Paradise's hand, and they walked back to his truck with Drew on their heels. Drew practically vibrated with his need to find out what had happened. His detective mindset might actually solve this mystery. Blake couldn't wait for the load to be off Paradise. The danger felt ever present, and he wanted it to end.

His phone sounded, and he answered a call from Rod on the dash. "Hey, Rod."

"Good news, Blake. The state agreed with us on keeping the lemur in your care at The Sanctuary. But be aware that Creed is back in town early. He'll be coming your way when he hears the news."

"I'll be ready. Thanks for the help, Rod." Blake ended the call and his gaze met Paradise's. At least they had the law on their side.

Stilts elevated the white bay cottage with its hipped metal roof. A white SUV sat in the drive in front of an open garage door that revealed a blue car parked inside. Blake didn't spot anyone moving around the yard or in the garage. He pulled his truck into the double-width drive and parked beside the SUV. "Let's see if we can find them."

"I hope her husband is home," Drew said.

Pink azaleas bloomed along the front porch, and a large stand of rhododendrons blocked the view to the neighbors on the left. The breeze carried the scent of salt and fresh paint to his nose. Maybe they were working on the house.

"Wait here," he told Paradise and Drew. "I'll bet they're outside." Blake went up the steps to the porch and pressed the doorbell. After two more tries, he rejoined them. "Let's check around back." He sensed Drew's impatience to go first, but to his credit, the detective let him take the lead.

The white paint on the side of the house still glistened. In the backyard he spotted paint trays filled with soapy water and brushes by the back steps. An elevated deck had a view of a pier with a boathouse at the end of it. Two figures sat on the pier with their legs dangling toward the water.

"There they are," Paradise said.

The three of them walked down the sloping backyard, but the Millers didn't spot them until they stepped onto the boards.

Wes Miller's face turned their way. He was in his sixties with a neatly trimmed graying beard. He was mostly bald with very short gray hair at the temples. His gaze darted from Blake to Paradise and then to Drew before focusing back on Blake. He nudged his wife, and they both stood to face them. Trisha had white paint on her hands and arms, but Wes was mostly paint free.

Trisha's welcoming smile was stiff on her face, which was pink and perspiring from exertion. "Blake, Paradise, this is a surprise."

Paradise stepped closer to them. "We stopped by the shop first and saw it was closed, so we came by hoping to catch you for a few minutes. This is Drew Bartley. Andrew Bartley, my brother."

The pink washed out of Trisha's cheeks, leaving her pale. "Y-your brother." Her gaze lingered on Drew's face. "You and Paradise both look a lot like Becky, same coloring and all."

"So we've been told," Drew said. "I'm sorry to bust in on you like this, but Paradise and I are trying to find out who murdered her parents and my father."

Trisha blanched more. "Your father is dead too?"

"Right before our mother and Granger died. Peculiar, don't you think?"

Trisha wet her lips. "Coincidence."

"Unlikely. Especially now that Paradise has remembered an argument her parents had a couple of days before they were killed. A PI was looking for information about me and my father. Did he contact you?" Drew quirked an eyebrow in Wes's direction. "Either of you?"

Trisha shook her head, but before she could speak, her husband placed his hand on her forearm. "There's nothing to protect now, honey." His voice was a deep Southern drawl.

"But I promised—"

"And the truth is already out about Drew. There's no longer a promise to keep." Wes nodded toward the house. "I hear some sweet tea calling my name. Let's settle on the deck and we'll tell you what we know."

Trisha set her jaw in a mutinous scowl, but Blake knew her husband would spill it all if she refused. They might get somewhere today. He took Paradise's hand, and they all trooped toward the sprawling deck on the back of the house.

A white cat came down the steps to greet them and curled around Paradise's ankles. "Who's this beauty?" She scooped the small feline into her arms and followed their hosts up the steps.

"That's Bunny, named by our granddaughter. She was a stray who wouldn't leave once Trisha fed her." Wes headed for the door. "I'll be right back with sweet tea."

An awkward silence descended until Trisha gestured to the chairs. "Have a seat." She perched on the edge of a blue Adirondack chair. "I'm not sure what you think we know. It's probably not as much as you hope."

Drew sat across from her. "Do you know my father's name?"

"I know his first name, but that's all. I know he came from a wealthy family. In Louisiana I think."

Blake exchanged a dismayed glance with Paradise. That wouldn't narrow it down much. Paradise started to speak, then shut her mouth. They'd let Drew handle the questions. He was the expert at interrogation.

"What was his first name?" Drew asked.

"Ben. Becky called him Benny, and he didn't let anyone else call him such a silly name. He was eight years older, but she didn't care. I tried to caution her against him, but she wouldn't listen. Until the day his wife showed up."

Paradise gasped and put her hand to her mouth. "He was married?"

"Very married. With a three-year-old daughter. It devastated Becky, and she broke it off. Two weeks later she found out she was pregnant. As far as I know she never told Ben."

Drew gulped. "Was he looking for *me*?"

Wes came through the door with a tray of ice-filled glasses and a pitcher of tea. “Here we go.”

“I told them everything I know,” Trisha said.

Wes set the tray on the table and began filling the glasses. “Then I’d better tell them the rest.”

CHAPTER 10

PARADISE'S PULSE KICKED AT the thought that Wes might know more than Trisha. She took a sip of the sweet tea. It was delicious and tasted like it had been brewed by the strong Alabama sun on their back deck. "You went to college with my dad, too, didn't you?"

Wes lowered his bulk to the love seat beside his wife. "We roomed together. Granger's death gutted me. A close friend like that doesn't come along every day." He shot a glance at his wife. "I've kept this bottled up for decades, even from my wife."

Trisha gave a start and stared at him.

He patted her knee, and she put her hand on top of his. "Granger had been 'off' about a week before the murders." Wes glanced at Drew and Blake. "Guys don't share stuff like women do. I figured if it was important enough, he'd say something."

Paradise searched her memories for any hint that her dad hadn't been himself and came up empty, but she'd been a kid and unlikely to notice. She had so many questions, but she kept silent so she didn't stop his flow of words.

"He called me a couple of hours before he died."

Trisha gasped but said nothing, and Wes continued. "Granger talked to the PI who left the message. Guy by the name of William Fletcher. He said he was trying to prevent a tragedy." Wes's eyes were wet when his gaze went to Paradise. "I guess he failed."

The enormity of the revelation dried her tongue. "So William knew someone planned to hurt my parents?"

"Granger said this Fletcher guy warned him to take you and your mom away on vacation or something until he had a chance to find out more. That's why your dad came home early. He called me from the road. He'd asked your mom to pack for a trip, and she refused. She told him she was going to leave him." Wes's Adam's apple bobbed in his neck. "It's hard to hear a grown man cry."

Paradise's eyes burned. Her dad had been so strong, so loving and kind. "I saw a man kiss my mom. I couldn't remember much of what happened until recently when it started to come back. I found an October entry in my diary about it."

"Do you remember what he looked like?" Drew asked.

"Not really. I only saw the back of his head. He had dark hair and was taller than Dad maybe. That's it."

Wes shifted in his chair. "Your dad suspected her first boyfriend had come back, but the bigger piece of news for you is that Fletcher said the guy had a lot of money and was connected. Granger wasn't sure if that meant a mob connection or power. He suspected the guy might be from an influential family in politics though. He didn't tell me why he thought that. Maybe it was something Becky said."

Drew leaned forward. "So let me get this straight—Fletcher basically told Granger someone wanted to prevent Becky from getting back together with my unknown father and might harm them to make sure it didn't happen."

"That's the gist of it."

"Who hired Fletcher?" Drew asked.

"The PI told Granger he was hired by an 'interested party.'" Wes put air quotes around the words.

"That could mean anyone," Drew said. "A spouse, a parent running for office who didn't want his kid to ruin his reputation. Even a partner who thought it could derail their business. Any idea where this Fletcher lived? I'd like to talk to him."

"His phone number was from Pascagoula. That was all Granger knew."

Drew pulled out his phone. "He might still live there. It's worth checking out." He tapped on the screen. "I'll have my partner check on the man's whereabouts."

"I should have told the cops about it, but I didn't want to drag Becky's name through the mud. She was a good friend even though I hated what she was about to do to Granger."

"The cops might have brought their killer to justice if they'd had any idea where to look." Drew's clipped voice and tight jaw revealed his disgust. "Fletcher might not even be alive now. I read the investigation files, and there was no mention of Becky having another child. That direction was never checked out."

"I—I can't believe it." Trisha set her glass of tea on the table in front of her. "I never would have dreamed Becky would get back with him when he had deceived her like that. And she never told me she'd been in contact with Ben."

"She was getting a little older, and maybe the pull of her first love was stronger than she realized when he showed back up." Paradise had never gotten over Blake either, and it hadn't taken long for her to realize she still loved him. The minute she looked into his blue eyes again, she'd been swept up in a cauldron of emotions from her teen years.

She wiped the moisture from her cold glass and swallowed the last of her tea before she rose. "Thanks for your honesty, both of you. We'll let you get back to your day."

Drew rose and handed Wes his card. "Call me if you think of anything else." Wes nodded and slipped it in the pocket of his tee. "I'll be in town awhile."

Paradise took Blake's hand and tried to think of the next move. This changed everything.

Blake had watched Paradise through dinner and her interactions with the boys at Mom's house. She'd tried to keep up a good front, but he'd seen the shadows in her amber eyes.

They kissed the boys good night and headed for the back deck. Drew was holed up in Blake's apartment over the garage, and Blake had been waiting for some time alone with Paradise. They stepped out into the night lit by stars and a sliver of moon. The scents of grass and camellias wafted on the breeze. An owl hooted in the distance, and monkeys chattered in response.

He spotted one of her hair ties on the floorboard and picked it up. "You have a hard time hanging on to these things."

She took it from him. "They flip out of my fingers."

A tiger chuffed, and he turned that way. "Sounds like Evan is feeding the big cats."

She leaned against his chest. "There's nothing like the sound of the park at night. The animals moving to rest or to prowl around their acreage. There's a feeling of contentment—that all is right with their world and ours. I can't imagine living anywhere else."

"I can't imagine having anyone but you to share it with." He kissed her, relishing the taste of her lips and the way she leaned against him with total trust. She pulled away and rested her cheek back against his chest.

He'd gotten a text that her ring was ready for pickup, and he was awed when he saw it. Hez was going to return the favor of taking pictures when Blake asked her to marry him, but he still couldn't decide where or how to do it. Aboard a Gulf dinner cruise? On a walk through the park? Here at home with his little brothers so she realized how much the whole family loved her?

There were so many choices. Now that the park was on stable financial ground, thanks to Governor George, nothing was standing in the way of looking for a house of their own. He loved his family and knew Paradise did too—but the thought of having their own place to start a new life together was an amazing thing.

His mother poked her head out the open door. "The governor texted. She's sending her aide over tomorrow to arrange another visit with her grandson and the press."

Paradise lifted her head. "That's great news! We'd better prepare for another surge in visitors after the media gets here again."

"I need to hire a few more people. Another employee or two for the gift shop and maybe more tour guides." Jenna ducked back inside.

"It's so great to hear the optimism in her voice," Paradise said. "You have both been under so much pressure lately. It's hard to believe things are on the upswing here." She fell silent. "Today was . . . interesting."

"How do you feel about what you learned?"

"Shocked. The thought that Mom would leave Dad and take me with her doesn't sound like her. She was so much about family." Paradise took a step back. "If she would do something like that, she must have loved Ben very much."

"Want to take a walk?"

She nodded. "Stretching my legs might let me absorb everything we've learned. What if that PI is still alive? We might solve all of this very quickly."

Blake didn't want to burst her bubble, but he had an uneasy feeling it wouldn't be that simple. He took her hand, and they went down the steps into the thick grass. It was time to mow again. The list of things to do seemed never-ending, but he loved the continual activity.

Right after sunset was his favorite time of day. The air smelled sweet and fresh, and the darkness softened the edges, hiding the maintenance that needed to be done on some of the buildings. One thing at a time. They were getting there. The bills were paid, and they had enough money to tackle more urgent projects.

He spotted Evan strolling the tree line and nodded toward him. They reached the side of the building and an engine growled its way angrily into the parking lot. Tires squealed as the driver stomped on the brake and brought the vehicle to a halt. "Someone sounds upset," Blake said. "Maybe you should go inside."

"It's probably Creed. Evan mentioned he saw him in town. I was expecting him to come here the minute he got back."

Blake paused and exhaled. "You're probably right." He stepped ahead of her into the parking lot and spotted the detective.

Greene's face was set and angry under his sandy hair, and his hands were fisted at his sides. Still in his uniform, he stomped toward them and stopped three feet away under a glow from the security light. "I want my lemur."

Blake stood ready for a sudden move from Creed. "King Julien was a danger to people and was transferred to our care, Deputy. He's adjusting nicely. You can come by and check on him tomorrow if you like. He's sleeping now."

"What I'd like is for you to put him in the cage I brought. I'll take him home."

Paradise stepped to Blake's side. "He was in bad shape. He wasn't being fed properly, and he's diabetic. He has some other problems as well, including malnourishment. We got an order from the state allowing us to remove him from your custody. He's ours now."

"You have no right to do that." Greene started to move past them.

Blake stepped to his right to bar the deputy's progress. "Keeping him in good health won't be cheap. He needs diabetes medicine and more fresh fruits and vegetables. He's a primate and shouldn't be penned in a crate. We'll take good care of him and you can visit whenever you like."

Greene's green eyes narrowed, and he hesitated before stalking back toward his truck. "You haven't heard the last of this," he shot over his shoulder before he got into his pickup and drove off.

"I think I'd better let Rod know so he's prepared to deal with Creed," Paradise said.

"I think I'll put up a security camera in the lemur habitat too. Greene is unpredictable."

She took Blake's hand. "Forget about him for now. Let's take a walk down by the pond and listen to the frogs and katydids. I don't want to think about anything right now but being with you. It feels like we haven't had any time together in weeks. Tomorrow we can decide our next steps, but not right now."

The pond was a nice, long hike, well away from other people. "That's the best idea I've heard all week."

CHAPTER 11

SPRING RAINS HAD FILLED the pond to its brim. Paradise stood at the water's edge with her hand in Blake's and took in the idyllic view of moonlight on water and the little footbridge on the right side of the pond. She inhaled the sweet scent of flowers mingling with the loamy aroma of the pond and exhaled the last of her tension. The light glimmered on a tangle of white honeysuckle blossoms along the left side of the pond and bounced off the smooth surface of the water. She let the symphony of crickets chirping and frogs croaking wash away the anxiety that had steadily crept in over the past few days.

Blake put his arm around her waist and pulled her against his side before he pressed his lips against her temple. "Better?"

She watched a fish splash in the middle of the pond. "Much. Sometimes it takes nature to put everything into perspective. God created all this and keeps the world ticking along. We humans complicate things so much. I'm glad we live here and not in a big city where it's so easy to lose touch with what really matters."

"You have a way with words," he murmured against her hair.

She turned toward him and lifted her face up for a kiss. His lips came down on hers, and the passion in his kiss sparked her own. She wrapped her arms around his neck and kissed him back in a promise to him and herself that she'd never let go of this love they'd found. No matter how long it took for things to get sorted out, this was where she belonged.

His breathing was ragged when he lifted his head. He wrapped a long strand of her light brown hair around his finger. "You ever wonder why things work out the way they do? I never dreamed when you left all those years ago that you'd be back in my arms again. That we'd have such a single purpose in working together for a future."

"God knew. I think it takes some years to get perspective on the bad things that crash into our lives and send us barreling off in a different direction. Without the experiences we've had, we wouldn't be here."

His phone sounded with a text message. "I don't think I'll get that."

"You should. It's late, and it might be important."

He grimaced and dug out his phone. "It's Mom. There's a leak in her bathroom sink, and she can't turn the shutoff valve."

Paradise gave him a small push. "You run ahead, and I'll be right behind you. Your long legs will get you there quicker without me slowing you down."

"I don't want to leave you here alone."

She gave him another push. "Go. I'll be right behind you."

He gave her a quick kiss before jogging off. She watched him disappear into the trees lining the pond, and the sound of his steps faded into the sudden chorus of frogs. Their little interlude was over, but it was okay. It had given her the peace she needed.

She started to follow him to the house and spotted something glittering on the little footbridge. It almost looked like gems sparkling. What on earth? Skirting the edge of the water, she walked through the bullrushes toward the bridge and stepped onto the first board. It shuddered under her weight, and she paused. Blake had cautioned her about walking on it because it was for charm only until he shored up the joists, but she wanted to see what still sparkled in the center of the bridge. The moon retreated behind the clouds, and she would need to get closer to determine what it was.

She gripped the handrail and decided it felt solid enough, so she sidled along the floorboards, which felt soft underfoot. Just four feet and she'd retrieve the item. She inched along until she was a foot away and leaned down to pick it up as the moon emerged in full force. She stared down at a collar embedded with stones. The musky big cat odor hit her then. This collar had been on the leopard watching her from the trees a few days ago.

She picked it up and looped it around her wrist, then started to retreat to the shore when a board cracked beneath her.

She grabbed for the railing, but the floorboards under her split open, and nails pulled loose from the handrail.

Still holding the board and the collar, she hurtled into the murky water in the middle of the pond.

The water went over her head until she found her footing on the slimy bottom of the pond. She bobbed up with the water reaching her chest. She swiped the water smelling of algae and moss out of her eyes.

A gator slithered into the water toward her. Its tail splashed as it propelled toward her with its eyes barely peeking above the surface.

She wasn't in danger of drowning but in danger of being eaten.

Adrenaline shot through her, and she moved as fast as she

could toward the safety of the land, but it was slow going with the mud so slippery on the pond's bottom.

Fear dried her mouth. Those giant teeth would clamp around an arm or a leg any minute, and the gator would have her in its death roll.

The handrail board was still in her hand. Maybe it would do as a weapon.

The gator was coming fast, and she turned toward it. Its mouth opened, and she jammed the board in as far as she could and turned to scramble onto the grass. She spared a glance behind her and saw the gator retreating. Shivering and wet, she scurried away from the water before it changed its mind.

Something moved in the tree to her right, and she stared up into the blue eyes of a leopard.

At least the boys hadn't awakened while Blake repaired the bathroom plumbing issue. His mom worked on mopping up the floor while he found plumbing flux and a soldering iron to reconnect the pipe under the bathroom sink.

He backed out from under the musty-smelling bathroom counter. "I might need to replace the cabinet floor. It's already swollen from the water. We'll let it dry before I replace the contents and see if it returns to normal. But it won't be too expensive if I have to put in a new cabinet bottom."

His mother's hair was still wet from the dousing with water while she had tried to turn off the supply valve. "It's a good thing you're a jack-of-all-trades."

"And master of none?" he teased.

"You're the master of all of them. I hated to interrupt your evening with Paradise. The two of you have gotten so little alone time."

He washed his hands in the sink and dried them. "Plumbing waits for no one. Is Frank good at plumbing?" His mom had been dating a former classmate, Frank Ellis, a well-known land developer. Blake liked him.

His mom's cheeks grew pink. "I haven't asked him."

He quirked a brow and smiled. "It's important to know these things before your relationship progresses any further. When are you seeing him again?"

She made a show of picking up the wet towels strewn on the floor. "I invited him to the cookout on Sunday."

"Ah, is that sort of like walking through fire to meet everyone involved in this complicated family? Well, Paradise's complicated family, at least. Ours is straightforward."

"Her family will be part of ours. Did you pick up the ring?"

"Sure did. It's gorgeous. Want to see?" He tossed the towel onto the sink. His mom followed him to his room where he dug out the black velvet box. The two-carat emerald sparkled in its setting of diamonds that accentuated its perfect square shape. "The jeweler said it came from Zambia. Do you know where Dad bought it when it was in a necklace?"

She touched it with a reverent finger. "I have no idea. We didn't have much time to talk about it before he left on that final tour of duty. I waited to wear it until he came home, but he never did. It stayed in the safe all these years. It's much prettier in a ring. I think Paradise will love it."

"I hope so." Blake closed the lid of the box and put it back in his drawer under his socks, then glanced at the bedside clock.

"Whoa, it's later than I thought. It felt like fixing the plumbing only took a few minutes, but it's been half an hour. Where's Paradise? I didn't hear her come in."

"I didn't either, and she would have come to check on your progress to see if you needed help." His mom clutched her hands together. "This is worrisome. Maybe she's talking with Drew."

"Let me go check." Blake headed for the kitchen door and walked to the garage to climb the steps to the apartment on the second floor. Music played from inside, and he rapped his knuckles on the door. "Drew?"

The door opened almost immediately. Drew was alert and still dressed. "Everything okay?"

"Is Paradise with you?"

Drew's eyes widened, and he shook his head. "You've lost her somewhere?"

"I left her at the pond to rush home to fix a leak, but she shouldn't have been more than five minutes behind me. It's been half an hour." Fear gripped Blake and he turned to run down the steps. "We have to find her," he called over his shoulder.

Drew's footsteps pounded down the stairs behind Blake. "Where's the pond?"

"Out near the swamp. It will be faster to take the Gator. Come on." He grabbed the tranq rifle, then they ran for the parking lot. Why hadn't he paid attention to the time?

They reached the utility vehicle, and Blake barely waited for Drew to land on the passenger seat before he turned the key and accelerated to the pond.

A smooth path extended through the field and stopped at the ring of swamp tupelo trees circling the pond. He parked the Gator. "We'll have to walk from here." He cupped his hands to his mouth. "Paradise!"

A lion roared behind him in the predator enclosure as if his shout had startled it. He ran along the narrow flagstone path with swamp privet grasping at his clothes. They broke through the last of the vegetation into the clearing around the pond, and he spotted her at the same time Drew gasped. Why hadn't she answered him?

Paradise stood motionless on the right side of the pond, staring into a tree. Something glittered on her wrist.

"There's a leopard," Drew whispered. "Above her head." He reached for the tranq gun and aimed.

"It's got a collar on. It didn't attack her before." But the way its tail lashed told him the leopard was agitated and might make a different choice this time. Could he scare it off? "Don't look it in the eye. Drew, you have your real gun?" When he nodded, Blake exhaled with relief. "The tranq works too slow. Shoot your gun off in the air after I start yelling."

Blake snatched a fallen tree branch beside the trail and held it aloft. "Hey, you there! Get out of here. We don't want you here." He spread out his left arm and waved the branch in his right as he approached the tree where the leopard crouched.

The animal's blue eyes watched Blake advance, and it flinched when a gunshot sounded. It pinned its ears back and backed away before vanishing into the canopy of trees overhead.

Paradise whirled and ran straight into Blake's arms. He held her trembling shoulders. "He's gone. And why are you soaking wet?" She smelled of pond and mud. Had the thing chased her into the water?

She stepped away and held up her arm with something circling her wrist. "It's a long story. I need to warm up and I'll tell you what happened."

CHAPTER 12

WITH HER WET HAIR draped over the towel around her shoulders, Paradise sat on the floor in front of the fire crackling in the fireplace with all the kittens on her lap. The aroma of her plumeria shampoo had replaced the stink of pond water. She'd finally stopped shivering and warmth crept through her muscles. Blake, Jenna, and Drew had listened in silence as she went through what had happened out at the pond.

Blake settled beside her and showed her the pet collar in his hands. "Someone put this on the bridge to lure you out."

Drew paced the floor beside them. "While you were taking a shower, I went out there. I retrieved some of the boards. The bridge was sabotaged to collapse when you got out there. This was no accident."

Paradise flinched. "I could have broken a leg."

"Or worse," Blake said. "That gator could have kept on coming." He pointed to a small button of plastic. "There's a tracking device on this collar too. It connects to someone's smartphone."

"Did you try easing away from the leopard once you saw it?" Drew asked.

She nodded. "Every time I tried to move a few inches, the leopard's tail lashed even more. I kept an eye on him but didn't challenge him with direct eye contact. I'd used the board I had on the gator, and I wasn't close enough to any tree limbs to arm myself that way. I knew you'd come."

A lump formed in her throat at those minutes of terror. She would never be at ease around big cats, especially jaguars. She wasn't frozen in fear now, but she had a healthy fear and respect for them in the wild.

She rose and headed for the kitchen. "I'm going to make coffee. I don't think I'll be going to sleep anytime soon. Anyone else want a cup?"

"Me," the men chorused behind her.

Blake followed her and crossed the kitchen to the fridge. "Mom made brownies too."

She nodded and got the coffee going. "Someone seems determined to frighten me." She turned at Drew's footsteps.

He took down three mugs and set them by the coffeepot. "I'm the catalyst that started it all, Sis. The killer knows he's in the bull's-eye of our investigation. He's afraid the truth is going to come out. Whoever killed your parents—and my father—is still out there. He lives nearby and has been able to observe everything we're doing to get to the truth."

The word *sis* on his lips brought a lump to her throat. This wasn't only for her to figure out. They were all in this together—Blake, Jenna, Drew, even Abby and her cousins. The truth would have to come out when faced with such a formidable force as all of them bound by love.

Blake set the plate of brownies on the counter and whipped out his phone. "Let's make a plan of attack. Trisha and Wes were helpful. We need to talk to Donald Phillips, the HR manager who used to work with your mom at Tupelo Grove University. We could go see him tomorrow after the governor's aide leaves."

Drew snagged a brownie. "I'd like to talk to the detectives on the original case. I know the lead investigator died, but others would have been working it too. I'll talk to Jane Dixon tomorrow while you're with the governor's aide."

"And we have the family picnic on Sunday," Blake said. "That might give us some new leads."

"We need to track down neighbors who lived on the street back then," Drew said.

"One of them works here," Paradise said. "Evan lived on the block. He was in his teens then. I've talked to him, but you're trained at interrogation. He might remember something he didn't tell me."

She took a brownie and bit into it. The soft, chewy chocolate taste was heaven after swallowing too much pond water. She kept remembering the leopard's blue eyes fixed on her and the way its tail lashed. "I just thought of something. What if the leopard belongs to Creed? If he had a pet lemur, he could have a pet leopard. I think we need to check out his premises."

"He'd never let us on the property," Blake said. "But we could have Mason send a drone over it."

Their teenage volunteer at the park was obsessed with his drones. "That's a great idea," Paradise said.

Drew pulled a notepad from his shirt pocket and scribbled in it. "You remember anyone else who lived nearby?"

"Doris Martinez lived next door to us. I don't know where she is now though."

Jenna came through the doorway, her dark brown bob tousled and her blue eyes sleepy. "Doris lives at an independent-living place in Pelican Harbor. I didn't remember she was your neighbor, Paradise. And I know her well. We can all go visit her when we can. And interrogate me. Maybe I'll remember something I've forgotten." Jenna yawned. "But not tonight. I heard you all talking and was afraid I was missing something. Seven will arrive before we know it. You should all go to bed. Coffee at midnight is a terrible idea."

But the aroma was more than Paradise could resist. "We'll quiet down so you can sleep. The boys will be crawling in bed with you before you know it."

"I won't get much sleep on the sofa anyway," Blake said.

Paradise was sleeping with Levi tonight, and he tended to sprawl crossways. She was wired enough not to sleep even without coffee. In spite of the close call tonight, she had hope they might get to the bottom of all this.

Blake raised the pot in his hand toward the governor's aide, Angela Burns, seated on the sofa in the park's reception room. "Coffee?"

She'd arrived promptly at nine in a short-sleeved navy dress with sensible pumps. He knew she was in her mid-fifties, but she looked younger and her arms were toned and muscular. Her soft white hair accentuated her angular features and youthful skin. She must have gone gray early.

Angela crossed her ankles and smiled. "I'd love some, thank you." Her shrewd blue eyes narrowed on Paradise, who carried a plate of brownies toward her. "I'm glad you could join us, Ms. Alden. I didn't get a chance to talk to you last time, but the governor is very interested in your role here at the park."

Paradise set the brownies on the coffee table in front of the sofa and took a seat in a chair opposite the governor's aide. "I was trained in exotic animal veterinary science, and I'm privileged to take care of the many animals here at the refuge."

Angela reached for her cup of coffee and thanked Blake. "I hear you're originally from this area and returned after many years away. Where did you live?"

"In Nova Cambridge, four miles away across the Kate Norris Bridge. I left when I was fifteen."

Blake caught Paradise's haunted expression. "She's been a terrific asset. She knows so much about all the animals, from the lemurs to the snakes."

Angela shuddered. "I abhor snakes. A run-in with a copperhead is what finally drove me inside to the gym instead of running along trails. Terrible creatures."

Paradise shot Blake a smile of thanks. "Most people hate snakes. I find the boas fascinating."

"I'll let you deal with them."

Blake glanced at his watch. "When would Governor George like to come to The Sanctuary, and what does she want to do while here?"

Burns smiled. "Keeping us on topic, I see. We'd like to come in two weeks. The governor would like to have a special tour with the tigers with details about their majesty and strength. We'll have media here to record the animals in the background while she talks about her determination to fight for high-paying jobs and adequate housing in Alabama. Since her first visit, supporters have been calling her 'the Tigress.' Seeing the big cats in their natural habitats will enhance her messages about fighting for constituents. She's happy about the exposure her ad will give to the park, but even though her presence will lift up The Sanctuary, she's donating a hundred thousand dollars to the park and will present that check while the reporters are here."

Blake exchanged an excited glance with Paradise. "That's very generous, and we're happy to assist the governor."

Burns took a final sip of her coffee and rose to gather her handbag. "I'll let Governor George know. She and I will arrive with the crew at 8:00 a.m., and we plan to begin shooting at nine. We'll start with video of the big cats in their dens or whatever you call where they sleep. That will be used for clips about housing. I think we should be done by lunch or a little after."

Blake walked her to the door and opened it. "Thank you again, Ms. Burns." He shut the door behind her and did a fist pump before picking up Paradise and twirling her in his arms. "A hundred grand! We can expand some of the habitats. I'd especially like to enlarge the range for the big cats."

She wrapped her arms around his neck and held on. "I can't believe how quickly things have changed. A month ago we were in danger of losing everything, even ownership and what you and your mom invested. God is good."

"He's good all the time, even when things look bleak. Even if we lost it all, he's still good." He set her back on the ground and kissed her, lingering over the softness of her lips and the sweet scent of her breath. "Someone sneaked a brownie when no one was looking," he teased. "I think this is cause for a celebration and I'll have one myself."

He kept possession of her hand, and they walked to the plate of brownies where he snagged the largest piece. He ate the sweet chocolate reward with thankfulness welling in his chest. It was like Paradise had said—their circumstances had changed so quickly it almost gave him whiplash.

Paradise reached for her coffee. "I liked Angela. She seemed genuinely engrossed in what we do here. I wonder if her initial interest is what led the governor to come here in the first place.

Had she ever visited before she brought Governor George here?"

"She looked familiar, so maybe she came with her family. I should have asked her. People tell people who tell people, and the cycle continues."

The door opened and his mother entered. "How'd it go?"

He grinned at the hopefulness in her voice. "The governor is going to use the park as a backdrop for some of her new campaign ads. They're calling her 'the Tigress' now." He held up his hand when his mother clapped her hands. "That's not all. She's donating a hundred thousand dollars to the park!"

His mom put her hand to her mouth and her eyes filled with tears. "Blake, you have to be kidding me."

"No joke, Mom. I wouldn't do that to you. I'm already planning how to spend it."

Tears spilled down her cheeks. "I'm so thankful. Wait until I tell Frank."

"I can't wait to tell Drew. He's heading this way." Paradise motioned through the window for her brother to join them.

Drew entered a few moments later. "You're all smiling so I assume it went well."

"It couldn't have been better." Paradise told him what had happened. "Did you talk to Jane Dixon?"

"I did. There's one other officer around who might know something about the case. He lives out on Fort Morgan Road. I called him and arranged for us to talk to him tonight after dinner if you want to come along."

Blake's spirits soared even more at the hope in Paradise's face, but he worried that solving the murders might prove harder than saving The Sanctuary.

CHAPTER 13

FORT MORGAN ROAD WAS Paradise's favorite place in the Gulf Shores area. She watched for glimpses of the Gulf of America on one side and Mobile Bay on the other. Many of the homes were on stilts, and the sugar-white sand was a dream to see and to walk on.

Detective Booker Lewis lived out on the peninsula along Mobile Bay across from The Beach Club. The small ranch-style home had a killer view of the gentle waters of the bay. The large yard was nicely manicured with a small vegetable garden. Blake parked, and the three of them got out to the sound of voices on the water side.

Drew gestured to the walkway that skirted the side of the house. "He said they were working on the new deck out on the water. Nice place."

"Cute," Paradise agreed. Their shoes crunched on the crushed oyster shells as they rounded the house to the front. She spotted a man and a woman sitting on a small pier. The salty breeze lifted Paradise's hair and blew it in her face. She should have pulled it back today.

Drew took the lead and walked ahead of them. Even in shorts and a tee, he appeared in charge and professional. Every time she'd had to ask questions, she felt out of her element, but her brother was used to this.

Blake took her hand, and she laced her fingers with his as they fell behind Drew a few feet. "I hope Lewis has some unseen files for you."

"Me too. I was trying to remember if I'd ever talked to him. My memories of that time are still faint."

The pier shuddered when they stepped onto the new boards, and the man turned their way. He wasn't much taller than Paradise, but his thick muscles flexed with power under his tee. His cropped Afro highlighted intelligent brown eyes that narrowed when he spotted them. Paradise was filled with a distinct memory of him putting his hand on her head and telling her he was sorry.

He held out his hand. "Detective Booker Lewis, and you must be Detective Drew Bartley." He gestured to the woman standing to one side with a shy smile. She was softly rounded with dark brown hair. "My wife, Chantel."

Drew shook her hand and made the introductions to Blake and Paradise.

Booker's expression softened. "You were just a little thing when I saw you last."

"You were the first officer to come that night," she said. "You had tears in your eyes when you led me out of the bedroom."

"We have a daughter about your age. When I got home that night, I went into her bedroom and kissed her while she was sleeping. You went through a terrible thing, Ms. Alden, just terrible."

"Call me Paradise." She glanced Chantel's way. "I think you came to the funeral?"

Chantel nodded. "We both did. I made sun tea if you'd like some."

"That would be great," Drew said. "We're still floundering on where to look for their killer."

Booker gestured to an outdoor seating area around a firepit, and they all took a seat. A worn notebook lay on a table next to one of the chairs, and he picked it up. "These are my notes, and I scanned them into an email and sent them to you, but I thought maybe we'd go over them together. They might trigger a memory for you, Paradise. Me too, for that matter." He placed the notebook on his lap and flipped open the cover. "The thing that struck me was that all the doors were unlocked even though it was late—11:01 p.m. to be precise. Did your parents commonly lock their doors?"

"Sure. Mom was kind of paranoid about making sure we were locked in tight, especially when Dad was out of town like that night."

"And you weren't expecting him back yet?"

"He was supposed to be gone two nights, and he'd left that morning before coming back in the night. I didn't see him though, not until h-he was dead."

"You were so traumatized you didn't tell us many details of what happened. You remember now?"

She nodded. "Mom was reading to me, and she sat up when she heard a sound. She whispered for me to hide in the closet, so I scrambled into it and hid in the back." Paradise could almost smell the vanilla sachet in her memory. "I peeked from under the clothes and saw her bare feet when she grabbed a baseball bat and turned toward the door."

Her mouth went dry, and she had to swallow before she could continue. "Mom screamed, and I heard the baseball bat smack into something. I didn't scream though, and the intruder never found me. We thought for a while it was Sheriff Davis, but the man I caught a glimpse of was slim and strong, not bulky like the sheriff."

Booker shot her a surprised glance. "You suspected the sheriff?" His wife returned with a tray of iced sweet tea and handed the glasses around.

Paradise accepted one. "His wife told us he and my mom were having an affair."

Booker shook his head. "It's interesting Bea would lie when she knew better."

"She said he'd asked for a divorce to marry my mom, then changed his mind."

Booker gave a disgusted snort. "She knew that wasn't true."

Paradise glanced at Blake and saw the same confusion on his face that she felt. "Then why was he over there all the time?"

"Gerald Davis was protecting you guys."

It took a second for the words to penetrate. "*Protecting* us? From what?"

Booker glanced from her to Drew. "The sheriff knew your dad, Drew. Once your dad found Becky again, that summer before the murders, he asked Sheriff Davis to watch out for her. He thought that when he told his wife he wanted a divorce, she might try to hurt Becky."

Drew leaned forward. "What's my father's name?"

"I don't know. I wish I did. Gerald wouldn't tell me. He spilled this much the night of the murders. He was talking crazy—saying it was his fault and he should have protected her. When I questioned him, he told me he was supposed to protect her, but then he clammed up. I was never able to get more out of him."

Paradise almost spilled the glass of tea in her hand. Blake put his hand on her knee and whispered, "Steady."

She set her free hand on top of his and gulped. This changed everything.

Paradise felt as though she might throw up the few gulps of sweet tea residing in her stomach. As they entered Pelican Harbor, she ran her window down in Blake's truck and inhaled the aroma of freshly mown grass and salt water. Booker hadn't had any other evidence to offer, but his bombshell had been enough to shake the foundations of all they thought they knew about the case.

Blake pulled into Bea's driveway. "You sure you want to do this now? I think we're all shell-shocked, and I'm not sure we'll have the right questions."

"I have plenty of questions," Paradise said.

Drew shoved open his door in the back seat. "And I want answers."

Blake shut off the engine and opened his door. "We can always come back."

Paradise hadn't called Bea because she wanted the element of surprise. She was relieved when she spotted Bea's curly salt-and-pepper hair from where she was bent over pulling weeds in the front flower bed. She wore capris and a sleeveless shirt. A wide-brimmed hat shaded her face from the bright sunlight. She stood and faced them when the truck doors slammed.

Her smile dimmed when they neared, and her gaze darted from Paradise to Blake before landing on Drew. "I-is something wrong?" Her soft Southern drawl trembled, and her hand went to her throat.

Paradise reached out and brushed cobwebs from Bea's hair. "Looks like you've been in the attic or the basement."

Bea leaned over and brushed her hair vigorously. "Going through Gerald's man cave in the basement." She straightened and planted her hands on her hips. "What's going on?"

"We learned some disturbing news today." Paradise gestured at her brother. "This is my brother, Drew. Andrew Bartley."

"You found him."

"Yes." Paradise forced her fists to unfurl. They were standing there like guards about to take the woman in front of a firing squad. Toning down the immediate accusations might get more answers. "I'm sorry to burst in on you without warning, but we just came from talking to Booker Lewis. We think whoever murdered my parents killed Drew's father first."

Bea put her hand to her mouth. "His father is dead? When did this happen?"

"The week before my parents were murdered. Your husband wasn't having an affair with my mother at all. Why did you tell me he was?"

Bea paled and took a step back. "I—I don't know what you're talking about."

Drew put his hand on Paradise's arm. "I'll handle it," he whispered. "Mrs. Davis, Booker told us the truth. The sheriff was trying to protect Becky. He didn't file for divorce—you did. I verified it in the court system on the drive here. You filed for divorce, then dropped the case. Why did you lie about it?"

Bea licked her lips and stared down at her feet. "That's none of your business."

"It could be relevant to our investigation. There has to be a reason you lied to Paradise and tried to cast the blame on your husband. He isn't here to defend himself, but we'd like the truth."

Bea's panicked gaze connected with Paradise's, and she wrung her hands. "I just wanted the case to be over. You were poking around something that was over long ago. There was no reason to be digging up all that old dirt."

"Justice is a good reason," Paradise said in a quiet voice.

Something about Bea's behavior struck her as odd. The woman kept glancing down the street as if she thought someone else was coming. "Wait a minute," Paradise said slowly. "Lloyd Adams was at your house several times. Does he know something about all this?"

Bea shook her head. "No, no, that's not it." She chewed on her lip and left a trace of lipstick on her teeth. "I—I can't say more. Can't you just let it go? You're making yourselves the targets of a very dangerous person."

"Was Adams here to warn you?"

The color washed out of Bea's cheeks. "I can't talk to you." She whirled and ran for the house. Drew followed her but she slammed the door before he could get there. The distinctive *click* of a lock snapping into place told them the conversation was over.

His expression grim, Drew rejoined them on the lawn. "We'll try again. This conversation isn't over. Lloyd Adams was your foster dad, right?"

"Yes. He's in jail awaiting trial."

Drew headed for the truck. "I think we should have a chat with him. He might know who's behind this."

Blake took Paradise's hand and followed. "I'm not so sure. He's a small-town punk with no power any longer."

"But he might know things," Drew said.

Paradise glanced toward the house and saw the curtains flutter. Bea was watching from inside. "She's terrified, Drew. I don't think she would be afraid of Adams. Whoever is behind this has killed three people. We can talk to Adams, but I doubt he knows anything, and even if he does, he won't tell us. It's his way of thinking he has power over me. He's small and mean and cruel. Bea was truly frightened. The sheriff took the threat seriously and was at our house quite a lot before the murders."

Blake stopped with his hand on the truck door, and his eyes widened. "Wait a minute. If the sheriff knew who was behind this, why did he let the scuttlebutt and rumors about his involvement stand? Clearly the police force didn't believe it. Booker dismissed it out of hand. The sheriff deliberately didn't correct the gossip. Drew, you might want to look at the sheriff's finances. Maybe he was paid to cover it all up. If that's so, we might be able to find out who paid him."

Drew opened the truck door and climbed in. "I'll check it out."

Paradise got into the truck and took Blake's hand after he slid under the wheel. *Thank you*, she mouthed. He always backed her up and rushed to her defense. She was beginning to get used to the sensation of being cared for and treasured.

CHAPTER 14

THE SCENT OF GRILLING burgers wafted in the air. Blake flipped them over and closed the lid to the grill. He glanced at Drew, who had paced the backyard after the explosive discussion with Booker Lewis and then Bea. Paradise sat on the deck reading a story to the boys, while his mother finished making potato salad to go with the meal.

They all appeared a little shell-shocked. Even his mother had been taken aback at Booker's bombshell and Bea's refusal to provide more information. They all turned to stare at Drew when his phone rang. Maybe it was the report on the Davises' finances, though they'd all thought it might be hard to track that down over twenty years after the fact.

Drew's expression was grim, and he talked in a voice too low for Blake to make out. Paradise finished the picture book and set it aside. The boys scampered over to the swings, and she descended the steps to stand by Blake. "Can you hear what's happening with Drew?"

He shook his head. "Whatever it is, it doesn't appear to be what he'd hoped to hear. You okay?"

She slipped her arms around his waist and leaned against his chest. "We knew it was a tangled web, but we didn't know just how convoluted it was going to become."

"I'm praying Bea's conscience starts bothering her and she tells us what she knows. She was clearly terrified. Maybe we should be scared too."

"Why would Drew's father ask Gerald to protect Mom? And that brings up my next question of whether Dad would have been killed too if he'd been gone. Mom appears to have been the target."

Blake rested his chin on top of her head. "We don't know who was killed first. Did the killer hit your mom first, then your dad came in and was collateral damage?"

Her arms tightened around his waist. "I'm ready to get life back to normal. I hate that you're sleeping on the sofa again. Drew and I could go to my place, and you could take back your apartment."

"Drew and I both think it's safer to all be together until the danger to you has passed. Besides, if the goal is to keep the truth of the murders hidden, Drew is likely in as much danger as you. He's safer here than by himself at your place."

Paradise nodded. "I suppose so."

"I don't mind sleeping on the sofa." It wasn't the most comfortable spot, but he'd slept on the ground in Afghanistan often enough while stationed overseas. Being near enough to protect the woman he loved was worth sleeping on a wire rack. "I'd better flip the burgers." He kissed her and stepped away when she let go of him. "Want to grab the buns? These burgers are ready to come off. The hot dogs are done too."

She wheeled toward the door. "I'm on it."

Drew had finished his call and strode toward Blake with his

jaw set and his eyes narrowed. He spared a glance at his sister and waited to speak until she returned with the plate of buns. "The bank doesn't keep financial records that far back. By law they have to keep them seven years, but some hang on to them internally for longer periods. This bank kept them for ten years, but that's still not long enough."

"What about tax records?" Paradise asked.

Drew blew out a huff of air. "Same situation. The IRS only keeps them seven years."

"What's next?" Paradise asked.

"I'll talk to Adams and see if he knows anything. And we can move on to the next item on our list." He consulted a note on his phone. "My partner found an address for the PI, William Fletcher. Seems to still be a PI, though he's got to be in his seventies."

"Road trip?" she asked.

Her brother nodded. "In person would be best, and he's in Pascagoula so that's an hour and a half away."

Blake put the burgers on the buns. "When do you want to go?"

"As soon as possible. Tomorrow if we can."

Drew wasn't letting any grass grow under his feet. Blake nodded. "I'd like to have Mason send a drone over Creed's property and see if he's behind the leopard scares targeting Paradise, but we wouldn't have to be here for that."

"Works for me," Paradise said.

"Before we go, I'll make sure Fletcher will be around. I have his number." Drew held his phone to his ear and walked a few feet away.

"I haven't been to Pascagoula in ages," she said. "I wish there was time to enjoy the trip."

"What would you like to do there?"

"I'd go to the lighthouse and maybe get pictures of the boys under the Gateway Oak. The town has probably changed a lot since we were in our teens. Remember when we went with your mom and you gave me that plastic ring?"

"How could I forget?" He'd thought she'd pushed it out of her memory along with so many other things. "You kissed me for the first time on the Ferris wheel."

She poked him with her elbow. "I remember it very differently. *You* kissed *me*, and I thought for sure it was over because I was so surprised I couldn't figure out how to kiss you back."

He chuckled. "Oh, you knew how just fine. I was ready for seconds but was afraid to scare you off."

"I still had that plastic ring until my cabin caught fire five months ago."

"Really?" A plan began to form. What if he gave her the real ring in Pascagoula? It would take some arranging to get pictures and the family involvement he knew she'd love, but it would be worth it to bring their relationship full circle.

Drew turned. "No go for tomorrow, guys. Fletcher's in California and won't be back until late Sunday evening. I snagged a lunch appointment on Monday though. Let's talk to Mr. Phillips instead. And I still want to talk to Lloyd Adams."

Which would give Blake time to make those plans.

It felt like every prisoner in the place was staring at them. While Blake tugged on his collar, Drew didn't appear to be uncomfortable at the jail in Bay Minette. Blake assumed he was used to interviewing suspects as part of his job.

They waited on their side of the glass for Adams. It wasn't long before the man came through the door with a guard. His light brown hair was stringy and greasy. He took a seat and grabbed the phone with a meaty hand. Drew reached for the one on their side.

Adams's gaze went from Blake to Drew and puzzlement lingered in his hazel eyes. "You look like Paradise."

Drew stared back. "I'm her brother."

"Didn't know she had one. Where were you when she needed a home?"

"I didn't know about her then. I'm Detective Drew Bartley, and I have some questions for you."

"Can't say I have answers."

Blake clenched his fists and wished he could smash one into the man's insolent face. Jail hadn't improved Adams's attitude. Blake drew a deep breath and resolved not to let his anger control him. Drew knew how to handle men like this.

"You know Bea Davis."

Adams snorted. "Doesn't sound like a question. Everyone knows Bea."

"Why were you at her house before you landed in here?"

Anger flashed in Lloyd's face, and he let out a string of curses. "So now it's against the law to visit an old friend? She and the sheriff were best friends with me and my wife for thirty years. I was just checking in while I was in town. And she's always been good about helping me out on occasion."

"We know you were trying to get information about Paradise. Was there any other reason you were at Bea's house?"

A crafty expression lurched onto Lloyd's face. "I don't have to tell you anything."

"No, you don't, but I can let law enforcement know you cooperated in an ongoing investigation." Drew stood. "But that's fine. Go back to your cell if you don't want to help us out."

"I didn't say I wouldn't help. What's this all about?"

"We're investigating the deaths of Paradise's parents," Blake said.

"I never met them so I can't really give you any information."

Blake could tell this wasn't going anywhere. Paradise was right. "Bea's husband was the sheriff when it happened. She led us to believe he was having an affair with Paradise's mother, Becky. It wasn't true. If you were such good friends, maybe you know why she'd tell us that."

Amusement crinkled Lloyd's crow's-feet. "You'd better look elsewhere. It's all your fault I'm in here. Yours and hers."

What a dud of an interview. Their time was up, and the men walked to the parking lot in silence. The fresh air cleared away the stink of the jail.

A truck rumbled by, and Wade Greene's eyes went wide when he spotted them. He turned around at the next drive and drove in beside them. Smiling, Wade got out and walked toward Blake with his hand out. "I was on my way to the clerk's office and couldn't believe my eyes when I spotted you. I've been meaning to stop over and see you, buddy. Thanks for coming to Elowen's rescue the other day. That was a tight spot, and I couldn't get to her."

Blake gripped his hand, and Wade clapped him on the shoulder. Drew came around to join them, and Blake introduced him to Wade. "We were glad to be able to help. King Julien is doing well now. He's enjoying being with other lemurs."

Wade's smile faded. "Creed was livid. Our relationship has been strained for a long time, but I'd guess it's beyond repair for the moment."

"I'm sorry. He came by demanding the lemur back, but we refused. Julien was in a bad way, and we couldn't do it. Rod backed us up, and the state gave us custody."

"Glad to hear it. Since we aren't speaking, Creed hasn't updated me on the lemur's situation. He sure hates you guys."

"Do you know why? We've never been able to figure it out. It all started when he made a pass at Paradise and she turned him down. When that activist Danielle Mason was found murdered on our property, he was determined to find me guilty."

Wade shook his head. "We had different fathers, and his was awful. Creed showed up after visits with bruises and injuries, but Mom was never able to get those visits stopped. He has always taken his unhappiness out on other people. Any slight has to be punished forever. If Paradise rejected him, he'll never forget it. You're likely collateral damage and lumped in with her. Try not to take it personally. Just stay out of his way and hope he moves on to another victim."

"Kind of hard to do when he keeps showing up to investigate."

Wade's gaze swung to Drew. "You have to be related to Paradise."

"I'm her brother. I'm in town helping her try to find out who killed our parents, and someone seems determined to drive us away," Drew said. "Maybe once we get to the bottom of the murders, there won't be any incidents Creed has to check out. If he comes to the park again, I'll handle him."

But Drew had no authority in Alabama, and Blake couldn't see Creed backing down. They'd have to deal with him until this was over.

CHAPTER 15

DONALD PHILLIPS LIVED ALONG a quiet street in Magnolia Springs. On the way to his house, they passed people mowing and trimming shrubs on this beautiful Saturday morning. The Creole-style home was set back off the street toward the back of an acre lot with moss dangling from the live oak trees lining the driveway. Rhododendrons and azaleas threw out an extravagance of color under the trees along the west side of the house.

Drew had checked records on the man. Donald's wife had died two years ago, and he was nearly eighty. Paradise's call asking to talk to him had probably been a bright spot in his week.

Blake parked in front of the garage door. "Looks like he's waiting for us."

The man rose from the porch swing with a broad smile. His gray hair was neat and trimmed. A pitcher of lemonade and a package of store-bought iced oatmeal cookies were on a table. "You must be Paradise Alden. You're just as pretty as your mother." He gestured to the chairs as the three of them stepped to the porch and took a seat. "It's a warm day so lemonade sounded good even if it's from a mix." Donald poured the drink into glasses and handed them around. "I love the sound of ice tinkling in glasses, don't you?"

"I sure do." Paradise sipped the lemonade, which wasn't bad. "Thanks for seeing us." She introduced Drew and Blake. "Did you know my mother well?"

He tore open the bag of cookies and retrieved one. "I hired her, and we often ate lunch together in the cafeteria. Her pottery was beautiful. I still have the coffee mug she made me. And she was a dedicated fine arts teacher. Students loved her. My, how she loved you. I saw many pictures of you as a child."

A lump formed in Paradise's throat. Her cousin had said the same thing, except when it spilled off Lily's lips, it had been with derision. "I loved her very much."

"I'd heard you were looking into what happened. It's about time someone did. I said all along the detectives weren't investigating very hard."

Glass in hand, Drew leaned forward. "Why did you believe that?"

"She was afraid," Donald said. "Someone had been following her. They broke into the house a few times and moved things around as if to let her know she wasn't safe."

"Did you tell the police about this after the murders?" Drew asked.

"Of course. They made note of it, but there was no call record of her reporting a break-in, so I think law enforcement dropped the thread."

"Did she say who she thought might be targeting her?"

Donald demolished the cookie in two bites before shaking his head. "She admitted she'd reconnected with a former lover and thought the harassment was someone in his family discouraging the affair. I'll admit I was shocked she would betray her husband when it would hurt her daughter."

Drew set his lemonade on the table. "I think that man was my father. I was adopted and never met him, but hearing about his death and then the way Paradise's parents died triggered my interest in whether the deaths were connected."

A tiger cat leaped onto Blake's lap, and he stroked it a moment. "One thing we've heard is that Drew's father was well-to-do. Did you ever stop to think you might have more siblings out there, Drew? We're assuming the murderer wants to stop our investigation because of the fear of discovery, but it could be something else."

"The thought has crossed my mind," Drew said. "Maybe I was the firstborn and there were provisions in a will. Until we discover the man's name, we're at a dead end. Did our mother ever mention anyone by name?"

Phillips pulled a pipe from his pocket. "You mind?" When they shook their heads, he lit it and puffed out a plume of cherrywood-scented smoke. "I overheard her on the phone about a month before the murders. I caught a glimpse of her phone with the name 'Benny' on it. She quickly left the cafeteria and went outside to sit on a bench by herself. I could see her through the window, and she appeared agitated. At one point she stood and paced while gesturing with her free hand. She was perspiring when she came in and put her things away with angry movements. She was on the verge of tears the whole time."

"Did you ask her what was wrong?" Paradise asked.

His rheumy blue eyes stared at her through the smoke, and he finally nodded. "She said it was personal. I asked if she thought it had anything to do with someone harassing her. She just shook her head, but I saw fear flash into her eyes."

"Were there any other incidents?" Drew asked.

"Just one. The day before she died, she gave me a file of pictures and told me to give them to her son. I was going to give them to you, Paradise, because I didn't know where to look for a son. But they belong to Drew." Donald reached under the wicker coffee table and pulled out a folder, then handed it to Drew. "I was quite happy when you called. I'm happy to finally be able to complete my promise to your mother."

Drew's eyes widened and he slowly reached for the folder. Uncertainty flickered in his eyes, but he shook the pictures out onto the table. There were four pictures—one of Drew in his early twenties. The other three pictures were of two boys and a girl. Paradise reached for Drew's picture and looked at the writing on the back. "This was in 2011. You would have been twenty-one." She read the numbers on the other pictures. "One is a year older than you, and two are younger. Your siblings?"

Drew's expression was hard to read. "If they are, they're suspects." He reached for the photos. "I can run these through facial recognition and try to find out who they are and where they live, though I'm not hopeful since they're children and these were taken so long ago."

The thought of sharing her newfound brother with more family stirred something in Paradise's chest. Jealousy was an ugly feeling.

"Donald, are there any other people you think might know more about Mom's private life?"

"Did you speak to Greta Welch?"

Paradise shook her head. "She knew my mother well?"

"The two of them worked together at the college, and Greta was torn up about Becky's death. She wouldn't talk about it, but I always thought she knew more about the guy than anyone else did."

Paradise glanced at her watch. There was plenty of time to talk to Greta before they had to get back. But first, lunch.

The guys had been all for grabbing lunch at Jesse's Restaurant in Magnolia Springs. They opted to eat outside at one of the tables with the lively blue-and-white chairs. The weather was gorgeous with a light breeze that carried the scent of roses. The setting felt like being cocooned with beautiful trees and plants. The men had spilled most of what Adams told them on the drive back.

She ordered shrimp and grits and a club soda with lime. Both guys got Jesse's burgers and iced tea. Her stomach rumbled in spite of her need to talk. "I'd hoped Adams would tell us something important. We still don't know why he went to see Bea."

Drew reached for a piece of bread and buttered it. "Maybe he was blackmailing her. He seems the type to poke around and learn things."

The server brought their drinks to the table, and Paradise squeezed her lime into her club soda. "It feels so hopeless right now."

Drew set his hand over hers and gave it a gentle squeeze. "Take heart, Sis. We're getting more and more information. Who knows where the ripples will take us? I think we're close to finding out my father's surname. The floodgates will open once we find that out."

She ran her finger around the beaded moisture on her glass. "Drew, if your adoptive parents talked to our mom through the years, why didn't they give you the information? You had to wait to find it through DNA."

"I've always wondered that. The last time I pressed them, we had a big blowup and things were tense for weeks. I decided to find out on my own. I think they didn't want me to search for my birth family."

"Do you think they were worried you'd be in danger?" Paradise asked.

He lifted a brow. "I'm a police detective. I face danger just shaving every morning."

She chuckled but he wasn't wrong. For a moment she was tempted to tell him she was worried about him finding his father's family. What if she lost him just as she'd found him and grown to love him? It felt selfish and probably was, so she took another sip of her drink to swallow down the confession.

The modest mid-seventies home in Foley matched many others on the block. Meticulous landscaping and a plethora of azaleas and rhododendrons. Blake hadn't called first.

The woman answered the door on the first ring and stared at them for a long moment. "You have to be Paradise Alden," she said finally. "You look just like Becky." Her blond hair was a sleek bob, and he guessed her to be in her fifties.

"We're sorry to drop by with no call, but I have some questions about my mother, and I hoped you wouldn't mind."

Greta stepped out of the way. "Come in."

They followed her deeper into the home's interior, past the living room and kitchen, to a family room with light streaming through patio doors. The glass looked out on a desk nearly bursting with color from flowers arranged in clay planters. The wood floors were spotless and nothing was out of place.

Greta perched on an armchair in the family room. "How can I help? I still think about your mom. She was a good friend."

Paradise settled on the sofa between Blake and Drew. "We spoke with Donald Phillips today, and he mentioned you worked with my mother."

Greta's blue eyes brightened. "Your mother was a wonderful person, full of life and fun. And her art was gorgeous." She pointed out a large floor vase filled with dried pampas grass. "She made that for my birthday, and I treasure it."

"We're investigating the murders," Drew interjected. "She was my mother too. Do you know anything about her affair with my father?"

Greta pursed her lips. "So you're the child born out of wedlock."

"Do you know when Mom and Drew's father started seeing each other again?" Paradise asked.

"It was the October before she died."

Paradise leaned forward. "Do you know how that meeting happened?"

"I saw him," Greta said. "He came to the university. Maybe he was looking for her, or maybe it was accidental. Your mother never said. I saw them together at the charity function, and wow, he was handsome. He wore a tux like it had been made for him. Becky's expression when she looked at him was like he was a god. Her eyes were luminous and she didn't stop smiling. I caught him kissing her in the hallway. When I pressed her about it the next day, I was able to get more details out of her, though she didn't like that I'd seen them."

Blake knew this had to be hitting Paradise hard, and he took her hand. She'd always thought her parents had a great marriage, and maybe they did until this Ben person came back. "What did she say?"

"She told me he was her first love, the one she'd never been able to forget." Greta stared at Paradise. "She and Granger were having some problems. She wanted another baby, and he didn't. He said you were the perfect daughter, and he didn't need any other kids."

Paradise's grip tightened on Blake's. "I asked for a sibling all the time. Did you notice if this Ben wore a wedding ring?"

"First thing I looked for. And yep, he sure did, along with a flashy set of cuff links with a *C* on them. Becky said he wasn't happy in his marriage and was going to divorce his wife."

Blake exchanged a glance with Paradise, and she pulled the plastic bag with the cuff link out of her bag. "Did it look like this?"

Greta stared at it and nodded. "I can't be sure because it was a long time ago, but it appears very similar. I wondered if his wealth swayed her, at least a little bit. Granger's company was struggling, and his pay had been cut, which was why she went to work for TGU in the first place. Having a wealthy, powerful man can be very tempting, but Granger was worth ten of a man who had pursued her when she was only seventeen and he was married."

Drew scowled. "Just like that, she's going to leave Granger and go with the man who lied to her in the first place? Seems foolhardy to me. Money isn't everything."

Greta nodded. "To me too. I pointed out that he'd lied to her once before, so why should she believe him now? Becky didn't have a good answer for that other than she had always loved him, and she felt guilty that she didn't tell him about his son. And she had *Granger*. She didn't even appreciate what she had. Granger was such a great guy. Not just handsome, but kind. He never even looked at another woman, and he was the best father I ever saw, always doing things with Paradise. He never went on a trip without bringing her something. There aren't many men like him out there."

"He was the best," Paradise said in a choked voice.

"Did she ever tell you she was afraid because someone was stalking or harassing her?" Blake asked.

"Yes. I think fear was one of the things that made her decide to tell Granger she was getting a divorce. She believed if the relationship was finally out in the open, the danger would be gone."

"Do you know her lover's full name?" Paradise asked.

"I'm sorry, but I don't. She referred to him as Benny. His family was in politics though, that much I do know."

Drew moved restlessly. "In Alabama? Or maybe Georgia?"

"I don't think it was here. He lived in another state. Mississippi or Louisiana I think."

"Did she ever say if this Ben told his wife he was divorcing her to marry Becky?" Blake asked.

"She said he did, but could she trust that? I'm not so sure."

Blake wasn't either. What a mess Becky had made of her life, and the result had ruined three lives, maybe more since no one knew what had happened in Ben's family.

"What was your take on Greta Welch's information?" Blake asked.

They'd run through a drive-through to get an iced tea, and Paradise stuck her straw in the top of her drink. "You think she's hiding something or lying about it?"

"She talked about missing your mom, but her tone when talking about your dad went in another direction. I think she was jealous of Becky. I'm not saying Greta was lying, but I think she was happy to trash your mother by casting her in as negative a light as possible. And I suspect she didn't tell us everything."

"I have to say there wasn't anything good in Mom's actions, but you're right. Greta kept referring to my dad in very complimentary terms. Is she married, widowed? We don't know anything about her."

Drew looked up from his phone. "I was checking her out. She's been a widow since her daughter was small, and she got a job at TGU to make ends meet. So if she worked with your mom, she might have been eyeing your dad and wishing she had him."

Drew sipped his drink. "Do you suppose she ever made a play for your dad?"

"I'd sure like to find out. I think I'll text Wes and see what he knows." Paradise shot off a quick message to Wes.

The screen on her phone lit up with a reply from Wes. *Greta told your dad to listen to the answering machine. She and Becky had a huge fight, and she didn't even go to the funerals. I forgot all that until you asked.*

Paradise read it to the guys. "Wow, you're a good judge of character, Blake."

"Don't I know it. I had the good sense to snatch you right up." He took a self-satisfied sip of his tea.

CHAPTER 16

PARADISE'S CONDO APPEARED TO be in order when they dropped Drew off at the park, then headed for town. Blake scoped out the fridge for anything that needed to be taken to his mom's house until someone moved back in here and retrieved pepperoni and several cheeses. Paradise was in her bedroom gathering a few more items of clothing.

He zipped the cooler and put it by the door before going in search of her. She sat on the edge of the bed with an open suitcase at her feet. "You about ready?"

She stared at her phone and sighed. "Drew didn't get any hits on the facial recognition.

"This is hard, Blake. We take one step forward and two steps back. I never seem to get anywhere with this investigation, and now here I am sleeping in Levi's bed instead of my own with everyone disrupted again. I want to stay here and find some sense of normalcy."

He knelt in front of her. "I'm sorry, babe. But look at all the leads we've uncovered. Staying together is safest, plus we can talk through the things we're discovering. I mean, finding those pictures of Drew's siblings was a huge development. With Drew's connections he'll find out the identity of his father in no time."

"Maybe. I'm just discouraged tonight." She swept her hand around the room. "All my cozy things are here—my books, my soaps, my candles—everything that feels like home."

He could have told her to bring anything with her she wanted, but it wouldn't be the same as having her own space, and he knew it. He stood and held out his arms. "I'll be your haven whenever you need a hug."

Paradise managed a smile before she stood and stepped into his embrace. He could feel the rhythm of her heartbeat against his chest as he held her and inhaled her plumeria scent. She'd been through so much, but she kept plugging along until circumstances slapped her hard. Even though he knew she'd be her chipper self tomorrow, he ached for her pain and longed to go straight home and slide that ring on her finger. They could start searching for a home together and making plans.

But the timing wasn't right. If he hoped for her to have peace and closure, they had to stay focused. With new clues dropping into their laps, he hoped closure was right around the corner.

She sighed and stepped back. "Let me grab another bottle of shampoo. What I have at your mom's is almost gone."

He watched her cross the room to the small attached bath. His phone dinged with a message, and he glanced at it. Hey, Blake, I found something at Creed's this afternoon. "I heard from Mason." Blake quickly tapped out a response. Can you send me the file?

Sure.

Paradise returned with the shampoo in her hand. "He found the leopard?"

"He didn't say what he found. He's sending the file." His phone dinged with another message. "Let's open it on your desktop." He forwarded the file to her email, and they went to the office down the hall.

He flipped on the computer. "I'd feel a lot better if we found that leopard."

She perched on the edge of the twin bed in the room and hugged herself. "I keep watching the trees and shadows. I'll be glad when I don't have to do that any longer."

The computer screen illuminated, and he settled on the chair in front of it and called up her email, found the file he'd forwarded, and opened it. It took a minute to orient where the property was located. Greene lived out near Elberta, and Blake spied a pond circled by trees. In the woods he glimpsed a metal roof. "Looks like a shed in the woods by the pond. It's enclosed by high fencing like we have at The Sanctuary."

She stood and leaned over his shoulder to look at the video as the drone moved and the camera panned over the site. Her finger touched the screen. Her breath whispered against his ear. "Blake, that's a tranq rifle."

He saw it then. "You're right. And are those chunks of raw meat just inside the fencing?"

"I think so. It's hard to tell for sure. He's got a predator behind that fence though. I'm sure of it."

"We can talk to Rod about it at the cookout tomorrow. Maybe I can get permission to go look when Rod knows you seem to be the leopard's target. That can't be an accident. Creed has had his sights on you since you arrived."

"I wonder what would happen if I talked to his wife. Maybe she'd rein him in."

"Or it would infuriate him so much that you'd be in more danger. Let's talk to Rod before we do anything else."

She put her arms around his neck from behind and leaned against his back. He relished the feel of her against him and the kiss she pressed against his cheek. They'd weather this and find their future.

CHAPTER 17

THE AROMA OF OLD Bay seasoning in the shrimp boil bubbling away wafted on the breeze. The yard bustled with family members greeting each other. Paradise hung back with Drew, waiting for the hubbub of laughter and initial excitement to die down, though she was eager to introduce him to everyone. She wished Blake was by her side, but he was tending to the food.

As they waited she pointed out various members to Drew. "That's Mom's cousin Lily." Lily's lustrous shoulder-length salt-and-pepper hair gleamed in the sunlight. "And that's Rod. He's the sergeant in charge of the Bon Secour sheriff's substation and is Lily's son. You'll have a lot in common with him. His wife is Sheila." She motioned to the smiling woman with red hair and brown eyes. "His sister is Molly, the one with brown hair and hazel eyes. You can't miss her because she and Rod look so much alike. She's a schoolteacher."

Drew stood with his hands in the pockets of his khaki shorts. "They seem happy to see each other. Who will be most helpful for me to learn more about our mom?"

"Probably Lily. She was always a little jealous of me for some reason and has been less than forthcoming, but there's a good chance she'll open up to you. Let's start there." Paradise walked with him across the freshly mowed grass to intercept her cousin. "Lily, I know you're as eager to meet Drew as he is to get to know you. This is Drew Bartley."

Lily's hazel eyes narrowed before she smiled. "I heard you found him, but I didn't expect the two of you to look so much alike. You both take after your mom."

Drew gave her a quick hug when she opened her arms, then stepped back. "I heard you and our mom were very close."

Lily nodded. "First cousins. We were more like siblings though. Her death devastated me."

But not so much that Lily had been willing to spare Becky's child from foster care. Paradise kept the words locked behind her teeth. The past couldn't be changed now, and she'd forgiven Lily.

"What was she like?"

"Becky was wonderful. Terribly creative—she made pottery and quilts. Any kind of craft interested her. She did a lot of baking and took pies and cookies to neighbors."

"Who was my dad?"

Paradise tensed when Drew spilled the crucial question. Lily had always claimed she didn't know, but if she was like a sister to their mother, wouldn't Mom have told her things she didn't tell anyone else?

Lily thought for a moment. "I don't know his name, but I saw him pick her up in a shiny new Camaro after volleyball one night. He had to be ten years older than she was. At first I thought it was a friend of my dad's, but she leaned over and kissed him before she shut the car door. The interior lights showed it was no friendly peck on the cheek."

Paradise was already aware of those details. "We heard his first name was Ben and Mom called him Benny. Did you ever hear that name?"

Lily hesitated before inclining her head. "I really can't say. It was a long time ago."

"I appear to have some siblings from my father's marriage as well," Drew said.

"I'm not surprised. I always wondered if he was already married. He was old enough to be."

"There's one thing we've been puzzling over." Paradise pulled out the baggie holding the cuff link. "We found this mixed in with Drew's baby clothes. Does the *C* ring a bell on Ben's name?"

Lily pursed her lips. "That man she was seeing wore a fancy suit, so I would imagine cuff links might accompany one. But I don't know Ben's last name."

Paradise quelled the shaft of disappointment. She should have known better than to get her hopes up that Lily would be more forthcoming. "I'd love to get that box of items that belonged to my parents. You mentioned it a few weeks ago."

"I brought it with me. It's in the trunk. Here comes Rod. I'll have him get it."

Rod came their way and stopped to extend his hand to Drew. "So you're the new cousin. I could have picked you out anywhere. And I heard you're a police detective in Atlanta. You must get a lot of interesting cases."

Drew gripped his hand. "We see our fair share. I deal with homicides, and we have way too many of those. We've been working to get drugs and gangs off the streets, and our homicide rate has been falling." His hand fell back to his side.

Paradise glanced over at the food table and caught Blake's gaze. He gave a nod as if to say she should go ahead and ask her cousin about Creed. "Um, Rod, Creed came out here mad as a hornet. He wanted his lemur back, and we didn't give it to him."

"He came to me about it too, and I told him to let it drop or face charges. He stomped out of my office, and I haven't heard any more out of him about it."

"That's a relief. There's one more thing though. We've seen a loose leopard roaming here on park property. It wears a collar and isn't ours."

Drew folded his arms across his chest. "And what Paradise is not saying is that she seems to be a target. We have drone footage of Creed's property that shows some interesting fencing and possible meat chunks behind an enclosure that make us think Creed might be the one keeping the leopard as a pet. We'd like to get on the property and find out."

"No pictures of leopards, no indication he actually has one?" Rod shook his head. "I don't think I can get a court order without more proof. And you know he won't agree to letting you roam there."

"What if you urged him?" Paradise asked.

Rod lifted a brow. "You've met Creed Greene, right? I keep hoping he'll quit, but he hangs in there, and I don't have grounds to fire him."

And that would be the end of it unless they could get more proof. Maybe a drone video at night with an infrared camera would be in order.

"Rod, would you get that box I brought for Paradise out of the trunk?" his mother asked.

"Be right back with it."

Paradise had to check the impulse to go with him. There would be no time to look through it until late tonight or tomorrow.

The food had been eaten, and one by one family members said their goodbyes and left. Blake hadn't been able to keep his attention off Paradise as she moved from person to person. She'd changed so much since she arrived nearly six months ago. She'd been wary, a little angry, and a whole lot off-putting. Now her place in the community was firmly established, and it showed in the glow of her amber eyes and the confident smile on her face.

Twilight softened the edges of the trees and buildings, and the scent of impending rain hovered in the air. Paradise sat on the deck glider with a little boy on each side of her as she read them a story. Her presence had been a balm for all of them.

She closed the book and caught his intense gaze. A blush settled in her cheeks, and she smiled. "Isn't it time to feed the predators?"

"It is. Want to come with me?"

"I'd love to." She hugged his brothers. "Time for you guys to take a bath and brush your teeth. I'll be back in time to tuck you in." They protested but slid off the cushions and headed for the door. She descended the steps to where he stood and took his hand. "What a great afternoon. Thank you for making it happen."

"I saw you talking to Rod. Did you get anywhere with searching Greene's property for the leopard?"

She shook her head. "Not enough evidence. I'd like Mason to try the drone at night with his heat-seeking camera."

"I'll text him." Blake released her hand to tap out a quick request to Mason, who answered immediately. "He's already on the road near the house waiting for full darkness. Good kid! Let's hope if he's got a big cat, it's roaming outside and not in the building."

Hand in hand, he and Paradise fell into step to head for the park. By the time they reached the predator area, the darkness had deepened. They neared the small building where the food storage fridge was housed, and he peered through the darkness. "Someone left the door open." Blake held her forearm. "Wait here."

He tried to flip on the light, but nothing happened. A power outage? He turned on his phone's flashlight and shone it around the space. Everything looked normal in the sweep of the light. He stepped to the breaker box and opened it. The breaker was off, so he flipped it and the overhead light came on. Nothing appeared out of order. He unlocked the cabinet for the tranq guns and found them safely nestled inside. The predator food appeared intact inside the fridge.

"Blake?" A tremor shook Paradise's voice.

He ran for the door and found her staring into the trees across the lane that meandered to different buildings. "What's wrong?"

She pointed. "Aim your light into the branch of that tree."

He didn't have to do that to catch the gleam of a big cat's eyes. It lay stretched out on the hefty branch with its gaze fixed on Paradise. The cat's tail wasn't twitching though and its ears were alert and interested, not laid back. "Back away to the building. Text Clark."

Evan had gone home for the day, but Clark Reynolds lived on the property. He'd quickly become an indispensable part of the park workforce and a man as dependable as his twin brother, Kent, who had served with Blake in Afghanistan until his death.

"I think it's best if I don't move. I can text Clark though. Get the gun."

Stubborn woman. Blake returned to the storage building and unlocked the gun cabinet to retrieve a rifle, then grabbed several darts preloaded for big cats and loaded the weapon as he returned to her side.

The big cat hadn't moved, but its tail had begun to lash, and its eyes tracked movement to their left. Clark eased along the fence with his rifle in one hand and a tranq pistol in the other. He stopped and dropped to one knee, then aimed the pistol at the big cat.

The dart struck the leopard in the right shoulder, and it growled as it bit at the offending object sticking out of its skin. It would take at least ten minutes for the tranquilizer to take effect.

Clark motioned for them to move away, so Blake took Paradise's arm and pulled her behind him while they waited. He could have shot a dart as well, but he didn't want to overmedicate the animal. The overdose might kill it.

Paradise stirred behind him. "It's the same cat."

"I noticed the collar looks like the one you recovered from the footbridge." The leopard stood and stretched, then leaped from the tree to the ground, falling awkwardly and heavily into the high grass. It curled up and closed its eyes, but Blake didn't approach. Not until he was sure it was completely out.

Clark moved closer though, his pistol loaded with another dart. His expression radiated satisfaction at a job completed.

Paradise moved to Blake's side, and he put his arm around her waist, relishing the feel of her in his arms. His idea of a romantic stroll in the moonlight had been obliterated. "We might not know who it belongs to, but we'll have the cat safely penned and can check it out. It's possible the owner tagged it." But not likely. Whoever owned it wouldn't want their identity revealed.

Blake glanced at his watch. Ten minutes. It might be safe to approach, but he readied another dart before he walked toward Clark and the prone cat. Paradise walked with him, but he restrained her from going to the leopard first. "Let me."

"I'm the vet."

"And I'll let you take over once I'm sure he's out." Blake reached the big cat and grabbed a fallen stick to prod it with. It didn't move so he tried its muzzle. Still no reaction. "It's out. Good job, Clark."

"I was scared I'd miss." His voice trembled.

This close Blake realized it was a huge male, bigger than he'd thought. He guessed the cat to be five feet long, not counting the tail, and easily 100 pounds. "I'll get a crate and we can load him. You saved us tonight, Clark."

At least the huge cat wasn't stalking Paradise any longer.

CHAPTER 18

THE WARMTH FROM THE leopard's prone body radiated through the gloves Paradise wore. She managed to control her fear enough to remove the collar and hand it to Blake. "He's in good shape. Well fed with strong muscles." She pulled back its lip. "Good teeth too. Someone knows how to maintain a leopard well."

He examined the collar. "So probably not Greene. If he couldn't even take care of a lemur, it's doubtful this guy would be in such good shape. We have an empty enclosure for him."

She nodded. Leopards were loners. "Let's move this big guy to his own space. I do want to point out that Creed only had King Julien a couple of weeks. His poor condition wasn't necessarily Creed's fault."

She turned to Clark, who had been quick to answer Blake's request for help. He had also fed the restless predators while Paradise worked on the leopard. "You guys can use a backboard. It's only a minute or two to get there, and he'll be out a while yet."

Blake and Clark lifted the inert animal onto the backboard while she ran ahead to open the door. The men carried the leopard down the lane to the empty enclosure. Paradise opened the gates as they went, then grabbed straw to throw out for a more comfortable resting place for the leopard.

She did a final check of the cat's heart rate and respiration. "He's doing fine."

The three of them left the enclosure, and Blake made sure both the inner and outer perimeters were locked and secure. "It's fair to say we have a new leopard. The owner wouldn't dare admit he'd trained a big cat to stalk a human."

She exhaled with relief. "I won't have to keep watching the trees."

Blake shook Clark's hand. "Job well done, buddy. Thank you."

"I'm glad I was close." Clark headed for his trailer.

Paradise took Blake's hand to walk back to the house. His firm grip lifted her fatigue, and she slowed her steps to prolong the time with him. "Anything from Mason?"

"I haven't checked my phone." He pulled it out and made a sound of surprise. "He said his camera picked up a couple of predators, but they were wolverines."

"So that would explain the meat left for them."

"I guess so. We're back to square one on finding the owner. I'll give Drew the collar. It matches the one out on the bridge over the pond. Maybe he can track down where they were purchased and see if any were bought in our area."

"It's a long shot."

"It is." Blake stopped and embraced her. "But hey, I got to spend a few hours with my girl, even if she was focused on another male."

"A strong one too. Did you feel that guy's muscles?" She ran her palms down his biceps. "On second thought, you have him beat any day."

"Does that mean it's okay if I rescue you on occasion?"

His teasing grin made her smile. "I'm learning to like it just a little. Your strength doesn't have to make me weak. We complement each other."

He cupped her face in his palms, and his lips met hers in a slow exploration that left her legs trembling. Her breath caught in her throat when she pulled away. "No fair," she whispered. "You have to hold me up."

"I think I can manage that."

He gathered her closer until she couldn't tell where his heart left off beating and hers began. Her fingers tangled in his hair at the back of his head, and she deepened the kiss until her legs were rubber.

He gulped in air when he pulled away. "I'd charge a whole prowl of leopards for just one kiss like that."

"I think it would be worth more, way more." Her lids were heavy, and she didn't want to move from her comfy position against his solid chest. "We should get some sleep."

"You mean you'd rather wrestle with Levi's stretched-out arms and legs than make out with me?"

"I wouldn't say that." She chuckled. "It's way past my bedtime."

He nuzzled her neck. "Clark texted Mom and told her what was going on."

Shivers ran down her spine at the feel of his lips on her neck. She wanted nothing more than to stay right here for the rest of her life. But there was work to do before she could let herself think about what their future might look like. All she knew was that home was wherever Blake was. His faith and strength of character were a beacon she could follow even as she learned more about her own walk of faith. It felt so puny next to his. He'd been through so much, and his steady progress forward never failed. Maybe it had only been a forward progression of inches at times, but he never gave up.

It was hard to think with his warm lips trailing along her neck and jaw. "How do you do it?"

"Do what?"

She smiled. "Stay so strong and focused."

"The only focus I have right now is the taste of your lips."

"And I haven't had chocolate-covered peanuts in days." Paradise gave a little push on his chest, and he let her move him back a few inches.

He grinned and swiped his hand through his dark hair before his expression grew somber. "It's all God, babe. But for him I would have done nothing with my life. So follow him, not me. I'm just a guy with lots of flaws."

Blake could be hardheaded and determined to wrap her in cotton, but he was the only man she'd ever loved like this. With her history that said a lot.

Paradise managed to abort her yawn. "I know it's late, but since we're going to Pascagoula tomorrow, there won't be time to look through that box I got from Lily. You game to stay up and see what's in there?" She sat on the sofa with all four cats touching her, either on her feet or on her lap. They wouldn't take kindly to being disturbed.

Blake got up and headed toward the kitchen. "Sure. I'm a little hungry. I think I had two bites of my shrimp boil before Mom asked me to do something, and then I forgot about it. Want any leftovers?"

"I only got a taste of your mom's pecan pie—it was awesome.

If there's any of that left, I'll have a piece." She swept her hand over her current feline situation. "I'd come help you, but they have me pinned down."

He grinned. "I can handle it by myself. I think Mom made extra pies for the family. The boys begged."

"Of course they did."

She heard Blake rummaging in the fridge, then the beep of the microwave. She smiled at how content she felt in this small, yellow, shotgun-style house filled with the people she loved. If she'd gotten her way about staying at the apartment, she wouldn't be experiencing this right now. She'd be alone in her tiny space listening to the hum of souped-up cars spitting gravel in the street outside. By now she'd be in bed listening to the hum of a fan she used to drown out the arguments of the next-door neighbors at midnight. Contentment like this was found in small moments that created the foundation of security and belonging.

Blake returned holding two plates. "I cut a big piece of pie, but I can help you with that if it's too much."

She eyed the humongous slice. "I think it's safe to say I'll need help." Levi's kitten, Selah, was always the most interested in food of any kind, and she sprang up from Paradise's lap to push her nose toward the plate. "Oh no you don't." Paradise lifted it out of the black-and-white cat's reach.

"Shoo them off, and I'll get the box. You'll need your various appendages anyway." He put his plate on the fireplace mantel out of reach of the cats and went to grab the box they'd left by the front door.

Selah meowed a complaint when Paradise put her down, but black Merlin and white Luna wandered over to the cat tree by the window. Bailey's gray body was a streak as she sprinted in hot pursuit of a fly. Paradise smiled. Another one of those moments too inconsequential to matter, yet it did.

Blake returned carrying the enormous box and set it by her feet, then he grabbed his plate and took a bite of the shrimp. He settled beside her with his food. "Did Lily say what all was in it?"

"She didn't. I wanted to ask her about the answering machine, but I thought it might be more fun to discover what's in the box on my own." Paradise had already had a couple bites of the pie and pushed the rest of it toward him before she reached down to remove the box's lid.

She reached for the brightly colored fabric on top. "I think it's a quilt top!" She spread it out on the floor, and Bailey made a leap for the dangling threads on the end. Paradise pushed the kitty away with her bare foot. "Oh no you don't."

The various shades of blue and gray interlocking rings were overlaid on a black background, and the contrast was stunning. "It's a double wedding ring pattern. I remember Mom saying she was going to go blind if she had to finish it. But it looks complete. And it's big enough for a king bed. I think she was making it for herself and planned to enter it in a 4-H contest."

Blake touched one of the rings. "It's beautiful."

She scooped it into her arms and pressed her face into it. It still held the faint aroma of her mom's perfume, and tears rushed to her eyes. Her mother's face swam so clearly into her memory, and she wished she could remember the name of the citrusy, fruity scent. It would be a way to hold her close, even now.

Paradise sniffled and laid aside the quilt. "I'll see if I can find someone to attach the backing and quilt it."

He set his hand on her knee. "I can stitch up a cut, but I'm hopeless with a sewing machine."

The thought of Blake bent over a sewing machine made her

even more misty-eyed. He'd do most anything for her. She dove back into the box and pulled up the black backing. "I think all the parts are here, even the batting." Deeper into the box she found a bottle of Princess perfume by Vera Wang. "This is what she wore! I couldn't remember the name." She lowered her voice before she woke the boys. "Trying to remember the name of her perfume was driving me crazy."

A memory hit her and she gasped. "When Dad surprised her he brought her a gift. It was a bottle of this perfume." Was this the bottle Mom had held that day? Paradise swallowed hard and bent over the box again. A notebook filled with recipes was the next item out of the box, and she flipped through it, remembering her mother's ham tetrazzini. The recipe was in here. She was going to enjoy trying the foods from her childhood.

She reached back into the box. At the very bottom was the answering machine, but the elation she'd thought she'd feel felt a lot like dismay.

She wasn't sure she was ready to hear what it might hold.

CHAPTER 19

BLAKE PLUGGED IN THE answering machine. It was a Casio PhoneMate with digital recording capability, and he'd already skimmed the booklet. "This thing must have been the bomb back then. It didn't use a tape and had eighteen minutes of storage for messages. As long as Lily never used it, whatever was recorded on it at the time of the murders should still be on it."

Paradise stopped his hand when he started to hit the Play button. "I'm afraid, Blake."

"You don't have to listen to it. I can do it and write down anything important."

She pulled her hand back. "I'm being childish. It's not like it's going to be Mom screaming as she's dying or anything." Paradise gulped and nodded. "Go ahead."

"If it's too much, we'll hit the Stop button. It may not even work." But his intuition said it would work fine and might hold some important information. He pressed the saved messages button with one hand and clutched her fingers with the other.

"December 12, 2005, at 2:00 p.m." Then the beep. *"I'm trying to reach Becky Alden. This is William Fletcher, and I've been hired to*

track down the child you gave up for adoption. You can reach me at this number." He rattled off a phone number. *"It's very important you call me back."*

"The PI," Blake said.

Paradise nodded and clutched his hand tighter. "Just a couple of months before they died."

The machine moved on to the next saved message. *"January 25, 2005, at 11:00 a.m."* A beep came, then a male voice. *"Becky, it's me. I—I don't know how to tell you this, but I think you're in danger. I want you to get out of town for a little while. Be careful, sweetheart. We can't be together right now. Be patient."*

A week before the murders. Why hadn't Becky listened and gotten out of town?

"January 25, 2005, at 6:00 p.m." A beep sounded and the next saved message started. *"It's Sheriff Davis, Becky. I just received some terrible news. I hate to give it to you over the phone, but I can't get home for another hour or two. You need to get out of the house. Ben is dead, and I think whoever killed him is coming after you next. Tell Granger the truth. Take Paradise and hole up somewhere. Take this seriously, please."*

"The sheriff was protecting her like Booker Lewis said," Paradise murmured.

"I'll play the more recent messages. I thought maybe there wouldn't be any." He jabbed the button.

A mechanical voice spoke. *"February 2, 2005, at 8:00 a.m."* There was a beep, and a female voice spoke. *"Your cable repair is scheduled for today at 10:00 a.m. If you need to reschedule, please call us back."*

"The day they died," Paradise whispered. "When I got the monkey music box."

Blake reached for his phone. "I'm going to text Drew. The

dates might help Drew figure out the name of his father." He tapped out a message. *"End of messages,"* the machine intoned.

Paradise's grip tightened on his hand. "Why didn't Mom do what he said? Did she think he was lying?"

"It's impossible to say, babe. Maybe she thought the sheriff was overreacting. I don't get why Becky was a target."

Paradise pulled her hand away and stood to pace the living room floor. "None of it makes sense."

The front door opened, and Drew stepped in. He crossed the floor to embrace his sister. "You okay, Sis?"

"Sheriff Davis warned Mom to leave the house, that whoever killed your dad was coming after her." She rested her head on his shoulder and swiped at the tears on her face. "She didn't listen! Why didn't she pay attention? Life would have been so different if she'd left the house. And your dad warned her a week before she died too. She ignored everyone."

Blake wanted to hold her, but he let Drew comfort her. He had the right to. "But would it have changed anything, babe? How long could she have stayed gone? You had school, she had a job, and life would have to resume at some point. The killer could have come at any time. There are always what-ifs in any situation, but we can't change what is. You're brave and strong. Nothing has broken you. I know you miss them though. That's the worst part of all of this."

She nodded and stepped away from Drew. "I think I'll go to bed. I can't think about this any longer tonight. It hurts too much."

Blake didn't try to stop her. Pain like hers sometimes required being alone with God, who was the only true comfort. He hoped his plans for tomorrow would help her focus on the future and not a past that couldn't be changed. He said good night to Drew, then reached for his Bible to help his own heart.

The boys chattered with excitement as they lugged their fishing poles and tackle boxes from the van to the beach at Pascagoula. Mom went with them to check out the pier. Blake scrolled through the checklist in his head. Water, snacks, swimsuits, towels, and a change of clothes. He handed Paradise a stack of towels and watched her carry them toward the water to stake a spot until Mom got back with the boys.

Paradise glanced back and he held up five fingers to let her know they needed to leave shortly. She gave him a thumbs-up and picked up the pace. She seemed fine this morning after the trauma of listening to the answering machine's messages last night. She'd told him she'd prayed and wrestled with it all for about an hour until she fell asleep.

He patted his pocket to make sure the ring was still there. Yep. Hez and Savannah were meeting them at Lighthouse Park at five to catch the afternoon light. He'd made reservations at Brady's Steaks and Seafood to celebrate after pictures were taken and she hopefully said yes.

Was he making the right choice about how and when to propose? He'd been tempted to do it privately, but love had been in short supply after her parents died, and his family had gone a long way toward healing the hurts in her heart. This felt right.

Drew lifted the cooler out of the back of the van. "More food."

"You've never seen my brothers eat after swimming. Their stomachs are endless pits."

Drew eyed him. "You look nervous, but you don't have to worry. She'll say yes."

"I hope you're right." Blake kept remembering her stricken

expression when she proposed and he said not yet. He'd been sure she was doing it out of pity when they were about to lose the refuge, but he wasn't so sure now. He glanced at his watch. "Fletcher is still expecting us at lunch?"

"I got a text from him. He's at the restaurant. I told him we'd be there in ten minutes."

Blake spotted Paradise hurrying back from the beach. "We're ready to go."

He held the door open for her, and she slid in. "I can't wait to get in the water myself. The boys were sure they'd be able to catch all our dinner, and I didn't have the heart to tell them they'd have to do catch and release today."

As far as Paradise knew, they were grilling burgers later, and Blake's palms grew sweaty on the steering wheel. What if he slipped up and spilled the secret? What if Hez and Savannah came early and Paradise figured it out? He swallowed and focused on the short drive to the meeting place.

The café was on a quiet street off the main drag in downtown Pascagoula, and he quickly found a parking spot. Paradise was a little pale when she climbed out of the van. "I'm trying not to get my hopes up that we're going to crack the case today."

Drew slid the van's back door closed. "Me too."

They entered the small eating place and Blake glanced around. It was eleven thirty, a little early for a big lunch crowd, and he spotted an older man at a back booth with papers spread out on the table. His gray hair was parted low on one side to comb over the bald spot on top. The waitress had already brought him iced tea and a plate of fried oysters.

The man looked up and brightened before waving them over. He stood as they approached and held out his hand. "William Fletcher here, but everyone calls me Fletch." He reached for

Blake's hand. "You must be Blake. I recognize you from the pictures on The Sanctuary website." His gaze went to Paradise. "This pretty lady must be Paradise Alden. You look like your mother." He stared hard at Drew. "And Detective Andrew Bartley. You were hard to find. Impossible, really." He gestured to the benches. "Have a seat."

Paradise slid in first, and Blake settled in beside her while Drew sat across from his sister. Fletch sat in front of his computer and papers. "I brought everything I have on the case and copied every scrap of evidence I found."

Drew angled his back into the corner by the window to stare at Fletch. "The first thing I'd like to know is who hired you."

"The person wanted to stay anonymous. I never liked working that way so it didn't take me long to track her down."

Paradise straightened. *"Her?"*

"Yep. It was a woman by the name of Pamela Collins."

"Was her husband Ben?" Paradise asked.

Fletch raised a brow. "You already knew?"

"We discovered the first name of Drew's father, but that was all we'd found out." She pulled out the onyx cuff link and showed him the *C*. "This makes sense now."

"I was unable to give her much information about you, Drew. Becky refused to give up the names of your adoptive parents."

"There's more you might not know." Blake told him about the messages on the answering machine.

"How did my father die?" Drew's voice was a monotone.

"He was killed on January 25, 2005, a week before the Aldens. His body was discovered at just after 5:00 p.m., but time of death was placed right after lunch based on stomach contents. We know he ordered a pizza at 11:00 a.m. The police assumed it was a robbery gone wrong. Ben owned a huge building full of collectible vehicles, and his family was wealthy. One of the cars, a 1970 yellow Hemi Barracuda, was missing. It's never been found." Fletch studied Drew's expression. "Strangely enough, Pamela Collins died from a fall down the stairs a week later. She died the day before the murders in Nova Cambridge."

Paradise gasped and leaned forward. "She was killed?"

"I have my suspicions, but it was ruled an accidental death."

Blake didn't buy it. That was way too coincidental. He reached for Paradise's hand, and she laced her fingers through his.

Drew raked his hand through his hair. "This is a very convoluted case. I'd like to see those case files. Pamela's death is too coincidental for my liking. Paradise remembers seeing Becky kissing a man."

"Was politics involved at all?" Blake asked. "Maybe someone was trying to avoid a scandal?"

"I suggested that angle to the police. Ben was planning to run for the Mississippi Senate. He comes from a long line of politicians."

"Who's his family?" Drew asked in a tense voice.

The name *Collins* had been rolling around in Blake's head. "Is it the Holden Collins family?"

"Bingo," Fletch said.

That Collins family just happened to be one of the most prestigious families in Mississippi. There had been multiple governors and senators and even a Collins who'd run for president. Blake let out a low whistle. The pool of suspects just got a lot bigger.

CHAPTER 20

THE MINUTES TICKED BY as they pored over the documents Fletch had provided. Paradise had already downed two coffees, and the acid roiled in her stomach. She called up the information about the Holden Collins family and ran through the list of politicians and founders of large companies as well as several large nonprofits. "I've never done a deep dive into the family, though I've heard of them, of course."

She glanced at her brother and saw him absorbed in something on his phone as well, and it hit her how personal this information was for him. "Did you look up the obit?"

Drew glanced up, his expression intense. "Yeah. I have the names of my half siblings. One of them lives right outside town, about five minutes away. The estate looks palatial." He turned his phone around to show her a large white mansion set off from the road by a vast green lawn.

"The children were all too young for me to contact," Fletch said. "I'd let it all go years ago, but when you called, I started digging. Taylor is a Mississippi state senator now. She's married to an oilman, Troy Murphy. I thought you might want to talk to her, so I checked her schedule. She's in residence for the week. We could try to get in to see her."

"Is the estate gated?" Drew asked. "I could flash my badge."

"That should work," Fletch said. "The guard will want to comply with law enforcement. As part of the government Taylor would look bad if she turned you away."

Paradise turned off her phone screen and stood. "Let's do it."

Blake glanced at his watch and nodded. "We have time."

Time for what? Were they on a schedule? Maybe he'd promised the boys he'd go swimming with them or take them fishing. He treasured his time with his little brothers, and they adored him. This was important though and the reason they'd come. It would take however long it would take.

"You want to come with us, Fletch?" Drew asked. "You could explain what you know."

"I didn't want to intrude, but I hoped you'd ask." The PI closed his computer and followed them out the door.

Blake paid for their drinks and lunch on the way out, and Paradise waited for him by the van. Drew and Fletch took the middle row. Paradise watched them talk through the window. Her brother was in his element—focused and determined to get to the truth.

Blake exited and walked toward her with a smile that lingered on his face. "You look happy," he said when he reached her.

She nodded toward the men in the van. "I think this investigation is in good hands. Those two know what they're doing."

"Hey, we haven't done too bad ourselves figuring out who was attacking The Sanctuary."

"True. We make a pretty good team." She slid into the van, and he closed the door behind her and went around to the driver's side, where he paused. "Hey, Drew, maybe you should drive.

You can flash that badge from the driver's seat, and it will seem more official."

"Good idea." Drew slid open the door, and they exchanged seats.

They drove out of town and Fletch directed them to the estate. Drew stopped the van at the guard gate and held out his badge. "Detective Drew Bartley to see Senator Murphy."

The guard was young, probably mid-twenties, but his brown eyes were alert and focused. He stubbed out a cigarette, but the smoke wafted into the van. "Are you expected?"

"No, but I believe she can help with a case I'm working. I won't take up too much of her time."

The guard nodded and turned his back to grab the phone. He spoke for a few moments before pressing a button that opened the gate. "She'll see you on the back patio. She's working in her garden."

Drew drove through the open gate toward the house in the distance. Magnolias, rhododendrons, and azaleas dotted planting beds bordering the brick driveway. Paradise admired the water view and the lovely old oaks festooned with moss. The mansion was a huge two-story Greek Revival with massive white Corinthian columns. Roses bloomed in flower beds along the porch.

Drew parked the van in front of the steps and got out holding a green folder. The group converged in front of the van. "You take the lead, Drew," Paradise said. "We'll all hang back. If she doesn't know about you, this could be a shock."

"I assumed she knew about me, but you could be right. They would have been raised by a relative, probably their grandparents, after their parents died. I was fifteen when my father died, so Taylor would have been sixteen. She's the oldest, so they were all too young to be told much, especially if our father's death was never solved."

Paradise followed her brother along the oyster path bordered by moss rose. A woman standing in a vegetable garden turned toward them with a questioning expression. Her blonde hair was windblown, and her pale skin was flushed from the warmth of the sun, even in her shorts and tee. She'd be thirty-six now.

She yanked off her cotton gloves and approached them. "I'm not really dressed for company, but I'm always available to our law enforcement. Sweet tea will be out shortly." She gestured to the expansive seating area on the brick patio. "Have a seat and tell me how I can help."

Blake felt Paradise trembling beside him on the glider. She jiggled her left knee, and he reached over to take her hand. Her fingers gripped him like a lifeline. The revelations today had been confusing and upsetting to both Drew and her.

Drew and Fletch sat in chairs across from them. Taylor handed out glasses of sweet tea before she took a seat beside Drew. The confusion in her blue eyes grew when she took in Paradise's distressed expression.

Taylor turned to Drew. "What's this all about? It's a little odd that a police detective would bring civilians along."

Drew set his glass on the table between them. "I'm investigating the murder of your father."

Taylor's smile froze. "Why now after all this time? Is there new evidence?"

"I think so. Are you aware your father had a child out of wedlock?"

"That's ridiculous." She glanced at Paradise. "Are you here trying to get some of Dad's money?"

"I'm that child, Senator Murphy, not Paradise," Drew said. "I'm sorry if this is distressing news. I'm your half brother, and I have no interest in money or anything else the family owns. I'm solely after the truth of what happened. Paradise Alden is my other half sister. Her mother was Becky Alden, a Bartley at the time of the affair that produced me. She was seventeen and still in school when she met your father. He was already married to your mother and was also much older." He gestured to Fletch. "This is William Fletcher, a PI your mother hired before she died."

Taylor went white and shook her head. "This is a lot to take in. Why would Mom hire a PI?"

"I can answer that," Fletch said. "She found a box of letters from Becky one day when she was cleaning the garage and wanted to find out more about her. And Drew." Fletch leaned forward with his hands on his knees. "I tried to get Becky to tell me Drew's new surname, but she wouldn't do it. When your father was killed and then your mother died, I tried to warn Becky, but it was too late. She and her husband were both murdered."

Taylor put her hand to her head and stared at Drew. "Wait, wait. Your mother was killed too?"

Drew nodded. "Bludgeoned to death like our father. Her husband, Granger, came home unexpectedly and was murdered the same way. In the space of a week, our parents were all dead. I believe your mother's death was not an accident. There has to be more."

"Who on earth?" Taylor murmured.

Paradise had a death grip on Blake's hand, but he managed not to wince. "Did you hear any rumors that your father planned to leave your mother? Could that have been a motive to stop him from derailing his run for governor?"

"I—I overheard a fight between my parents just the day before

Dad died. He had asked her for a divorce, and she screamed at him that she would make sure his political aspirations never came about. He stomped out and took off with tires screeching and didn't come home that night."

"Did you tell the police about it?"

Taylor stared down at her hands. "I was sixteen and wanted to protect my mother."

Paradise leaned against Blake and exhaled. He wished he could spare her hearing all this and having to relive the night her parents died too. These deaths had to be related, but for the life of him, he couldn't see who would want them all dead. Unless . . . "Would your dad's family have tried to talk him out of divorce? Could it have been a disagreement with one of them that got out of hand?"

Taylor reached for her glass of tea and took a sip without answering for several moments. She set the beverage back on the table and laced her fingers together. "The only family member Dad ever argued with was Uncle Bear. He was older than Dad and never had much success with politics, though it was his passion. Tempers could run high between them since they often disagreed on policy or election strategies. But in spite of those differences, they were tight. I can't see Uncle Bear ever hurting my dad."

"Bear?" Paradise asked.

"His real name is Arthur, but we all call him Bear. I was never sure where he got the nickname."

Paradise pulled her hand from Blake's and rubbed her head. "I was there the night my parents died, and I blocked out most of it until recently."

"I understand your loss." Taylor glanced down at her clasped hands. "I—I found my mother at the bottom of the stairs. She'd just gotten up and was still in her robe and slippers. It was very traumatic, and I try not to remember."

Drew reached over and touched Taylor's hands. "That had to have been very hard."

She moved slightly so that his hand fell away. Blake tried not to dislike her for it. She'd taken a hard hit with this news, and she already had two brothers. She wouldn't welcome the unknown addition with open arms. At least not yet.

Drew returned his hand to his chair's armrest. "I'd like to speak to your brothers too. And your uncle of course. Are there any other siblings? A-are your grandparents still alive . . . ?" His voice trailed off and betrayed how much that final question meant.

Grandparents were important in any kid's life, and Paradise had keenly felt the lack of any in her life. Blake had too. Visits with his maternal grandparents had been few and far between since they lived in Scotland, and his paternal grandfather had died in the Korean conflict. His paternal grandmother had died in childbirth.

Taylor looked down at her hands again. "My grandparents live here. I mean, with me. This is their home, really, and I just come when I need to get away from the hubbub of the legislature."

Drew's eager gaze darted to the door. "Are they home so I could ask them some questions?"

Taylor gave a jerky nod. "Give me a few minutes to explain the situation. They raised us after our parents died."

CHAPTER 21

BLAKE WATCHED DREW PACE the brick patio. Blake didn't blame him for the agitation. He took a glance at his watch. Three o'clock. Hez and Savannah were due to meet them at Lighthouse Park in two hours. Maybe he hadn't thought this engagement idea through as well as he should have. He hadn't expected an entire family meeting to open up to them. Hez would wait though. This was important.

Paradise linked her fingers through his. "Think I should try to calm him?" she whispered.

"No. He needs some time to process what he's learned." Blake had already figured out his soon-to-be brother-in-law was a deep thinker, which was why he was such a successful detective. Another person's thoughts were just noise when he was trying to sort things out.

Blake studied the yard to distract himself. Tiki lights lined the oyster walkway, and a small monument stood off to the right side. One dedicated to Ben? Way on the back side of the acreage he spotted a large building. He assumed it was the garage that housed the car collection.

Fifteen minutes ticked by before Taylor returned with her grandparents. Barely five-two, the older woman was as slim as a girl and her grayish-blonde hair was in a sleek bob. She wore yoga clothes and there was a slight sheen on her forehead as if she'd been caught exercising. She had the money to keep herself up and looked as if she always worked at it. Her husband was just as stylish in khaki pants and a light blue shirt. His white hair was as thick as Blake's but neatly styled.

The tiny woman behind Taylor didn't wait to be introduced but came barreling past her granddaughter. Her inquisitive green eyes flashed from Drew to Blake, then back to Drew. She held out her hand. "You must be Drew. Your nose is like my Ben's."

Drew's only indication of emotion was the way his Adam's apple bobbed when he swallowed. "I'm glad to hear that. I never met him."

"I knew about you, of course. Benny told me everything after he reconnected with Becky and heard about your birth. He didn't know she was pregnant when they broke up. She'd found out he was married and ended it. They never spoke until they happened to run into each other at a charity function at TGU, of all things. I sometimes wondered if he secretly hoped to find her there. I was supposed to make an appearance, but I got the flu at the last minute, and he quickly volunteered."

Drew blinked as the torrent of information poured out of her. "I wasn't sure what had happened. I didn't catch your name."

"I'm Victoria, but the grandchildren call me Pippy." She turned and gestured to her husband. "This is your grandfather, Percy, but you may call him Duke like the other grandchildren. Percy tried to find you after Ben died but didn't have much luck."

Drew shoved his hands in his pockets as if he wasn't sure what to do with them. "Pleased to meet you."

Blake hadn't thought things would go this well. It helped that they already knew about Drew's existence. He watched them all shake hands, but he noted the way Victoria checked the impulse to hug him. She would be easier to win over than Taylor.

She and her husband settled on a love seat, and she folded her hands in her lap. "We're happy to answer any questions. Taylor says you suspect Pamela's fall was murder. Do you have any proof?"

Drew perched on the edge of a chair. "Only the fact that it's way too coincidental that she had hired someone to find me and then died around the same time as my father and Paradise's parents."

Victoria spared a sympathetic glance in Paradise's direction. "Taylor didn't mention that part, but then, we got a very abbreviated summary of the situation. That's all very peculiar." Her glance settled on Fletch. "Pamela hired you to find Drew?"

"Yes, ma'am. Becky refused to give up his new family's name though."

Drew leaned forward. "I know these will be upsetting questions, but I have to ask. What can you tell me about my father's death?"

Percy placed his hand on his wife's clasped hands. "I'll answer that." His voice was like an orator's, deep and resonant. "Victoria usually cries when she talks about it. She found him in the backyard, right over there by the path to the large garage at the back of the property. January 25th, 2005. A day I'll never forget."

Drew glanced at the garage in the distance. "I'm sorry. I know this is hard. Could you tell what weapon was used?"

"A golf club. It was beside his body. A putting green used to be there, but Victoria couldn't bear to see it after he died, so we had the backyard redone. The club belonged to him, and he'd likely had it in his hand when he was attacked. Blood spatter was found near his golf cart parked out here and trailed across the grass when he tried to run. He didn't get far."

"Did he have any enemies?"

Percy shrugged. "All politicians have enemies, but they usually don't kill the opponent."

"Is there anyone who would have been furious that he was leaving his wife?"

"We all were, but we loved Ben. Pamela wasn't an easy woman to live with." Percy glanced over at Taylor. "I'm sorry, sweet girl."

"It's okay, Duke. I lived with her too," Taylor said. "She was manipulative. When she was being sweet and kind, you always knew she wanted something from you."

Percy sighed. "For all her faults I believe Pamela loved Ben."

Drew took a sip of his tea. "Pamela didn't want the divorce. It would have been motive for her to kill the Aldens, but she died before they did so we're back to square one."

Blake ran through the possible suspects now. The list was small. Ben's parents clearly doted on him. Neither of them would have wanted to see him dead. Someone else in the family?

Drew set his glass down. "How many siblings did my father have?"

"Just one brother, Arthur. We call him Bear. He lives in Texas, but I can give you his phone number. He wasn't in town when Ben died, but he came immediately when his mother called." Percy cleared his throat. "I expect you'll want to meet your two half brothers. They don't know about you, so we will need to inform them. They live in Texas near Bear. Gray and Parker run the business Bear founded, but they will all be here next week for Victoria's birthday party. It would be a good time to meet the family. All of them."

Drew's gaze sought out Paradise's, and her fingers tightened on Blake's. She nodded at him. Blake was proud of the way she was handling this. She'd only just found her brother and now had to share him, but she was doing it with class.

Paradise walked with Blake toward the gazebo at Lighthouse Park. They'd dropped Fletch off at his car, then stopped to pick up the rest of the family before heading to the park to take some family pictures with good light. They probably should have done it before because the boys had beach hair and pink faces, but they would still be fun memories to go over when they were older.

The round lighthouse had been decommissioned and moved to the mainland, and it stood tall and proud against the backdrop of green lawn and trees. She imagined the cute pictures with the boys mugging it up for the camera. Blake had brought his camera with the high-powered lens. She'd have to see if Drew or Jenna could take a picture of her with Blake. She didn't have a photo of just the two of them.

She swerved closer to Blake and slid her arm around his waist to walk in lockstep with him. "What a day." She smiled at Isaac atop Drew's shoulders with his small hands tightly gripping her brother's hair. He was going to make a good dad someday.

Blake squeezed her fingers. "You okay with how today turned out? Drew's grandparents seemed to welcome him with open arms."

"I loved that. Taylor will warm up to him. Everyone does." Blake always knew how she felt inside, so his real question was about fear. "I admit there's a twinge of jealousy to think he has a whole other family when I've just found him, but we already have a strong bond. We love each other, and there's never too much love."

"You're so right. The bond between you is unbreakable." Blake scanned the area around the gazebo as if he was looking for something.

She turned to look too. "Did you see someone?"

"Just getting the lay of the land for good pictures."

She stopped. "You forgot your camera."

"You're right. I'll grab it and meet you at the lighthouse." He turned and jogged back toward the van.

She hurried to catch up with Drew and fell into step beside him and Jenna. Levi had already reached the lighthouse and had his head tipped back to stare up the stairs. Seagulls pecked around his feet searching for food, and the air carried the scent of cut grass. When they reached the lighthouse, she dug in her purse for her hairbrush and tried to tame the boys' hair.

Levi jerked his head away. "Aw, Paradise, I don't want it brushed. I'm hungry."

"We'll do family pictures and then get our food out." When Drew set Isaac's feet on the ground, she took care of his windblown hair as well, but he held his tongue with his face set in determination.

When she looked up, the family had stepped away and left her alone in front of the lighthouse as Blake approached. His blue eyes held tenderness, and a slight smile of trepidation lifted his lips. Her gaze fell to his hands. "You didn't get the camera?"

"I passed it off to get a picture with you."

It was exactly what she wanted, but some other statement seemed to be hovering in the air, as if everyone was holding their breath to hear it. She spotted Savannah, then saw Hez with the camera to his face snapping photos. She couldn't look away from

Blake, and he dropped to his knees when he reached her and pulled out a black velvet box. She forgot to breathe as the love in his eyes swallowed her whole.

"Blake?" she whispered past the boulder in her throat.

He opened the lid of the velvet box to reveal the most beautiful emerald ring she'd ever seen. "Paradise, I've loved you for most of my life. Even when we were apart, the memory of you held me in its grip and I never got over longing for you. Your love is as necessary to me as oxygen. Being with you has made me better, strong and whole."

His other hand gestured toward where the rest of the family stood. "You've had a huge effect, not just on me, but on my family as well. *Our* family. Will you be my wife? Will you be a sister to Isaac and Levi and a daughter to my mother? Will you take us all as one?"

Her vision blurred, and she blinked quickly so she didn't lose sight of his eyes so filled with adoration and strength. These past months had been the happiest of her life. "I'm only whole when I'm with you," she whispered. "How could I say anything but yes?"

He took her left hand and slipped the ring on. It was a perfect fit. His grip stayed firm on her hand, and he rose to take her in his arms. She nestled against his chest, safe in his arms. His firm lips came down on hers, and she lost herself in the passion of his kiss.

In that moment she knew she was where she was supposed to be, as if God had ordained it just this way.

CHAPTER 22

THE AROMA OF SEAFOOD battled with the sweet scent of Brady's famous key lime pie. Blake headed for two seats together at the back table with Paradise. They were the last ones to enter the restaurant because he'd had to pause and kiss her in private. Euphoria surrounded him like a bubble, and he was almost afraid it might pop. He had to keep assuring himself it wasn't a dream. She'd really said yes.

They reached the table, and he grabbed Hez's shoulders and squeezed. "I hope you got some great pictures. And at least you weren't accused of being a gunman like I was at your engagement."

Hez turned in his seat and grinned. "Paradise never so much as glanced away from your face." He took Paradise's hand and stared at her ring. "That's some rock he got you." He winked at Blake. "You did good, man."

"I tried." They passed Savannah and Simon to sit on the other end across from his mom and the boys. Isaac and Levi had mobbed Paradise the minute Mom let them go. They were still smiling, and his mother's eyes were misty.

Mom reached across Drew and squeezed Paradise's hand once she was settled beside her brother. "I hope you didn't mind we butted in."

"It made for the most perfect proposal ever," Paradise said. "I'm so happy I can hardly think." She stared down at the ring. "I love emeralds."

"Tell her the story, Mom," Blake prompted.

"The stone was in a necklace Blake's father gave me before he left on his final tour. I hadn't worn it because I wanted him to see it on me for the first time. He never came back, and it sat in the safe all these years. When Blake mentioned wanting to get you a ring, I showed it to him, and he said you loved emeralds. Since you're such an integral part of our family already, it felt right that you should have it."

Blake traced the outline of the stone with one finger. "When I took it to the jeweler for him to design something, he said it was from Zambia. We don't know much about its history."

Paradise stared at her ring. "It's beautiful. I love it so much. I'll always treasure its history, Jenna. I'm honored to be part of its importance." She fingered her locket. "Family heirlooms are precious, and I'm going to treasure both the ring and the locket for the rest of my life."

"When's the wedding?" Drew asked. "I can get behind having Blake for a brother. My family is expanding by the second."

Paradise's gaze swung to Blake, and he took her hand. "The sooner the better as far as I'm concerned. Though we have to find a house and work out all kinds of details."

His mom cleared her throat. "About that. There's that one little point of land near the road that will likely never be utilized as part of the park. You kids are welcome to build on it if you like. Or not—it's up to you."

Paradise gasped, and her amber eyes shone. She reached over and squeezed his mother's hand. "I'd love to be close to you and the boys, but building will take some time." She glanced at Blake with a questioning expression. "We could live at my place until it's done."

At least she wasn't putting off the wedding until they had a house. He'd like to carry her across the threshold of a house that was uniquely theirs together, but he could already picture a home on that picturesque acre along the lane back to the park. "We'll go take a look at it tomorrow and see where we might put a house. You could pick out the style of home you want, babe. As long as I have you, I don't care."

She squeezed his fingers. "You might regret giving me full control."

"Never."

The server took their drink orders, then Paradise's attention swung back to her brother. "How do you feel about everything today, Drew, or have you not had a chance to process all of it?"

"My brain has been going a mile a minute." He glanced at the boys across from him. They chattered animatedly to Simon about riding lessons. Drew lowered his voice and leaned toward Paradise and Blake. "My father was the first target. I'd like to have seen that box of letters Pamela found, but I texted my grandmother after we left, and she said it was destroyed. Was everyone else wiped out to make sure no one had any idea of the killer's identity? Maybe Pamela figured out who killed Ben and had to be silenced too."

It was very confusing, and Blake didn't want to think about it right now with Paradise sitting beside him. All he wanted to do was stare at her and think about the future. He knew Paradise was concerned about the relationship though, so he asked what she'd hesitate to verbalize. "And you have new family."

Drew reached for his iced tea. "I'm glad my grandparents weren't angry, but Taylor wasn't what you'd call warm. I'll never be welcomed into their family." He reached for his sister's hand. "This sister is the one who has filled a void for me, and I don't know how you did it, Paradise. Even after all you've been through, you somehow dredge up love in your heart for other people."

Paradise's fingers curled around Drew's. "You're not 'other' people. You're my brother. If you knew how I've longed for a sibling, especially a brother, you'd get it."

"Aren't we your brothers?" Isaac asked.

"Of course you are, buddy," she said. "Now I have three brothers. I have a big brother and two little brothers. I couldn't feel happier or more blessed about that."

Blake put his arm around her. "Am I chopped liver? I think a new husband counts up there pretty high."

She leaned against him. "At the pinnacle."

He inhaled her sweet aroma. What a wonderful day. When they were alone tonight, he wanted to talk more about timing. He'd press for a quick wedding.

The morning sun slanting through the clinic window ignited the stones in Paradise's engagement ring, and she smiled before focusing on the work at hand. She activated her clicker to get King Julien's attention, and he came running for a treat of nuts. She fed him one at a time, praising him for listening. His bright eyes stayed focused on her, and he was a different animal than the one they'd rescued.

She fed him another nut through the wire enclosure. "King Julien looks really good," she told Warren. "You've done a great job training him."

His pale skin flushed at her praise. "I was hoping you'd say it was time. He's lived a lonely life, and I can't wait to see how he feels about seeing others of his kind."

The original conspiracy contained enough members that they'd decided to split them up. The plan was to introduce him to a female who'd lost her mate a few months ago. She had two juveniles with her on one side of the connected mesh enclosures. If it went well, they'd form a new conspiracy. "How have they behaved when catching sight of each other?"

"They're definitely interested. I haven't seen any signs of distress yet. The last two days they both stayed close to the connecting mesh."

She glanced at her watch. Where was Blake? He was supposed to join her for the momentous occasion of starting a new family group. She started to text him when the door opened and she spotted his broad smile. "There you are."

"Sorry, Levi had a meltdown, and I helped calm him. Isaac tore his new book, so we had to have a talk about accidents and forgiveness."

Blake was such a good role model for his brothers. "You made it in time." She gave Warren a thumbs-up. "Let's try removing the howdy door and see what happens."

Warren removed the separation between the lemurs. "It's going to go great. Lemurs are like people—they aren't meant to live without others. King Julien is about to experience a full life he didn't even know enough about to dream it might exist. We humans should be lucky enough to find our people and wash away the past."

They watched the vet tech open the door separating the lemurs. Julien was quick to rush through to meet Pixie, who immediately began to groom him, a good sign of acceptance. He returned the favor a few moments later.

"He's getting it," she said.

Since Julien hadn't grown up in a troop, he'd only been able to display instinctual behaviors and would have to learn what was usual in his new mate's conspiracy. The juveniles approached to be introduced, and he groomed them as well, an action they tolerated.

Paradise reached out to take Blake's hand as they watched the new little family. Warren left to get more food for the lemurs. Pixie's children began to groom Julien too, and the family unit appeared to be as tight as if they'd always been together. Julien was smart, and he quickly picked up the behaviors he'd been ignorant of when he came here.

Paradise blinked at the sting of tears in her eyes as she realized something she should have noticed already. She palmed Blake's face, relishing the scrape of what was left of his whiskers after his shave. "You're like Pixie," she whispered. "You welcomed me into your family and shared your mom and brothers with me without restriction. I was alone and lonely, without a real home. You taught me the meaning of family just like Pixie is showing Julien. He's a different lemur today. He's alert, happy, and at peace. That's how I feel now too. I've found my conspiracy, my home. And it's all due to you."

He brushed his lips across hers in a quick kiss. "I feel the same way about you. I always have. I thought I was doing okay without you, but when you walked in the door, all I'd missed about you hit me in the face. I'd deceived myself. A life without you wasn't complete." His hands went to her hair, but he didn't pull it from its holder.

She yanked her hair out of its ponytail. "You can groom me anytime you like, Blake. You can open doors, walk on the outside of the sidewalk nearest the danger. You can keep a keen eye out for anyone who might hurt me. I'll do the same for you. We're a team. I need you like air, like water. I realize that now." She stared up into his face and saw indescribable joy dawning in his blue eyes.

He plunged his hands into her hair and grinned. "Be careful what you say, babe."

"Do your worst and I'll do mine." She raked her fingers through his thick dark brown hair, and it stood even more on end.

She'd once been as unhappy and prickly as King Julien here, biting and snapping at anyone who might want to help her. Her battle cry had been "I can do it myself." And yes, she could do a lot herself, but *should* she go it alone?

She'd realized the answer was no. Just like lemurs, people needed community. *She* needed community, a purpose greater than shoving everyone away and living life as she thought best. Her life had been one of isolation and fear of what might happen next. She was always gearing up for the next battle. She'd always waited for the next shoe to drop, expecting life would get worse.

But that attitude was over. Even if Blake were taken from her someday by death, she'd never be the same. He had changed her forever. Family and love were what she'd needed, and they were hers, right here in front of her.

She wrapped her arms around Blake's waist and leaned against his chest. The steady beat of his heart under her ear was a soothing reminder that her place was here, in his arms. The old life was gone, washed away by love. Blake's love, yes, but even more by God's love. Blake had been a beacon showing her the way home in all definitions of the word.

CHAPTER 23

PARADISE STOOD IN NEARLY knee-high grass with her hand in Blake's and stared out over the rolling plot of land. "It's beautiful, Blake." She pointed out a knoll covered with native azaleas. "That reminds me of what the naturalist William Bartram thought when he first visited Alabama. 'Fire in the hills.' "

He watched her face light up as she checked out their future homesite. The sun sparked on the red highlights in her hair until it almost matched the eye-popping golds and reds in the blooms.

She pointed to the hillside. "What if we put the house there? It would have a great view of the refuge in the distance. How many acres are here?"

"A little over one. I like the setting. We'd have room to spread out here. It backs up to the African safari enclosure, so there wouldn't be too much danger if a giraffe managed to knock down a fence. Not that it would ever happen, but I'd rather have the safari area there than, say, a tiger enclosure." Neither of them had gotten on the zip line since he'd had to be rescued during the storm and flood. The hyenas had nearly gotten him.

She nodded and shaded her eyes with her hand. "The zip line

doesn't pass over our plot either, which is good. We won't be on display."

He tugged on her hand. "Let's walk up to the top of the knoll and check out our view." He led her to where rocky soil choked out most of the grass, and they wandered to the hill with azaleas all around them. He pointed out cows grazing in the distance. "It's almost as gorgeous as you are." He folded her in his arms, and she wrapped her arms around his neck. Her kiss tasted of promise and fidelity, and he wanted to relish it. So he did.

Her cheeks were pink when she pulled away. "I was looking online at floor plans last night. Do you like this?" She took out her phone and handed it to him, then stood close to point to the screen. "We'll need to stay on budget, and while this one isn't huge, it's got three bedrooms, enough for the boys to come stay and enough for kids down the road. I did some research, and a simple roofline helps to keep costs down. Plus this design has the plumbing close together so it cuts down on costs."

He flipped through the pictures. "I can see us on the porch watching the wildlife. And it reminds me of a shotgun house, and I like those."

"I do too! Very classic for this area." Her voice grew animated as she pointed out the kitchen. "I think I'd like painted cabinets, maybe in gray or blue. And high ceilings and wood floors if we can afford them."

He didn't want to deny her anything, but he was touched that she planned to keep an eye on the bottom line. The park was doing fine financially now, and his mother had raised his salary way more than he thought she should have. She'd assured him the park could afford to pay him a living wage now.

He handed her back her phone. "I like it. I'll start looking for a builder, but we really should set the date. We'll need some time to pull together the plans. It's not my area of expertise, but I'll help all I can. Do you know what venue you'd like? How about August? I think I can manage to wait until then." He chuckled when she blushed.

"I'd like a simple wedding with family and friends. We could put up a couple of tents in the backyard. I'd love to hear the animals wish us a happy wedding. We can order BBQ from Chet's along with sides, then have finger desserts. A happy day where we celebrate with people we love." She smiled. "But I still want a white dress."

"And I want to see you in one. You'll want Drew to walk you down the aisle? I'll ask Hez to be my best man."

"Would it be crazy to ask your mom to be my matron of honor?"

His throat tightened. "She'd be honored, babe. And would it be stupid to have both my brothers bring down the rings?"

"They might even be happy to fling flowers around. I know Isaac would."

She wasn't wrong. He grinned at the thought of his little brother tossing out handfuls of flowers. Neither of them had been to enough weddings that they would think that only girls did that job. "They love you, and I know they'll want to be part of everything." He wrapped her close. "Are you ready for the chaos?"

She kissed him. "I exult in it already."

Paradise's tummy was still warm with the chicken noodle soup and the brownie she'd had for lunch. She sat on the front porch with the diary from her childhood and listened to the monkeys' chatter in the distance. The subtly spicy scent of Jenna's bed of carnations filled her head, and the warm July breeze lifted her hair.

The screen door opened and Jenna stepped out. "There you are. Blake called from town and asked if we needed anything. He said you hadn't answered his text so he was making sure you were all right." She held up Paradise's phone and a hair tie. "I found these in the kitchen."

Paradise patted the spot beside her on the porch swing, then took the items and laid them on the cushion beside her. "Got time to sit a minute?"

"Of course." Jenna settled beside her and gave the swing a gentle push with one foot. "Any surprises in the diary?"

"I haven't started. The past few days have been a roller coaster, and I wanted to catch my breath first."

"I don't blame you. Lots of ups and downs."

"Big ups." Paradise held Jenna's gaze. "We haven't had a minute together alone, and I wanted to tell you how much this emerald means to me. You're the glue that holds this family together, Jenna. I want you to know how thankful I am for the man you raised and the little guys you're still shepherding. You're a wonderful example of what a mother should be. You have made me feel as loved and accepted as if you were my own mom." Her voice went hoarse, and she cleared her throat of the tears trying to clog what she wanted to say.

Jenna's blue eyes filled with tears. "Oh, honey, you've always been special to me. I mourn the years we lost with you, but God says he'll restore what the locusts have eaten. And here we are. You're back with us about to make a new life with Blake."

"And with you and the boys. I don't think I could have healed without having you in my life." Paradise embraced Jenna. When she released her, they were both crying. "Thank you for everything. I'm not taking your son—I'm joining your herd."

Jenna wiped her eyes. "I'm so happy, Paradise. You can always come to me with anything, even if it's a complaint against Blake. I'll be the wingman for both of you."

"I'll remember that." Paradise's phone sounded with a text, and she picked it up. "It's Blake. He's still at the grocery store and wants to know what's for dessert."

Jenna chuckled. "Tell him to bring home ice cream and I'll make apple pie. Frank is coming over too."

Paradise typed a quick message back. "I'm going to need all your recipes. The way to a man's heart is through his stomach." She lifted the phone. "And his text just proved it."

"You don't have to worry. You've had the key to Blake's heart since he was sixteen." Jenna stood. "I'd better get started on that pie." When Paradise started to join her, she held up her hand. "You have time to learn the recipe. See if there's anything important in that diary. If nothing else it's a trip down memory lane with your parents."

Maybe that's what Paradise was afraid of. She picked up the diary and opened the latch, then flipped through the pages. Most of them were mundane gushings of her eight-year-old self. She lingered over the details of her ninth birthday party and smiled when she remembered Abby at that age. How amazing that they were still friends. Her pulse rose as the date grew closer to the murders.

A dried leaf marked the spot of the page dated January 25, 2005, and her mouth went dry as she read her childish handwriting.

> I saw a yellow car outside when I came home from school. I asked Mommy who was here, and she said no one. She

> ran to the door to see the car and went outside. She asked me if a woman was driving it. I didn't see. She said maybe it was Pam. I don't know anyone named Pam. I don't know why she is mad.

Paradise tried to remember that day and the car, but she couldn't. Had the yellow car been the missing Barracuda? If that car had been parked in front of their house, who had driven it? Maybe whoever had killed Ben had come straight here to kill Mom. She flipped to the next page, February 2, the day of the murders.

> I love my music box. Mommy is mad I got it though. She asked if I saw the car bring it. I didn't see anyone bring it, but the cable guy said it was on the porch. Why does she keep talking about the yellow car? I don't know why she yelled. I didn't steal it.

The music box had shown up a second time as a way to rattle her when Roger Dillard was trying to coerce Jenna to sell the property, but they'd never addressed where it had come from in the first place. Just who had left it on the doorstep the day of the murders? Someone had known she loved *The Phantom of the Opera*. That narrowed the possible pool to family and a couple of friends.

She fingered the pages of the diary and forced herself to turn to the next one, the final entry. It was dated the day of the murders as well.

> Mommy said sorry. She said it didn't matter who left it. It was nice. I wish I could say thank you though. But

she looked scared. Why would she be scared? It's just a music box.

Unease rippled down her back. Had her mother feared the killer had left it? It wouldn't have been unusual for her to mention to Ben that her daughter loved *The Phantom of the Opera*. Maybe someone close to Ben had left it. Paradise rubbed her head. Maybe she was seeing connections that didn't exist.

CHAPTER 24

THE NEXT MORNING BLAKE parked on the street in front of Bea's house. "Who's taking the lead on this one?"

"I am," Drew said from the back seat. "This shouldn't take long. We just want to know if the sheriff ever saw that yellow car the week before the murders."

Paradise twisted around in the front seat to face her brother. "Be gentle with her, Drew. She was terrified when we were here last."

"I'll be kind. We aren't accusing her of anything—we need to know more about that yellow car. I suspect our mother might have called Gerald." Drew shoved open the door and got out of the truck.

Blake followed him and Paradise to the front door. Drew started to press the doorbell, then dropped his hand. "The door is ajar. Maybe she's outside."

"Go ahead and ring the bell. Maybe she didn't get it latched when she came in," Paradise said.

Drew pressed the button and the chime inside pealed. He sniffed the air. "It smells like burning bacon." He pushed the door open with his foot. "Don't touch the doorjamb or anything else." He poked his head inside. "Mrs. Davis? It's Detective Bartley, Paradise's brother." There was no answer, and he stepped through into the foyer. "Stay here. I think something is wrong."

"I'm a paramedic," Blake reminded him. "If she's been injured I can help." Without waiting for an answer, he followed Drew inside. He knew not to waste his breath telling Paradise to stay behind.

Black smoke billowed from the kitchen, and he coughed at the stench of burned bacon. Drew ran toward the kitchen with Blake on his heels. Flames erupted from an iron skillet, and Blake looked under the sink for a fire extinguisher. Paradise grabbed a hand towel and held it to her face. He could barely see her through the smoke.

He spotted the extinguisher behind the cleaning supplies and pulled it out. "Stand back."

Drew stepped away, and Blake aimed the nozzle at the fire. He had it out in less than a minute. Paradise went to the window and shoved it open. The smoke began to dissipate.

"Bea?" Paradise called.

"Stay near us," Drew said. "I don't like this. We'd better call it in."

Paradise pulled out her phone. "I'll call Rod." She turned her back to the men and placed the call.

Blake listened to her explain the situation to Rod as he poked around in the kitchen and dining room. "Maybe she's outside and forgot the bacon."

"Maybe." Drew didn't sound convinced. "I'll check the garage and see if her car is here." He went to the door on the other side of the dining room and peered into the garage. "Her car's there." He disappeared through the doorway and came back a few moments later. "No one's in the car and the garage door is down." He shut the door. "I'll check outside while you take the bedrooms and bathroom."

Blake nodded and began to search the house. Something bad had happened here, and he prayed he'd find Bea alive and well. The bedroom doors all stood open. The rooms were neat with the beds made. He made sure to check the main bedroom well, even under the bed. Nothing seemed out of place.

Her face pale, Paradise appeared in the doorway to the main bedroom. "Rod is sending someone out."

"Good." Blake moved toward the door to the connecting bathroom, which stood partially ajar. As he approached he saw a slipper-clad foot, and his gut clenched. "Get Drew, babe, and call for an ambulance." *Please be alive.* He pushed the door the rest of the way open.

Bea lay on her side on the floor beside the shower.

She wore a pink terry bathrobe and one slipper. The other lay over by the toilet. Her curly salt-and-pepper hair still dripped water, and she faced away from him toward the back of the room.

Blood pooled under her head. A lot of blood.

A coppery stench mingled with that of gunpowder, and beveling circled the wound where a slug had entered her head.

He knelt and felt for her pulse. It was faint but there. He grabbed a hand towel from the sink and folded it up to press against the head wound, which was still pumping blood. "Bea, can you hear me?" She groaned and flung out one arm. "Don't move. Help is coming."

He feared it would be too late. Her skin was pale and clammy, and her erratic pulse was weak and thready. The blood loss was slowing, but he wasn't convinced it was because of his attention. It might be because she was fading. "Hang on," he whispered.

Where was the ambulance? He prayed to hear the siren's warble heading this way.

Drew appeared in the doorway with Paradise behind him. "Sis called the ambulance. What's her condition?"

"Bad. Gunshot wound to the head. I don't see an exit wound either, and she's lost a lot of blood."

Drew let him care for Bea while he examined the room. "Don't touch anything if you can help it," he told Paradise.

She nodded and knelt on Bea's other side. "Bea, it's Paradise. Hang on. Blake is taking care of you."

Bea made a sound and tried to move her head.

"Don't move," Blake said. "I know it hurts, but try to stay still."

A moan slipped out of Bea's mouth. "Doris," she whispered.

"Maybe she means Doris Martinez who lived next door to us," Paradise said. "She's on our list to talk to."

"Doris," Bea said again. Her lids fluttered and she sighed out a long breath.

Blake held his breath to see if she would take the next breath. He couldn't find her pulse under his fingertips for several moments until it resumed its fluttery rhythm. Bea inhaled so softly he nearly missed it. She was still alive, but only barely.

Paradise stood close to Blake and leaned against him as they watched the ambulance tear off toward the hospital with lights flashing and siren blaring. It was lunchtime, but she wouldn't be able to eat a thing, and she doubted the men would either.

The ambulance turned the corner out of sight, and she blinked back tears. "I don't think she's going to make it."

Blake's embrace around her waist tightened. "She's in bad shape, babe."

Drew exited the house. "Rod says we can go. He may want us to come down to the station to go over our statements again, but we didn't see an intruder."

Paradise's sense of urgency rose. "Someone tried to kill Bea—and they might have succeeded. What was she hiding from us? I think we should try talking to Doris Martinez. There has to be a reason Bea mentioned her."

"Not necessarily," Blake said. "When people are semiconscious, they don't always make sense or have a reason for the things they say. But sure, I'm game to go see her. She's just over in Pelican Harbor."

They piled in the truck, and Paradise pulled up her phone's Notes app to see what other lines of investigation they might pursue. "Doris is just one possible source of information. We haven't talked to all of Mom's coworkers yet, just Mr. Phillips and Greta Welch."

Drew bent over his phone and started tapping. "I put in a request to get a copy of the files on Pamela's and my father's deaths. There might be something in them that will help us."

"We haven't talked to my dad's employer or any of his coworkers either. Maybe he had a good friend at work he might have confided in. He returned unexpectedly that day, and it's possible he told someone why."

Drew lifted his head. "I read the case notes. One of his coworkers said Granger got a call from the sheriff. I think Gerald warned him to get home after Pamela died."

If only she could remember more. Some memories had come back, but not all. And what she remembered felt covered in cobwebs. "Blake, your mom mentioned she knew Doris too. Jenna offered to be interrogated, but we haven't followed up on that."

"You're right. We can do it tonight after dinner."

They reached the outskirts of Pelican Harbor, and she pointed out the independent-living place on the left as they entered the city limits. "I probably should have called to make sure it was all right to come by. Since she's at Harmony Haven, she has to be pretty spry. They take residents on outings, and they aren't patients who need care. Back when I was a kid, she seemed ancient. Her husband had died, but Doris emotionally adopted all of the neighborhood children. When I got sent to foster care, she came to see me a few times, but the Adams family wasn't very welcoming, and those visits ebbed."

A clear vision of a round woman with her hair in a curly mop on her head came to her. She wished she'd thought of Doris before now.

Blake parked, and they trooped inside where Paradise asked to see her.

The nurse pointed down the right hall. "She's in room 114. It's on the left. Doris doesn't get much company, but she adores visitors. We love her around here. Are you family?"

"She used to be a neighbor when I was a kid. I thought I'd come find her now that I'm back in the area."

"She'll be so glad. Sign in here." The nurse pointed to the digital screen that recorded visitors' names.

Paradise entered all their names. Her pulse throbbed in her throat at the thought of seeing Doris. Why was she afraid? She'd loved the woman when she was a child, but trepidation slowed her steps and dried her mouth. It made no sense. She knocked on the door.

"Come in," a familiar voice called. It was scratchier and frailer than Paradise remembered.

Paradise's hand shook as she twisted the knob and opened the door. Doris's apartment here smelled just like the house where she'd lived all those years—a mixture of lemon furniture polish and vanilla from the candles she always burned. The first picture she spotted on the wall was one of Paradise with five other neighborhood kids. They were eating cookies and chocolate smeared their faces. Paradise's mother was smiling in the background. Paradise didn't think she'd ever seen this picture.

She gripped Blake's hand and blinked away the tears that gathered in her eyes. "Doris?"

Doris rose from the blue-and-yellow plaid sofa and smiled her way. The woman's curly hair was mostly white now, but her blue eyes still twinkled, and her skin looked soft and almost translucent. Her smile faltered. "Becky?"

Paradise took a step toward her. "It's Paradise, Becky's daughter."

"I knew you'd come eventually." And Doris promptly fainted back onto the sofa.

CHAPTER 25

PARADISE SPRANG TOWARD DORIS, but Blake moved her aside. "Let me check her. Call for a nurse."

Paradise pressed the button to summon the nurse and stepped to the side. Drew hovered nearby. Doris couldn't be dead. And why would she be expecting her? There'd been no mention of her being interrogated in the police files. Had she kept quiet for years about something important?

The nurse ran in and joined Blake at Doris's side. She administered smelling salts, and Doris coughed, then opened her eyes and pushed the vial away. "You trying to kill me, girl? Help me up," she commanded Blake.

He supported her back and eased her into a sitting position. "Take it easy."

"This has happened before," the nurse whispered. "Her heart."

Regret squeezed Paradise's chest. "Should we leave?"

Doris's hand shot out and clamped around Paradise's forearm in a surprisingly forceful grip. "No. I've been waiting to see you, Paradise. This old ticker will hold on a little while longer. I'm ninety-five, and when the good Lord calls me home, I'm ready to go. I'm tired of this crazy world anyway." She released Paradise and patted the cushion beside her. "You sit right here. Blake, you could start coffee. I don't have much of a kitchen, but it's enough."

"I'm on it." He walked to the minuscule kitchen, and the nurse brushed past him to exit the apartment.

Doris stared at Drew. "You look like Paradise. Are you Andrew James?"

Drew nodded. "You knew about me?"

"Shoot, Becky told me everything in that bright head of hers. She was a remarkable woman, your mama. I loved her like a daughter. She and Granger's deaths about took me to my grave too." Doris patted the sofa cushion again. "Sit in the chair there where I can see your face, Andrew James."

Drew looked confused but did as he was told.

The aroma of coffee began to overlay that of vanilla and lemon furniture polish. Blake returned with a glass of water that he handed to Doris. She thanked him and took a sip. "How's your mama, Blake?"

"She's great. Busy of course. She'll have my hide when she finds out I came to see you without her. The boys will too." He moved to sit beside Paradise.

She took his hand, relishing the rough calluses on his fingers and palms. She should have talked to him and Jenna about Doris as soon as her name came up. Paradise's pulse thrummed along her veins at the thought of what they might learn from her.

Doris's attention went back to Drew. "How'd you find your way here, boy?"

"I'm a police detective in Atlanta, and I knew I was adopted so I'd been looking for my birth parents. Paradise and I both had our ancestry done and I emailed her. We met a few weeks ago, and it feels like we've always been brother and sister."

Heat spread through Paradise's chest at the warmth in his tone. Any fears she had about him turning his back on her once this was all over vanished. Their tie was strong and unbreakable. "Why did you say you'd been waiting for me to come?"

Doris's eyes turned back to examine Paradise's face. "You're not a wallflower of a woman. I can see you're strong, and you're with Blake, aren't you?"

"I am." Was Doris stalling? Paradise turned her left hand so the emerald engagement ring winked in the sunlight streaming through the window. "We're engaged." The words were sweeter than chocolate on her tongue.

Doris clapped her hands. "That's lovely, just lovely."

"You thought I'd come eventually. Why?"

"I'd promised to keep Becky's secret about your brother until you came asking me for more information. She thought that might never happen, but even as a girl, you were the inquisitive sort—always sitting and staring at bugs and squirrels, examining tree trunks and flowers."

"I'm a wildlife vet now, so my curiosity about animals morphed into something useful. What do you know about Drew's father?" She could reveal they knew Ben's identity, but they might get more information if they let her talk.

Doris nodded in approval. "Drew is a great nickname. His name was Benjamin Collins. Yes, *that* Collins family. His mama found out he was having an affair and threatened to cut him off from the family money, but he might have divorced his wife anyway. Becky found out he was married, though, and broke up with him. I think Benjamin really loved Becky. And to be honest, it was right that he went back to his wife and honored his marriage. He already had a daughter he needed to raise. More children came along too."

This was nothing new and Paradise chafed at the lack of earth-shattering news she'd hoped to find here. "It's an old story, isn't it?"

"Not so old once he found your mama again. I think I know why she was killed, and I think I know who arranged it."

Paradise could barely breathe with the intensity of Doris's expression. Was that *sympathy* in her faded blue eyes? "What are you saying?"

"Your mama was pregnant. Benjamin was the father."

"No." Paradise licked her lips and shook her head, but she felt the weight of the truth in Doris's words. "How could she know? I mean, she and my dad weren't separated or anything."

"Your dad was overseas for a business trip when the baby was conceived. It was right after Benjamin came into her life again. She was distraught but determined to be with him. I had my misgivings."

Drew pulled his chair closer to her and sat with his knees nearly touching hers. "Who do you think killed her?"

"Benjamin said he was leaving his wife so he and Becky could be together, but I never trusted him. He wouldn't sully his own hands with murder, but he might hire someone to get him out of a difficult situation."

The news created a tsunami of emotion crashing into Paradise, and she hugged herself. "Did my dad know?"

Doris shook her head. "Becky told him she was leaving him for Benjamin, but I don't think she told Granger about the baby. It would have been cruel to tell him. He begged her to go to marriage counseling before deciding to leave, but her mind was set. I don't believe she ever got over Benjamin."

Drew's expression betrayed nothing. "You think my father hired someone to kill her to get out of a sticky situation? Do you have any evidence?"

"I saw the person who went into the house that day."

The words were dropped so casually, it took a moment for Paradise to process the information. "You recognized him?"

"I did. He worked for my husband before he died, and he always seemed the sneaky sort. I have good instincts about people. When he was a teenager, there was a rash of break-ins all over town. He was running with a bad crowd back then, and I always thought he was involved in those robberies. I watched him from the window when he went to the door the morning of the murders. He had something in his hand that he gave to you, Paradise, and you let him in. I saw him run from the house later that night too. It was before the murders, but he had been back inside."

Paradise remembered someone coming from the cable company. "What's his name?"

"Warren Gibson."

Paradise and Blake gasped at the same time.

"Who's Warren Gibson?" Drew asked, glancing from Paradise to Blake and back again.

"He works for The Sanctuary," Blake said.

"He's my vet tech." Since Warren was new, Paradise hadn't gotten to know him well. She'd always thought he was shy, but he probably lived in fear that she'd remember him giving her the music box. "Did you tell the police about him and about the pregnancy?"

"I told them about Warren but not about the pregnancy. I know I should have, but I couldn't bring myself to betray your mama's confidence. I hoped if I pointed them toward Warren, he would lead to the killer."

Paradise exchanged a glance with Drew. There'd been nothing in the files about an interview with Warren.

Blake parked the van in The Sanctuary lot. "I'll find Warren." He expected Paradise to object, but she nodded and opened her door. "He should still be in the clinic. We can all go."

Drew climbed out of the back seat and went to stand with Paradise. "You okay, Sis?"

"Just shocked. I can't believe Mom was pregnant and I never noticed."

"You were a kid. We both lost a sibling that day and never knew it."

The door to his mom's house opened, and Isaac and Levi came running to greet them. "You were gone forever," Isaac said, his brows drawn together.

Blake took a moment to scoop him up while Paradise hugged Levi. "I'm sorry, buddy. I can't play right now. I need to talk to Warren." His little brother smelled of banana.

Isaac clung to Blake's neck. "He's not here."

"He left already?" Paradise asked. "It's just after lunch."

Blake's mother opened the front door and stepped out. Her smile faded when her gaze landed on Blake. "Is something wrong?"

"Isaac said Warren left already, and we wanted to talk to him."

His mom frowned. "It was very abrupt. I'd taken the boys to see King Julien, and we were talking about how the lemur was doing. I got your text saying you'd been visiting with Doris and wanted to talk to him when you were done. He said he wasn't feeling well, then dashed off for his car. A stomach bug, I suspect."

"It's more than that." Blake jerked his head toward Levi. "Little pitchers."

She nodded. "Hey, boys, I noticed the GoodPops were frozen. You can each have two."

"Yay!" Isaac outran his brother in the race for the door, and they tussled at the entry before they disappeared inside the house.

"What's going on?" his mother demanded.

"Doris said Warren was the cableman who handed me *The Phantom of the Opera* music box." Paradise went over all they'd learned from Doris. "And someone shot Bea in the head. She was still alive when the paramedics took her, but she might not make it."

Mom put her hand to her mouth. "Poor Bea. And Doris never said a word to me in all these years. Pregnant. I was not expecting that."

"She said she told the police about Warren," Drew said. "But I've been over all those files several times and there aren't interview notes. It either slipped through the cracks, or someone took it out of the file. I've begun to suspect someone in the sheriff's department has removed evidence. It could have been Gerald Davis all those years ago or someone who works there now."

"Who in the sheriff's department would want to hide Warren's involvement twenty years ago? And why?" Blake would like to suspect his nemesis, Creed Greene, but he had no reason to think the obnoxious detective had that old murder on his radar. Could it be that Sheriff Davis was ordered to hide evidence as a favor to the Collins family? Or maybe he wanted to hide his involvement with Ben Collins. Ben could have been paying him to protect Becky.

"I assume you have Warren's address?" Drew asked. "We could try to intercept him." He turned to Blake's mom. "How long has he been gone?"

"About an hour."

They'd stopped to grab food in Pelican Harbor before heading back to the refuge. Blake doubted an hour's head start was enough for the man to clean out his apartment and escape town. Unless he headed out without taking his belongings. "Could you grab Warren's address for us, Mom?"

"You bet. It will be in the employee files. I think he lives in Foley. You can head that direction and I can text it to you." His mother hurried toward the office.

"I'm going to make a pit stop while she gets it." Drew headed toward the restroom.

Blake linked arms with Paradise. She'd been quiet and withdrawn since talking with Doris. "You doing okay?"

She leaned against him. "Talking to Doris brought back some sweet memories. I used to be at her house all the time. Mom once said Doris gave her the unconditional love she'd never felt from her own mother. I never understood her comment about how cruel my grandmother was until I found out about Drew. I wish I'd stayed in touch with Doris. Maybe I wouldn't have felt so alone."

"You'll never be alone again." He pressed a kiss on top of her head and picked up her left hand. "That ring sure is pretty on your hand."

She splayed her fingers. "I love it. Abby and your mom are going to go with me to look at dresses after the governor's visit. I verified that Chet's caters food, so we're good there."

"You're not wasting any time with the wedding plans."

"August will be here before we know it."

True enough. His phone dinged with a message, and he glanced at it. "Warren lives in Foley, on the same street as the library." He spotted Drew and motioned for him to hurry up. "Here comes your brother. Let's get going. Maybe we can intercept Warren."

They got in the truck. "Anyone want to put odds on whether Warren headed out of town without getting his belongings from his apartment?" Blake asked.

"I think he's still there," Paradise said.

"He's gone," Drew said. "His reaction was a dead giveaway that he's involved."

Blake started the truck and pulled out of the lot. "What if Sheriff Davis is behind the cover-up?"

"I'd sure like to see all the files on Ben's murder and his wife's death and how they might be connected to the Alden murders, but Pascagoula PD is dragging their feet on it," Drew said. "Police departments are often loath to share information."

"Speaking of the sheriff, we should ask about Bea once we see if Warren is around," Paradise said.

"I have an idea," Blake said. "The library director probably wouldn't mind checking to see if his car is parked there." He handed his phone to Paradise. "Text her and ask."

"I'm on it." She tapped out a message and sent it off. An answer came back immediately. "She's going outside to see if his car is in the driveway."

He increased his speed and turned right onto Route 98. He suspected Drew would win their wager, but he hoped he was wrong. His phone dinged with a message.

"His car is there!" Paradise pumped her fist. "I win!"

"As long as he doesn't jet out before we get there," Drew said.

The traffic wasn't helping. There was no way to pass, and Blake was stuck behind a slow-moving cement truck. He drummed his fingers on the steering wheel and resisted the impulse to lay on the horn. It wasn't the driver's fault his vehicle lumbered along like a turtle.

He finally reached 59 and got lucky enough to catch the light for his left-hand turn. Route 59 this time of year was always busy. Tourists packed the roads and slowed the traffic to a crawl.

"Almost there." Paradise gasped and pointed. "Wait, there he goes!"

Blake barely caught a glimpse of the blue Toyota Warren drove. He watched for a place to turn around. "Keep an eye on him. He's in a blue Toyota Corolla, Drew."

"He saw us," Paradise said. "When he spotted us, his eyes went wide and panicked, and he sped up."

Drew twisted in the back seat. "I don't see the car. Did he turn off?"

If Warren had seen them, he'd probably taken steps to vanish and selected an unlikely route. Blake turned around at the next light and went back south. But Warren had slipped out of the net.

CHAPTER 26

THE AROMA OF FRIED catfish mingled with that of baked mac and cheese. Paradise pushed away her plate. "Great meal, Jenna."

Isaac and Levi headed for the living room to get their iPads and their kittens for their screen time. They'd cleaned their plates like everyone else at the table.

"Best catfish ever," Drew said. "I'm going to take a look at the Alden murder files this afternoon. Since Bay Minette PD was kind enough to let me sign out the evidence kit, I want to study everything." He rose and put his hand on Jenna's shoulder. "Thanks for the meal and everything else you do around here."

She patted his hand. "You're welcome, Drew. We're all glad you're here."

"I'm glad too." He hesitated and his gaze locked with Paradise's. "Um, I wasn't going to say anything, but I can't keep it quiet. I'm applying for a job here. I don't really want to go back to Atlanta."

A surge of joy shot through her, and she jumped to her feet. "Drew!" She leaped into his arms and squeezed him hard. Tears sprang to her eyes and rolled down her cheeks. "I can't believe it."

His arms were tight around her, and he chuckled. "I have to get the job first, but I chatted with Rod while I was there, and he told me he'd walk it right through. I'll fill out an online application tonight and send it to him. They're short-staffed. Which is probably why they let me take the evidence. I'm sure Rod pulled some strings."

She released him and stepped back, wiping her eyes. "I'm so happy, Drew. I can't believe you're going to be right here where I can see you all the time. It's a dream come true." She wrinkled her nose. "You'd have to work with Creed, wouldn't you?"

"Probably." Drew swallowed as if he struggled with emotion too. "I can't leave you now, and I'd work with just about anyone to stay nearby."

"You'll need a place to stay," Blake said. "Consider the apartment your permanent abode until you decide you want a bigger place. Paradise and I are getting married next month, and—"

Squeals from his mother interrupted the rest of his sentence. "August?" Jenna clapped her hands. "We have to get to work on the wedding. And yes, of course, Drew, you can stay as long as you like. It's been wonderful having you here."

He grinned. "Nothing like a warm welcome to cement the idea. I'll keep you posted." He gave Paradise a final hug and headed for his apartment.

Jenna began to clear away the plates. "I'd like to hear what went on today, the full story."

Paradise grabbed plates too and began to tell her about finding Bea, seeing Doris, and barely missing Warren at his house. "You mentioned we should talk to you about Doris since you know her well too. Did you and my mother go to see her together?"

"We did, yes. She called us 'her girls.' Since she never had kids of her own, she spread her love around the neighborhood and at church." Jenna opened the dishwasher and began to load it.

"Did you know Warren back then?"

"That's why I hired him. He used to cut our grass when he was a teenager, and I'd always liked him. It's hard to wrap my head around Doris's belief that he might have something to do with the murders. He got that job with the cable company working under her husband."

"What did he do there?"

"He installed equipment. I'm not sure what he was doing at your house that day. Doris said she saw *The Phantom of the Opera* music box in his hands?"

"She couldn't tell what it was, but she saw him hand something to me. What exactly did you say to him before he ran?"

"I got that text about you guys needing to talk to him after meeting with Doris. That was all. But he clearly realized she knew something."

"How did he make the leap from cable installer to vet tech?" Blake asked.

"He went to school five years ago, supposedly because he wanted to work with animals."

"He's a good tech," Paradise admitted. "He's kind and gentle with the animals and has always listened to me. I don't think he's coming back though. He looked panicked."

"Rod checked out his apartment," Blake said. "It was a furnished apartment, but he took most of his things. He must not have had a lot."

"Did Warren ever mention friends or family who lived in the area?" Jenna asked. "His mom left when he was twelve, and his dad died a few years ago."

"He never mentioned a wife, and I didn't question him about

his family. He applied for the job after Lacey Armstrong went to jail for killing Danielle Mason. Do you think he wanted to work here to find out if we were getting close to finding who killed my parents?"

"It does feel as if he intentionally applied to replace her," Blake said. "Doris saw him running from the house the morning of the murders. Why would he be running unless something was wrong?"

Paradise wiped down the stove and counters. "I think we need to dig more and find out who he associated with."

Blake poured himself a glass of sweet tea from the fridge. "Maybe we could canvas his neighborhood and see if anyone knew him personally. I'm going to call Rod and see if he can dig up some information."

"We could ask our employees," Jenna said. "He might have opened up to some of them."

Paradise rinsed out the cloth. "Good idea. He's about forty, isn't he? We could start with Evan. He's been here the longest and might have talked to Warren on occasion. Warren sometimes helped him feed the animals at night before he left. They might have chatted about personal things."

After a dearth of clues to follow, it felt like floodgates were opening.

Blake stood in the shade of a large oak tree with Paradise and waited for Evan to finish the night feeding with Zach, the giraffe keeper. He planned to talk to both of them before moving on to other employees tomorrow. The lions roared their approval of being fed, and the tigers chuffed as well. The monkeys screeched deeper into the refuge, and their cacophony riled up the birds nearby.

Paradise stretched her arm around his waist and leaned against him. "It's a wonderful sound, isn't it? Contented animals sounding off. It's a special place, Blake. I'm so thankful I found it. And you." She turned her face up.

"It's amazing. We're blessed all the way around." He kissed her, lingering over the softness of her lips and her warmth against his side. He buried his face in her sweet-smelling hair. "I'm a lucky man."

A gate clanged, and he reluctantly released her as Evan and Zach, talking animatedly, came their way. "Hey, guys, glad we caught you."

Evan's brown eyes lost their mirth. "Something wrong, Boss? We did a head count, and all the animals are safe and happy. Even King Julien."

"Not really wrong, just puzzling. We needed to talk to Warren and he vamoosed, left town completely. It was very sudden. Do you have any idea where he might have gone? Does he have friends or family in the area?"

Evan glanced at Zach, who shrugged as if to say, *Don't look at me.* "He was always pretty closemouthed. Is this about the murders? You don't think Warren had anything to do with those, do you? He's so gentle, I can't imagine he'd even raise his voice."

There was no sense in hiding the truth. Blake studied Evan's expression. "You probably remember Doris. She saw him running from the Aldens' house a little while before the murders of Paradise's parents. She thought he knew something. And when he heard we wanted to talk to him after seeing Doris, he checked out early and went home. We passed him leaving town and were too late to see where he went. Did you hang out after he came to work here?"

"I have a family and don't have much time for hanging out. We were friendly here at work, but that's about it."

"Did he ever mention he was dating anyone?" Paradise asked.

"Not really." Evan glanced at his watch.

Zach shifted on his feet. "He invited me to go out for a drink once. He suggested College Social, but I told him I had to get home. Maybe check there."

The bar catered to college students and was in Nova Cambridge near University Grounds. Blake wasn't a drinker so he'd never been there, but they could check it out. The place was probably hopping about now, and someone might know. "Thanks, guys, we'll do that."

He let them head for their vehicles. "I think we should see if Drew wants to go with us to the bar. He'll know how to handle talking to a roomful of people."

"He might be done reading the files by now."

She started to follow him, and he realized she'd stopped so he turned. "What's wrong?"

"Abby knows everyone, and I think Warren's account was at her bank. She might know something."

Blake nodded. "We could swing by and talk to Abby before we go to the bar. She might want to accompany us. We haven't seen her since you were in the hospital."

"I'll text her." Paradise pulled out her phone and tapped out a message before they resumed walking toward the garage apartment. "We can go without Drew if he's busy. I don't want to wait. We might get lucky and find a lead to Warren before he's clear out of the state."

Her phone sounded and she glanced at it. "Abbs says she'll

meet us there. Quinn is studying with a friend, and she has to pick her up at nine, so she'll have time to hang out with us and talk."

He'd been tired before all this, but adrenaline put a spring in his step. Solving the murders felt so close. He'd once hoped Paradise would give up her quest because it seemed so hopeless. The turnaround felt destined, and he prayed God was opening the doors that needed to be kicked down. If Paradise could put all of it behind her, a new life awaited her. And him.

CHAPTER 27

COLLEGE SOCIAL WAS IN the same building as University Grounds but around the right side off a well-lit alley. Tiny lights dotted the ceiling of the large porch, and black iron tables and chairs added more seating than the bar's interior could hold.

Paradise spotted Abby at a table by the door. "There she is."

Drew opened his door first and waved. Paradise gave him a startled glance and spotted the animation in his face. Wait, wait, her brother thought her best friend was cute? She swung her gaze back to Abby and saw the same spark of interest. She wore a green dress that contrasted beautifully with her shoulder-length auburn hair and brown eyes. The ruffled cap sleeves showed off her shapely arms, and the skirt skimmed her hips and ended just above her knees, showing off her gorgeous legs. Had she dressed up hoping to see Drew?

When had this mutual attraction started? Maybe at Hez and Savannah's new house when Paradise had gotten out of the hospital. She hadn't seen their first meeting since she'd been inside resting, but there might have been sparks then.

Paradise just noticed her brother was wearing a different shirt than the brown tee from this morning. The blue looked good on him. She hid a smile and glanced at Blake to see if he'd noticed. His wide smile and wink her way confirmed he'd seen it too.

She bounded up the steps and hugged Abby. "I'm so glad you could come."

Abby glanced at her watch. "I have two hours. What's this all about?"

"We need to find Warren." She told her the situation. "I think he banks with you. Do you know anything about him?"

"Not much. He's quiet. I got the impression he hung out with the wrong crowd when he was younger, then decided to change his life." Her smile aimed over Paradise's shoulder. "Hey, Drew, looks like the party is about to get started with all of us here."

A group of college students spilled out the door, and Paradise herded her group out of the way. "It sounds raucous in there. How are we going to tackle this?"

"I'll handle it," Drew said. "Abby, you want to come with me? A guy with a beautiful girl on his arm is less intimidating to the bartender than me barging in asking questions by myself."

"You bet." Abby's smile increased in wattage, and she took the arm Drew offered.

Paradise stuffed down the laughter that wanted to bubble up. She linked her arm with Blake's. "I hope nothing interferes with their budding romance. It's a fabulous turn of events."

"They both seem interested." He leaned in so his breath whispered across her ear. "There's only one beauty here tonight, and she's on *my* arm."

"I think you're highly prejudiced."

"Could be, but it's still the truth." He held the door open for her, and she released his arm to step into the bar.

Light brick walls contrasted with dark wood floors and a

gleaming mahogany bar. A mirror reflected the rows of liquor bottles. Servers carried drinks and bar food through the crowd, and Paradise spotted a tower of onion rings with cocktail sauce. Music filtered through speakers, but she couldn't follow the melody with the flow of conversations around her. She and Blake shouldered through the throng to reach seats at the bar beside Drew and Abby.

Drew nodded to them and turned to the bartender. "I've got the tab for the four of us."

They all ordered sodas, and Drew ordered chips and queso for all of them. Paradise added that tower of onion rings she spotted.

"Food will be up shortly." The guy grabbed glasses and began to fill them with their drinks.

"Have you seen Warren Gibson around tonight?" Drew asked in a casual tone. "He works with us out at The Sanctuary."

The guy shot them an interested glance. "You guys work out there? Me and my wife love that place. My son likes the lemurs." He slid a Sprite Paradise's way. "I've seen your picture. You're the new vet in town too."

"Guilty." Paradise took a sip of her drink. "Warren helps out in the wild animal clinic. We stopped by his place, and when he was gone, we thought he might be here."

"You could ask his girlfriend." The bartender jerked his head down the row of stools toward a blonde who sipped on a beer. "She'll know where he is."

"Thanks." Drew lifted his glass of Coke as a toast and took it with him.

Paradise followed with Blake and Abby. Could it really be this easy to find Warren?

Drew slid onto the seat next to the woman, who appeared to be about Paradise's age, and gestured to Paradise, who quickly stepped over to stand by him. She had seen plenty of false eyelashes that were tastefully done, but this woman's were at least half an inch long and as thick as curling spider legs. She suppressed a shudder.

The woman turned a lazy glance toward them. "'Elp you?" she slurred.

Her breath blew the stench of beer to Paradise's nose, but she forced a smile. "Hi, I work with Warren, and I need to ask him a question. He left work early and isn't home. Do you happen to know where he is?" Was the woman sober enough to answer?

The woman's bleary eyes studied Paradise's face. "The new vet. Better find a new tech. He skipped out. Prob'ly halfway to Florida by now."

"Does he know someone in Florida?" Drew asked.

She swore and took another gulp of her beer. "Shot me a text and said he'd be in touch. *Suuuure* he will. Wish I could meet a good man, just once." She clutched Drew's forearm. "You taken, honey?"

"Sorry." He eased her hand off his arm. "You have any idea where he might be holing up? We really need to talk to him."

She shrugged. "His aunt has a condo in Perdido Key. Took me there once. Beach Colony Resort."

"Do you know the condo number?"

She sighed and reached for her purse. After digging in it for what felt an eternity, her hand emerged with a crumpled paper. "3D," she announced. "Nice place."

Drew put it in his phone. "We appreciate your help." He pulled out a card and pressed it into her hand. "If he contacts you, would you let me know?"

She glanced at the card. "You're a cop?"

"I'm Paradise's brother and I'm just helping her find Warren." He stood and took a step back.

It felt like a dead end, but Perdido Key wasn't that far. They could check it out. "Anyone up for a Perdido Key beach stroll?"

"I'm in," Abby said. "Let me arrange for Quinn to spend the night at her friend's." She headed for the exit.

Paradise caught Drew's expression and tried unsuccessfully to hide her smile. He was too smitten to notice.

The Beach Colony Resort was gated, and they didn't have a code. Blake tapped his fingers on the steering wheel. "We might have a problem."

Paradise glanced ahead at the gate. "Hang back. The oncoming car has its turn signal on. We can slide through behind them."

She was right. He eased his foot off the accelerator and let the oncoming car turn in front of him. He pulled his truck in behind it, and sure enough, he was able to tag along with the car ahead. "I knew I brought you along for a reason other than you're beautiful and I love you."

"Hey, we're back here watching," Abby said. "Let's stick to business."

Her voice held mirth, and when Blake glanced in the rearview mirror, Abby was only inches from Drew's side, and they were both laughing. Were they holding hands? Sure looked like it to him.

Blake turned toward the west building. "It appears you're watching each other, not us."

Drew and Abby burst into chuckles behind him, and he

exchanged an amused glance with Paradise. It was like being a teenager again and going on a double date.

He parked the truck at the end of the lot. "That's his car." He pointed out a Toyota Corolla.

They went inside the open-air lobby and the elevator refused to take them to the third floor. "I'll bet we need a code here too," Paradise said. "But it's only three floors. Let's find the staircase."

He'd much rather take a stroll on the beach, but they hadn't come here for fun. They caught another break when someone exited the door and held it open for them. They filed up the stairs to the third floor and found the D door. He rang the bell but no one answered. He tried the door. "It's not locked." Entering felt wrong, so he pushed the door open with his foot and peered inside.

A familiar backpack with a tiger's face on it lay just inside the foyer. "That's one of our logo backpacks. He's here somewhere." Blake leaned inside the door. "Warren, you in there?" No one answered, and the place felt empty.

"Let's try the beach," Drew said. "I'll bet the elevators work going down."

Moments later they were on the ground floor, and Drew pointed out the path around the well-lit pool to the beach. Blake followed the sound of the waves mingling with laughter. He took Paradise's hand and led the way across the boardwalk to the white sand dunes shimmering in the moonlight. There weren't many people here, and none of them were Warren.

"Let's stroll along the beach and see if he took a walk," Drew said. "We can check the condo one last time before we leave. He might be back by then."

They kicked off their shoes and carried them along the sand

with the water foaming around their feet. Paradise paused to run into the water up to her knees. Blake stopped and watched the breeze blow her glorious brown hair around her face. He was a lucky man.

She darted back to him. “It’s beautiful here.”

He kept his gaze on her. “It sure is.”

Amusement lit her amber eyes. She tucked her arm into his. “Let’s catch up with Abby and Drew.”

He fell into step with her and put his arm around her waist. They should come back when the sun was hot and they could stretch out on the white sand. Which brought up a good question. “Where do you want to go on our honeymoon? With the refuge on good footing, we can go somewhere fun.”

“I hadn’t thought about it. I’d assumed we’d be at my apartment and plan something later.”

He squeezed her fingers. “I’ll take you anywhere you want to go.”

“Since I’m an Alden, I’ve always wanted to go to England.” She swept her arm toward the water. “But I love the beach.”

“There are beaches in England. I’ve heard Bournemouth Beach’s microclimate makes for warmer water than most. It should be nice in August. Let’s see what we can find out. And if it’s too cold, we can explore England, then go to the South of France for a few days.”

“That sounds incredibly exotic.” She stopped. “Maybe a cruise! Let’s check it out.”

He loved seeing her so happy and animated. They started walking after Drew and Abby again. “He just kissed her.”

“He’s moving fast, and Abby’s still raw and hurting from her divorce. I’ll have to get Abby alone and see what she says.”

She stopped and they turned around to walk back toward the

complex. The wind picked up and she shivered. "That breeze is a little cool."

He put his arm around her again, and they picked up the pace to hurry over the boardwalk to the condo. Drew and Abby were right behind them. As they rounded the pool and got close to the outdoor lobby, he gasped. "Warren just got into the elevator. He didn't see us."

Blake ran toward the stairs and took the steps two at a time. His lungs labored as he pushed himself to go faster. If Warren got to the condo and locked the door, they'd be shut out. He wouldn't open it to them—not after trying to elude them all day. Breathing hard, he crashed through the third-floor door and raced to door D.

It was closing so he stuck his foot inside. "Warren, we need to talk to you."

The door banged farther open, and Warren backed up with his eyes wide. His red hair dripped water. His gaze darted from Blake to Paradise right behind him. "What are you doing here? Leave me alone."

Blake stepped into the condo. "We won't keep you long. Doris thinks you know something about the murders of Paradise's parents. We don't think you hurt them, but you might know something that would help us find out who did."

His brown eyes were wild, and he backed away with his hands in front of him. "I can't tell you anything. Bea is dead, did you know that? I'll be next. Look into Ben's history. The truth is there. Just leave me alone." He turned and ran to the sliding door out onto the balcony.

Blake didn't have time to dwell on the news about Bea but instead went after him. Warren swung one leg over the railing, then the other. He began to sidle along the edge of the balcony toward the wall, and Blake knew he planned to try to swing himself over to another condo. "It's windy out there, Warren. Come on in and we'll just talk."

Uncertainty twisted Warren's lips, and he edged back toward Blake. "I realized what they were going to do, and I ran away. I didn't want to hurt anyone." A thunderous roar grew, and a formation of low-flying fighter jets from Pensacola shook the building. Wind gusted around the balcony and yanked on Warren's shirt.

Blake darted forward to help steady him, but Warren lost his grip. He stared up into Blake's eyes as he plummeted toward the ground.

CHAPTER 28

PARADISE STOOD FIFTEEN FEET away from the group of officers and paramedics on the scene and hugged herself as the wind-driven sand stung her legs. Abby stood silently beside her with her auburn hair whipping around her face. The sound of the ocean should have soothed Paradise, but she was too uncomfortable here in the wind and the dark.

She craned her head to stare for a moment at the brilliant stars, then inhaled the salty tang of the wind and tried to calm her racing heart. Even though it felt like everything had spiraled out of control today, God felt close in this moment. He was in control.

Everything had happened so fast. Paradise had been right behind Blake, but they were both helpless to stop the terrible tragedy. The scene played out in her head over and over. Warren's wide, panic-stricken eyes, his mouth moving with words she couldn't hear, then that final terrible moment when the wind buffeted him and tore him from the railing.

Blake separated from the group and walked toward her. "You okay?"

She nodded. "He's dead?"

He put his arms around her and pulled her to his chest. "Yeah. Broke his neck in the fall." His voice vibrated with tension. "He was really scared of someone."

She nestled against his warmth and listened to the steady thump of his heart under her ear. "I couldn't hear what he said to you."

"He said, 'Look into Ben's history. The truth is there.'"

"And we have no idea what that means."

"If he's right, someone connected to Ben is at the heart of the murders. We have to dig into everyone's connections. It's a big job, but we have direction. Here comes Drew."

She moved away from the comfort of Blake's embrace and turned to face her brother. His grim expression tugged at her emotions. How did he handle being faced with death every time he turned around?

He shot a glance at Abby. "Sorry you had to witness all this. The police want to question each of us separately. It's standard policy. They'd like to talk to you first, Blake. You were the tip of the spear, so to speak, the one closest to Warren when he fell." Drew pointed out an officer with an unruly mane of black hair. "Go see him. I'll stay with the girls."

Blake nodded and headed that way. Would the police think any of them had killed Warren? But no, there were four witnesses to the accident. The stories would all line up to the truth.

Drew took Abby's hand. "You look cold."

"Just tired of the wind." She bit her lip and moved closer to him. "Do you think they suspect any of us pushed Warren off the balcony?"

"No, I think the scene is clear enough. They seemed to accept the recounting of events. I was right behind Paradise and saw it all. I gave them Rod's phone number so they could verify we were pursuing leads in a cold case. They'll probably come to the refuge and ask a few questions as well. People can verify that Warren left work suddenly. I also told them about his girlfriend who can verify he'd left town."

The tension eased out of Paradise's shoulders. Hopefully this wouldn't take long and they could get out of this wind and head for home. "Did you hear what Warren said to Blake?"

"I was too far away, and the wind was blowing through the open patio door. I saw his mouth move, but that's all."

She told him what Blake had said. "So it sounds like we need to find out everything we can about your father's family."

"It's a large one with a lot of tentacles in every direction. They're so involved with politics, it's going to be a huge pool of suspects. If we can figure out why Ben and his wife were targeted *and* your parents, it would help us narrow in on the killer. It's a puzzle."

"What do we do next?"

The breeze lifted his light brown hair, and he tried to palm it down. "I think another visit with my father's family is in order. I want to meet the other siblings and see what they know. Victoria's birthday party is Friday. We'll all go down."

"I'm not so sure about that. Maybe you should go by yourself."

"I want you with me. Blake too. We can wander around and see what we find out. It sounds like it will be a big party. I'll verify with Duke whether it's okay to bring you, but I'm sure it will be. I'm also interested in finding out more about Pamela. Even her own daughter says she was manipulative. Some connection to her could have led to the murders."

What a tangle of threads to try to unravel. "The governor is coming on Sunday. It might be worth talking to her about it. Even though she's the Alabama governor, the Collins family is a powerhouse even in national politics. And though Warren said to look at Ben's family, we can't ignore the other avenues of investigation. They might know something about Ben's family."

"True enough."

Blake came back her way. "The detective wants to talk to you." His warm hand pressed hers. "Just tell him what you saw and what we were doing. It won't take long, and we can get out of this wind."

She headed for the unsmiling detective to get this over with.

Blake let his brothers run ahead of him to the corral at the Dillard Ranch while he walked beside Paradise. The distinct odor of horse mingled with the scent of newly mown hay from the field to their left. "They were so excited I don't think they slept last night. I see Savannah and Simon." He pointed them out by the barn, where they stood talking to Abby and Quinn.

"Abby's looking for Drew," Paradise said. "She must not know he went to talk to Rod at the Bon Secour sheriff's station."

The boys reached the corral and stopped to stare at the horses. "They're bigger than I thought they'd be." Levi took Blake's hand.

"I want to ride that guy." Isaac pointed out the biggest one, a black gelding. As if the animal understood, the horse clopped over to bump the boy's hand with his mane.

Smiling, Abby's daughter, Quinn, walked toward them and met them at the gate. Her long red hair hung down her back in a braid. "Come on in and meet the horses. Some people like to start with ponies, but our horses are so gentle. Ponies can be mischievous." She opened the gate to let them in, then fastened it behind them.

"Glad you could make it," Savannah said. "This is Simon's

fourth lesson, and he loves it so much." She touched Isaac's hair. "You ready to learn to ride?"

"I've wanted to do this since I was a baby."

That wasn't far wrong. Isaac had watched horse shows on TV since he was a toddler. Levi hung back, clinging to Blake's hand. Though at seven he was the oldest, he wasn't as daring as his five-year-old brother.

Paradise leaned over and whispered to Blake, "I should have come prepared to ride myself, but I didn't want to make more work for Abby and Quinn. I remember my first lesson in this very spot."

"Next time," he told her.

Though Quinn was only ten, she was tall with an assertive manner. Blake knew she'd been riding since she was two, and it showed in her practiced movements bridling and saddling the horses. When all five horses were ready to go, she demonstrated how to mount and swing their legs up into the saddle. "You'll all need mounting blocks at first. It's hard to mount when you're way shorter than the horse." She patted the black horse's nose. "This is Onyx. He was born at the ranch, and he's super sweet."

"I want to try!" Isaac approached the black horse and climbed on the mounting block. He mounted like Quinn had shown them in one smooth movement. He held hold of the pommel. "Look at me!"

"I see you," Blake said. "Listen to everything Quinn and Miss Abby tell you."

"I will."

Blake kept hold of Levi's hand and walked with him to a bay mare. "She's beautiful, isn't she?" He stroked her nose, and Levi let go of his hand and did the same.

"Her name is Cinnamon," Abby said. "She's a good girl." She fed the mare a sugar cube, and the horse nickered.

"Ready?" Blake asked Levi, who nodded and approached the block with confidence. He made a false start once, then got his seat in the saddle. His huge grin warmed Blake.

Simon, Abby, and Quinn got mounted, and Savannah moved outside the corral to watch. The kids began to relax, and Blake wished his mom could have come to watch. Next time he'd stay home and work so she could watch the boys.

Savannah put one foot on the bottom rail of the fence. "Hez told me what happened a couple of nights ago. That had to have been traumatic."

Paradise shuddered. "I keep seeing it in my head."

"I understand. Hez had a thought this morning. Maybe Warren did business at the local bank where Abby works. She might take a peek at the records and see if any unusual deposits landed in his account in the past few months. She can't really give you any personal information, but she could suggest the police get a subpoena to see the activity. I doubt the police will probe too much since his death was an accident, but if there's a hint they could find clues to a cold case, they might do it."

Paradise settled on the grass and curled her legs under her. "I thought about that too, and when Abby gets back, I'll ask about it. Honestly, she might have already checked. It was a traumatic night for her too."

Savannah joined her on the ground. "We might as well get comfy. They'll be riding at least half an hour. You know Abby well. How's she dealing with her dad's death and his involvement in murdering Mary Steerforth?"

"We haven't talked about it much. She moved in here though."

"I heard her ex is getting remarried."

"It hit her hard."

Blake tuned out the discussion when movement at the barn caught his attention. Someone was inside the structure. A worker, or something more? He left the women chatting and slipped through the gate. The horses were on the other side of the corral, and he hurried to the barn before the riders came his way.

Sunlight streaming through the windows lit up the dust motes in the air. He walked through the space, stopping at the horse stalls along the way, until he got to the office in the back. He and Roger had chatted many times back here, and he'd never seen the door closed. He twisted the doorknob and a sound came from inside. He eased it open and stared at Lloyd Adams.

Before Blake could react, Lloyd barreled into him and knocked him to the ground. The older man rushed past him, and Blake jumped up to chase him. He caught a glimpse of the man's blue jeans as Adams exited the back door. Blake charged after him and got there in time to see him leap onto a dirt bike and drive off across the open field behind the paddock.

When had Adams gotten out of jail, and why hadn't they been informed of his release?

CHAPTER 29

PARADISE WRAPPED HER HANDS around the hot mug, hoping the heat would seep through the cold place inside her. "Why didn't they tell us Adams escaped? And what happened?"

Drew reached over and gave her forearm a squeeze. He'd left the sheriff substation to rush to the Dillard Ranch as soon as she texted him. "It's why Rod called me. I think he wanted to lay out what happened so I could tell you."

"Let's hear it." She wished Blake were beside her. He'd rounded up the boys once Drew got here so he could run them home in case Adams came back. He should be back in a few minutes. Savannah had taken Simon home, and Quinn was in her room.

Abby handed Drew a mug of coffee, and he thanked her. "He was being transported from the jail to prison and had a seizure. He was taken to a small hospital for emergency treatment. Rod now thinks the seizure was faked, but he hasn't talked to the doctor. Two men with guns showed up and broke him out. This happened the day before yesterday."

"And we just now heard about it? Why wasn't it all over the news?"

Her brother shrugged. "Good question. I'm wondering why he came here first." Drew angled a glance at Abby, who was pouring herself some coffee. "Adams was working with your dad. Did you ever see him here, Abby?"

She joined them at the breakfast bar. "I didn't. They were cousins, but he always gave me the creeps so I avoided him. Dad knew it too and always warned me if he planned to stop by. And remember, I lived in town until . . . until I moved here so the ranch wasn't empty."

Paradise's eyes filled with tears at the misery on Abby's face. They hadn't talked much about Roger's death other than right after the gators got him when he tried to escape from Swamp Island, where Blake had left him. Paradise had tried not to imagine the horror he felt in his final moments.

She reached over and took Abby's hand. "I'm sorry you're dealing with this. I'm not sure you should be here alone with him skulking around."

"I'll be fine. I'm a good shot."

"I think Paradise is right," Drew said. "You have a bedroom for me if I come hang out a few nights until he's found?"

Abby's brown eyes went wide. "The house is huge. There's plenty of spare bedrooms. But you don't have to do that." Her smile betrayed her hope.

"I want to. Blake will still be at the park protecting Paradise and the rest of the family. I don't like the thought of you all the way out here in isolation without anyone. I'll grab my things and come over."

Abby smiled. "You're the best, Drew. Quinn might drive you crazy. She's a talker."

"I like kids. And Quinn."

A car door slammed from outside. "That's probably Blake."

Paradise swung around at the doorbell and rose to step from the kitchen and down the hall to the living room. She unlocked the door and let him in. His presence calmed her agitation. Only he would understand how upset she was at the news of Adams's escape.

Blake embraced her. "Any sign of him?"

"Not that I know of. Rod and his men are combing the area looking for him." She raked her hands through her hair. "Why *here*, Blake? If he planned an escape, why not get out of the country? What could be so important he had to come here? He'd know the cops would be all over this area looking for him. There must be something in the barn."

Blake nodded. "I think so too. Let me ask Abby if it's okay to search the barn."

Paradise followed him toward the kitchen. "And we want to ask about Warren's bank account."

Drew released Abby's hand when they appeared in the doorway. "Blake, I'm going to run home and grab a few things. I don't think Abby and Quinn should be here alone."

"Good plan. Hey, Abbs, do you mind if we search the barn? Adams had to be out there looking for something."

Abby nodded. "I'll help too. I was just wondering why he'd be in the barn. Wouldn't incriminating evidence be more likely to be inside the house?"

"I would imagine the police extensively picked through things in here," Drew said. "What did your dad do in the barn office?"

"Mostly he met with his old cronies out there, talking politics and selling livestock. A lot of ranch business was done in that office. I rarely went out there though."

Paradise took the final gulp of her coffee, tepid by now. "And we wondered if you'd taken a peek at Warren's bank account.

I know you can't tell us anything, but do you think the police should subpoena his records?"

She hesitated, then nodded. "But you didn't hear it from me."

"Of course not." Paradise rinsed her mug and placed it in the dishwasher. Abby had already done the same to hers and Drew's cups. "Let's see what we can find."

Abby called up the stairs to Quinn that they were going to the barn. The girl called back, "Okay."

They exited into a warm, humid afternoon. Officers dotted the fields and Paradise spotted figures moving through the trees in the woods as well. She doubted they'd find him. Once Adams knew Blake had seen him, he'd be long gone from the county.

She hurried to the barn with the others. Blake ran on ahead and left the door open for them. She found him in Roger's office. The walls were barnwood, but he'd tried to liven it up with pictures of Abby and Quinn through the years. There was one with Paradise and Abby on horses. They were twelve. Her throat tightened at the memory of how good Roger had been to her over the years.

Blake yanked open the filing cabinet and pulled out file folders that he stacked on the battered desk. He and Drew began to go through them. Paradise picked up one also. She flipped through three pages until she realized she was looking at a list of pictures and names along with details of crimes and amounts of money in several installments.

She showed it to Blake. "I think Roger was blackmailing people."

Blake stood with Paradise off to one side of the Collinses' meticulously manicured lawn dotted with roses, azaleas, and rhododendrons. People he didn't know mingled, and their laughter and conversation flowed around him. Drew motioned to them from the drink table, where he stood with Abby, who had come along as his date. Blake caught a whiff of seawater in the breeze that blew in from the beach.

"Your brother wants us to join him. The people he's with look related." He took her hand. "I was enjoying watching, but our presence is required."

They walked across the soft grass. Drew appeared relaxed and comfortable with Taylor and the two men flanking her. Taylor wore a black cocktail dress and heels, and the men both wore sport coats. Blake felt underdressed in his khakis and polo shirt.

They reached Drew, who took Paradise's hand and pulled her closer. "This is my sister, Paradise. We share the same mother. Sis, this is Gray." He indicated the blond thirtysomething man with a receding hairline who stood expressionless with his hands in his pockets. "And this is Parker." Parker reached out and gripped Blake's hand. He was a shorter version of Gray with light brown hair. His open, friendly expression was in contrast to Gray's glower.

"I'm sure this was all a shock."

"Our parents had a rocky relationship, so it's not as surprising as it could have been," Parker said.

Gray hailed a server with a tray of champagne. He gulped back the liquid before turning steely gray eyes toward Drew. "You want money, I suppose."

Drew inhaled, then shook his head. "I don't want anything other than information. My birth mother and her husband were killed within days of both of your parents. That has to mean something. If I can figure out the connection, we might find justice for both of us. Did you ever know of anyone who argued with your mom or dad? Ben was running for the Senate before he was murdered, correct?"

"Yes, but I was too young to remember any of that. You should talk to our uncle Bear." Parker turned and hailed the portly man standing with Victoria and Percy.

Both of Drew's brothers resembled their uncle, but Bear's hair was gone except for a thin stripe extending from one ear to the other. His congenial smile was like Parker's as he walked over to speak with them. "Ah, my parents have been regaling me with what they know of my unknown nephew. You don't look much like Dad or Mom, do you?"

"Nope." Drew gave Paradise a side hug. "We both look like our mother, Becky Bartley. Have you ever heard that name?"

"Yes. Ben was head over heels for her. When Taylor was little, he was ready to get a divorce and marry Becky until the family put the hard press on him. Mom, Dad, our grandparents—they all talked incessantly until he gave in and broke up with her. Ben never said anything about a child at the time."

"He didn't know," Drew said. "Becky never told him."

Victoria and Percy said they'd been searching for Drew, but Bear must have been shielded from the knowledge of Drew's existence.

Drew must have thought the same thing because his eyes widened. "Your parents were looking for me. Weren't you and our father close?"

Bear's smile melted away. "Very close. Mom and Dad must have found out later, and they're less likely to share personal details than Ben was. I understand Becky and Ben met up again randomly, which was probably when he found out and told our parents. I've been living in Texas for the past thirty years, and once I moved, Ben and I didn't speak as often as when we were kids. There was no falling out or anything like that. I was glad he found success where I'd failed."

Drew snagged a glass of iced tea from a passing server and took a gulp. "We think it's possible some connection with his political aspirations led to the murders. He never mentioned an enemy?"

"Not to me."

"Did he have a campaign manager who might know more? We're particularly interested in who his supporters were."

"That was twenty years ago. But if anyone knows where those records are, it would be Octavia. She's Mom's best friend." Bear motioned to a woman talking to Taylor on the patio. "Octavia, come meet Drew."

The woman turned with a smile. She was the grandmotherly sort, softly rounded with pink cheeks. Her white hair was up in a French twist, an old-fashioned style that suited her.

She came toward them with a questioning expression, and as she neared, she glanced from Drew to Blake. "Drew?"

He cleared his throat. "Um, I'm Drew. This is Blake, who is soon to be my brother-in-law."

She switched her green-eyed gaze to Drew and surveyed him from head to foot. "You have your dad's build."

Bear gave an exasperated snort. "I'll leave you to it. I hear sushi calling my name." He headed for the food table with Drew's half brothers trailing him.

Drew crossed his arms over his chest and glanced at Abby, who moved closer to him. "Bear said if any of the campaign records still existed, you'd know where they were."

"I had them all backed up on an external hard drive. I still have some USB flash drives as well. I believe they should be in my office in a box of things I cleared out after your father's death. What possible use could they be to you now?"

He told her what Warren had said before he plummeted off the balcony. "So we're digging into anything to do with his campaign first. It makes sense a rival would be more likely to want him dead than someone in his family."

She lifted a thinning eyebrow. "You can have the files in my possession in case they're useful. I was going to throw them out anyway since I'm downsizing. Follow me to my house when this is over, and you can take them."

Blake glanced at the faces around the yard. The afternoon was still young, and they might come away with gold.

CHAPTER 30

PARADISE'S FEET HURT, AND she'd eaten too much. The potato salad had been the best she'd ever tasted, and the beignets were divine. Would anyone notice if she kicked off her shoes and walked down the path to the water? Blake was deep in conversation with Victoria and Percy. Their faces glowed with animation, and she could see their liking for that man of hers on their faces.

She waited until she left the green carpet of grass behind for the oyster path, then kicked off her shoes. The cool crushed shells underfoot felt soothing against the soles of her feet. The scent of the water drew her on past banks of azaleas, and she followed the sound of the gentle surf until the trees and flowers petered out at a stone wall with an opening to the water. She stepped through onto the beach and dug her toes into the warm, sugar-like sand.

She wasn't alone.

A woman sat on the stone wall, gazing out to where blue sky met blue waves. Her gauzy white dress fluttered in the breeze, and she pushed her long blonde hair out of her face. She appeared to be in her late twenties or early thirties.

A bird chattered angrily from somewhere, and she straightened, then caught sight of Paradise. "Well, hello." She patted the space beside her. "Most comfortable seat in the house."

"My feet could use a rest." Paradise had left the chairs scattered around the party for the elderly. Victoria was age eighty, and many of her friends were of the same generation, though Paradise hoped she looked as fit and beautiful as Drew's grandmother when she was that age.

The woman lifted her legs straight out to show pink-tipped bare toes. "Me too. I never feel like I fit into these things. I'm Gray's wife, Unity."

"What a lovely name."

"I try to live up to it, but it's hard in this family. Don't let their welcome fool you. There's a lot of darkness behind those smiling eyes."

Paradise blinked at Unity's candor. "I-I'm surprised. They've welcomed Drew with open arms."

"You ever hear the saying 'Keep your friends close and your enemies closer'? That's their motto. Drew seems like a nice guy, and I'd hate for him to open his heart to them only to see it trampled. Like mine."

"You don't have a good relationship with them?"

Unity stared at the blue water a long moment. "I probably shouldn't have said anything." She corralled her hair and tucked it behind her ears. "I'm divorcing Gray. He doesn't know yet. There are more secrets in this family than a scientist with unfiled patents. Layers and layers of secrets. Be careful when you go looking for one that you don't find something that knocks you on your heels."

"I'm sorry." Unity's despondency was so poignant that an unexpected moisture of film blurred Paradise's vision. There wasn't much she could say or do that would help, except one thing. "I'll pray for clarity for you."

Unity straightened. "That's kind of you when we're strangers."

"Do you have children?"

"I wish we did. Maybe it would have cracked open that shell Gray has around him. He's so closed off and remote. Being raised in that household would warp anyone though."

"Even Parker? He seems different."

"He's worse than Gray. My husband doesn't pretend to be something he's not. Parker sucks you in with smiles and warmth that's a veneer for someone who only cares about himself and what is best for him. He'd make a perfect politician. I'm not sure why he didn't choose that career."

Paradise shuddered with a chill, and it wasn't from the wind. "Thank you for telling me. Drew wants to find out who killed our parents, and that's our only goal."

But Drew would be hurt by this news. The initial welcome had warmed a place inside that longed for more family. It grieved her that he wouldn't find it here.

"There you are."

She turned at Blake's familiar deep voice that always accelerated her pulse. What you saw was what you got with him. No subterfuge, no masks. He was all kindness and encouragement.

Unity rose. "I'd better be getting back. Gray will be wondering where I am and what secrets I'm spilling." She paused by Blake before walking through the wall opening. "I'd suggest you hold the whole family at arm's length. Things aren't always as they seem."

Blake frowned. "What do you mean?"

"They're good at covering up the darkness inside."

Paradise rose and went to stand beside her. "Do you know who killed my parents?"

Unity held her gaze. "I have my suspicions, but I know better than to talk about them. I've said too much already." She brushed past Blake and walked up the oyster-shell path to the echoes of voices and laughter.

Blake took her hand. "That was weird. You think she was just blowing smoke?"

"I believe her. There's a deep strain of hurt and pain she didn't even try to hide. She warned us not to trust the welcoming smiles of the Collins family. I was already uneasy around them, but I told myself I was jealous and didn't dig into why I distrusted them."

Paradise wanted to get her brother and get out of here before the Collinses' tentacles wrapped them all up tight.

Blake parked behind the white convertible he'd followed from the Collinses' home. "Nice digs."

He'd seen more and more white homes with black window trim in the area, and the modern, clean lines appealed to him. This one was massive with beautiful landscaping. He got out of the truck and the four of them approached the door Octavia held open for them.

They filed into the soaring foyer behind her and followed her to the living room. The walls inside were white, too, and pale wood floors added to the clean feel. The furniture was white and shades of beige with a few teal throw pillows. The ceilings soared to twelve feet and the whole place felt open and expansive. It had to be new.

"Let me get those backups." Octavia disappeared into a hallway and a door opened somewhere.

"You like this place?" Blake asked Paradise. "I thought I didn't like modern, but it's nice."

She nodded. "It could use a little more color, but I love the floors and high ceilings."

Abby touched the top of a leather chair. "Once you start thinking about building a house, it becomes an obsession. This is beautiful."

Blake hid a smile when he saw the way Drew watched Abby. And she couldn't keep her gaze off him either. Drew's decision to move here and get a job could change a lot of things.

Octavia stepped back into the room. "I found one file folder in the cabinet as well as the backups. It's from Ben's final campaign." She held them out to Drew, who took them.

"Thanks for your help with this," Drew said.

Octavia's green eyes softened. "You're very welcome. Your father was a special man, Drew."

Paradise shifted beside Blake. "You've been around the Collins family a long time. Do you have any idea who might have wanted Ben dead?"

"Ben was one of those charismatic figures who drew everyone. Even women who should have been focused on their own husbands."

"Did Ben make a move on someone Bear loved?"

Octavia regarded her quietly a moment. "Did Unity say something? I saw you talking to her."

Paradise squared her shoulders and glanced at her brother. "She warned us the Collins family wasn't all it seemed. I met her on the beach." Paradise touched Drew's hand. "I should have told you on the way here, but it was such a short drive and I didn't want our conversation to be interrupted. She wanted you to keep your guard up—that the family isn't always what they seem."

A shutter came down over Drew's eyes. "I see. I'll keep that in mind."

Octavia settled on a chair and kicked off her shoes. "You might as well know that Ben was engaged to another woman when Bear started dating Pamela. Ben took one look at her and everything changed."

Paradise gasped. "Bear dated Pamela first?"

Octavia nodded. "Ben broke his engagement and married Pamela six months after he met her. Bear never got over it and has stayed single. Though the two brothers got along well, I think Bear moved because he couldn't stand to watch Ben live the life that Bear had wanted."

Paradise twisted the engagement ring around on her finger. "Marriage didn't seem to mean much to Ben. He was married when he pursued my mother. Pamela would have been better off with Bear."

Octavia relaxed in the chair and crossed her legs. "You're probably right. Pamela was beautiful. People compared her looks to Julia Roberts, and she was so sweet back then. The more years she stayed married to Ben, the harder she became to live with."

Blake rolled the words over in his head. "Did he have any other children besides the four we know about?"

She gave an elegant shrug. "Who knows? Victoria is my best friend, but some things she tends to keep very private. I had no idea she knew about you, Drew, until you showed up. But she knew all along."

"How did Bear find out?" Paradise asked. "About Ben and Pamela?"

"He'd noticed Pamela pulling away, being distant. Ben broke his engagement without any explanation, and that made Bear even more suspicious. He started following Pamela and the trail led to a hotel in Biloxi. Bear knew the hotel manager and got a key to their room. He caught them, um, red-handed, so to speak."

Drew winced. "That's about as sleazy as it comes. Did the brothers reconcile?"

"Oh yes. Bear always loved his younger brother, and he was a very attentive uncle to Ben's children. The year before Ben died, Bear lost a bid for state representative and decided to give up on running for office. He loved politics so much, but he never connected with the voters. After Ben died, he moved to Dallas and founded a polling company."

Octavia stared off into space. "I never believed Pamela's death was an accident. When she found the letters from Becky, she asked me for a PI recommendation and I gave her Fletch's information. We never told Victoria. We knew it would upset her, so Pamela talked to me about everything."

"What do you suspect happened?"

"I wish I knew. I don't believe Bear would hurt his brother, if that's what you're thinking. I'm not so sure about Percy though."

Paradise gasped. "His own father wouldn't have hurt him, would he?"

Octavia lifted a brow and shrugged. "Power is everything to Percy. Ben was about to throw away generations of a good family reputation. I'm not sure what lengths Percy might have gone to."

Drew stared at the folder and the USB drive in his hands. "We think Granger was only killed because he came home unexpectedly."

"I honestly don't know what happened. Nothing makes any sense to me."

Blake stared at the folder and drive in Drew's hand. They needed answers, but he wasn't sure where they'd find them.

CHAPTER 31

PARADISE FELT EVERYONE'S EXCITEMENT as they waited for the governor and her entourage to show up. The boys nearly vibrated with the anticipation of seeing the governor's grandson again. The news crew had already arrived with cameras ready, and she waited with Blake at the park entrance for the black SUVs to pull into the lot. It was a perfect summer day for the visit, with temps in the eighties and lower-than-normal humidity for July.

Dust swirled in the distance, and she spotted four SUVs heading for the refuge. "Here they come."

"The tigers are ready. I waited to feed them until she gets here. I'll let her use the feeder if she wants. It might play well for her constituents," Blake said. "I'm going to suggest a tour of the dens in case she wants to talk about housing with a backdrop of the animals. Her donation already came through too."

If she wasn't already a fan of the governor's, Paradise would have jumped on board with that news. She held Blake's hand and waited. The back door of the first SUV opened, and fiftysomething Governor George exited with her eight-year-old grandson. She wore white capris and a wraparound tunic with boots and chunky jewelry. The outfit looked elegant yet casual, and Paradise admired the governor's choices. The red-and-white top complemented her short gray-streaked dark hair.

The campaign manager, Angela Burns, exited behind her, but she'd opted for a pale blue pantsuit that played well against her soft white hair and brought out her blue eyes. Her smile emerged when she saw the welcome party. She waved the camera people over. "Get a picture of the group."

Levi waved. "Hi, Jackson."

Dark-haired Jackson glanced up at his grandmother, who made a shooing motion. "Join your friends," she said. The boys fell into chatter about the new additions to the park since Jackson had been here last.

Paradise let Jenna and Blake welcome the guests while she hung back and glanced at her phone. Drew was supposed to let her know if he'd found anything in the files. He'd made copies for all of them, but she hadn't had a chance to study hers yet.

Evan gestured her toward him. She veered from the path to the big cat enclosure to join him. "What's wrong?"

"One of the jaguars needs his right maxillary canine repaired. It's infected too. I didn't want to bother you on this big day, but the infection seems to be spreading. His jaw is swollen, and I don't like the way he looks."

Dread congealed in her gut, and her previously injured shoulder began to ache. The canines were what the big cats used to pierce the skulls of their prey, and she shuddered at the thought of working on one again.

Stop it! It was just a reaction to the last time she'd worked on a jaguar's tooth. She'd make sure it was completely sedated this time. It wouldn't happen again. But her hands trembled despite her self-talk as she told Blake she had to tend to a jaguar.

"Want me to come?"

"You're needed here. I can handle it." But could she? There hadn't been time to hire a new vet tech to replace Warren. She rejoined Evan. "Do you suppose Honey could come help with the anesthesia?"

"She's at a school meeting. She won't be free until later today. Maybe it could wait." His forehead creased with doubt.

"I'll do it now. I don't want to lose the jaguar." She walked the oyster path back to the clinic building. "Is he already caged?"

"Yes, I coaxed him into a crate with some meat. He was agitated though, so I tranquilized him, and he's sleeping in the clinic."

Her fingers curled into her palms when Evan opened the door to the medical facility. She could smell the big cat before she saw him. Watching him breathe in and out took her back to the moment she'd been injured. Her mouth went dry, and she nearly turned and ran. She held her breath and forced herself to take a step closer, then another.

"We'll need help to get him out of the crate to be examined. Can you get Clark and a couple more keepers?"

"No problem."

The big cat stirred, and she went to get the anesthesia to put him all the way under. She checked his weight and pulled the dose he needed into the pole syringe, then administered it. He didn't flinch.

Please, God, please. The constant prayer filled her head, and the longer she worked, the steadier her hands became. She didn't have to do this alone. This time she knew God was here.

By the time the men returned, the big cat was fully sedated. Paradise checked his vitals and they were perfect. The men got him situated on the table, and she inserted the general anesthesia through the breathing tube into his trachea. The gas and oxygen flowed smoothly. He was out so she went to work with steady hands.

An hour later she stepped back and exhaled. "Let's get him into his den to let him wake up. I hate that we had to take his tooth, but he won't need it for live prey anyway. I gave him an antibiotic to handle the infection. He should be fine."

And she was more than fine. She'd done the exact procedure that had caused her injury, and she'd made it through. This place had accomplished the healing she'd hoped and prayed for when she agreed to come here. It had brought more than that though—it had brought love and family in abundance.

Blake watched in fascination as the governor did take after take with seemingly endless patience and energy. Mom and Frank had taken the boys and Jackson off to see the lemurs and the otters. It was nearly lunchtime, and the camera crew started to pack up their equipment while the lunch crew set up tables and chairs upwind from the big cat smell.

He spotted Paradise heading their way and waved. She was out of breath when she reached him. "How'd it go?" he asked.

"Great. The tooth had to come out, but he'll be all right." She held out her hand. "Look, steady as a rock. I wasn't sure I could do it, but I prayed and remembered that I didn't have to do it alone. The jaguar is back in his den waking up. I'll check on him later, but I think I'm getting past my fear. I'll always use caution with the big cats, but I'm not paralyzed with terror."

"I'm so proud of you. I knew you could do it." He nodded toward the governor. "They're already done. I think the campaign ads will be great, and we'll get some amazing publicity out of it all. Want some lunch? They're setting the food out right now." He motioned to the crew bringing in barbecue and all the fixings on the nearby tables in the grassy area. The aroma had already begun to push away the stench of big cat.

"I'm starving. I was too excited this morning to have more than coffee."

He'd wolfed down a bowl of cereal, but it was long gone. "Governor George wants us to sit with her."

She slipped her hand in his. "I thought we should ask her if she knows the Collins family. She might have some political insight. I know they're in Mississippi, but it's not that far way, and it's worth a shot."

He prayed she didn't have her hopes up. It was all a long time ago, and he doubted neighboring states got that involved with each other.

The governor and her manager hailed them from the front table. Angela pointed to the spots across the table from them. The rest of the family sat farther down the table. He pulled out Paradise's chair and slid it in for her, then settled at the end chair across from the governor. "I think it went well. Are you happy with the spots?"

"Thrilled. Angela tells me she thinks they're fresh and innovative. I was able to articulate my policies as well, and who doesn't love big cats. You've got some beauties here."

"I'm going to vote for you," Paradise said.

The governor laughed. "Well, I should hope so! I heard you had to leave us for a little emergency surgery. Did the jaguar make it?"

"He did. He should be waking up about now." Paradise leaned forward. "I've never paid much attention to politics. Do you know the Collins power family in Mississippi? We met them over the weekend."

The governor lowered her barbecue sandwich to her plate. "Oh my, yes. Pamela and I were sorority sisters back in the day, and we stayed in touch until her death. How did you meet them?"

"We're investigating the murders of my parents and my brother Drew's father."

Governor George gaped, but she quickly recovered her composure and stared at Drew sitting on Paradise's right side. "Benjamin Collins was your father?"

"That's what I'm told."

The governor frowned in perplexity at Paradise. "How are you two brother and sister?"

"His father had an affair with my mother."

Both women wore shocked expressions, but Angela recovered faster. Maybe in her job she'd seen a lot of infidelity and secrets come bubbling to the surface. Blake took a bite of his sandwich while his thoughts ticked through possibilities. Paradise had been right, and if the two families had been friends for decades, was it possible Governor George might know something about this?

He took a sip of sweet tea. He'd slathered on the jalapeño sauce, and his mouth was on fire. "We learned Pamela Collins hired a private investigator before her 'fall'"—he used air quotes—"down the stairs. Did you ever suspect it wasn't an accident?"

The governor nodded. "I admit it seemed odd. If you knew Pamela, you'd question it too. She'd been a figure skater since she was a little girl. She was always so graceful and poised. She never rushed anywhere. I assumed there'd been something on the stairs she didn't see."

"I knew her well too." Angela glanced at Drew. "Do you have evidence her death wasn't an accident?"

Drew set his tea on the table. "No, but three other murders of people connected to her within a week is suspicious. I was surprised the police ruled it as accidental without a lot of investigation."

"Sometimes accidents happen," the governor said.

"We heard she was a difficult person. Maybe it's not too hard to believe someone wanted her gone."

"Ben was a womanizer, and that's putting it politely," Angela said.

"He seemed to really love my mother. He told Pamela he was divorcing her." Paradise leaned forward. "He was bludgeoned to death, just like my parents. The method ties them together."

"Your parents were killed with a golf club?" the governor asked.

"No, the killer used a ball bat on them, but clearly the murderer likes more personal, up-close killing," Drew said.

Blake could see the women were intrigued but not convinced. "We were told to take a close look at family members. Do you know Bear?"

The governor picked at her coleslaw. "Of course. I knew all of Pamela's family. I can't imagine him raising his hand to a man, let alone a woman."

"And what about Percy? Someone told me he would do anything to keep the family in power."

"Percy is always a gentleman. I can't see anyone in the Collins family committing such atrocious crimes."

The governor's manner grew frostier, and Blake smiled. "I'm sorry I brought it up. I can see it's upsetting you."

The governor managed a smile and picked up her sandwich. "I'm not upset, but I can tell you that family had nothing to do with this."

Blake moved the topic to King Julien. Maybe they were on the wrong track.

CHAPTER 32

PARADISE CHECKED ON THE black jaguar and saw him sleeping in the shade with no sign of facial swelling. He was going to be fine. She checked her phone. Drew and Blake would be waiting for her to discuss the contents of the files they'd gotten from Roger's office.

As she crossed the strip of grass, she spotted Angela leaning against a fence by the lemurs. She changed trajectories to join her. "Lemurs are great, aren't they?"

Angela turned with a smile. "I don't know why I find them so enthralling. Something about their eyes."

Paradise spotted King Julien. "That's the one I mentioned at lunch. He was held in a crate most of the time and never saw another lemur for years until we got him. Funny thing about lemurs is they're such social creatures. He was unhappy, antagonistic, and short-tempered. Once he saw others like him and was accepted into their conspiracy, he mellowed out. Now he's got a mate and a happy life."

"What a wonderful story. You said something about a conspiracy. Is that what a group of lemurs is called?"

Paradise chuckled. "Sounds odd, right? I've always wondered why they're called that when they're so social. Maybe it's because they conspire together to thwart predators. They also do something called 'mobbing,' where they leap out of nowhere to attack an enemy together. They aren't that tall, but they can jump six times their height so it can feel like the attack is coming out of nowhere."

"How fascinating! I don't know much about them except I love them." She studied Paradise a moment. "It sounds like you've been dealing with your own conspiracy for a lot of years. I'm sorry about your parents."

"Thank you. I've only recently begun to remember the night of the murders. I hope to remember everything eventually."

"So you were there." Angela gave a delicate shudder. "I'm sorry you endured something like that."

"I wish I'd had my parents all these years." Paradise watched the mama lemurs groom the new babies, and her eyes blurred at the memory of her mother's fingers in her hair, taming it into braids. Someday maybe she'd have the chance to do the same for her daughter.

She mentally shook herself to snap out of her fugue. "You've been with the governor a long time?"

"Twenty years. She was quite overtaken at the memory of Ben's death."

"I'm sorry we brought it up. We needed to know if she knew them. Blake didn't think she would."

"Politics is a funny life. Full of drama, friendship, enemies, and secrets."

Was the woman trying to tell her something? Did the governor know more than she'd let on? "You sound like you both love it and hate it."

"It's a challenge, but the governor is wonderful to work for. She's considerate of all her employees."

"Did Ben ever make a play for the governor? They're about the same age."

Angela blinked and frowned. "Of course not. Why would you ask something like that?"

"We know he was a player. Her reaction to my questions seemed . . . odd."

"It wasn't odd at all. She's been a friend of the family for decades."

"I assume you knew Ben as well?"

Angela waved off her question. "Not all that well. Acquaintances only."

Paradise studied Angela's defensive posture and decided to go with her gut. "I still suspect someone in the family, maybe even Percy."

"The governor told you he is incapable of violence."

"I'm not sure I believe her. Everyone is capable of anger and acting out of character."

Angela's expression of defensiveness made Paradise decide to dig into the governor's background a bit. Maybe there was more here than met the eye.

Paradise straightened. "I'd better get going to my meeting. Enjoy watching the animals. Oh, and if you want to drive the Gator to the parking lot, feel free. The keys are in it, and you can just leave it there."

"Thanks for the lemur education," Angela called after her. "I might do that."

Paradise thought her tone held a bit of relief. What could she be hiding about the governor?

The guys were on the back deck with the boys when she crossed the yard toward the house. Isaac saw her first and came running to jump into her arms. His thin arms clutched her neck and he clung to her like a spider monkey. She carried him to the deck and deposited him on the cedar boards.

Levi climbed into her lap when she sat beside Blake. "Mom's making lasagna. She let me add the cheese."

"I'm sure it will be delicious." She kissed him on the neck until he squealed.

"I wouldn't complain if you did that to me," Blake said under his breath.

Her cheeks heated and she shushed him. "Did you guys find anything interesting in the files, or were you waiting on me? I stopped to chat with Angela."

"She said she wanted to wander the park a bit and didn't leave with Governor George," Blake said. "I think she finds the refuge calming. But yes, we got a chance to examine the files."

She let Levi clamber down from her lap and go off to play in the tree house with his brother before dinner. "Anything of interest?"

"It's a blackmail list like we suspected. There was more darkness to Roger than we knew. But none of the names were familiar. I assume Adams wanted the list for his own personal use."

Drew reached for his glass of iced tea. "How were Roger and Adams acquainted? Maybe Abby would know. We could invite her and Quinn to dinner."

She smiled at his hopeful voice. "We don't need Abby to answer that. They were cousins. But I'd love to see her anyway. I'll invite them. Jenna always makes enough lasagna to feed an army." Paradise tapped out a quick invitation. She got back an almost instant acceptance. "They'll be here in an hour."

Drew's smile held eagerness. "There's been no more sign of

Adams. Rod tried for a subpoena of Warren's bank account but hasn't gotten it approved yet, but I'm hopeful."

"Things are going well over at the Dillard Ranch at night?"

"It's no surprise to you that I like Abby. We've had a lot of good chats in the evenings. She's been hurt and so have I, so we're taking it slow."

It didn't seem all that slow to Paradise, but she hid her pleased smile. Nothing would make her happier than having Abby for a sister-in-law.

Nothing smelled as good as his mom's lasagna. Blake leaned back in his chair on the deck and groaned. "I should have stopped at two pieces. That third one did me in."

Drew eyed the remnants on his plate. "Dude, you should have warned me. I was doing what you did. And those breadsticks . . . wow."

"Paradise made those." Isaac slipped out of his chair with his brother. "Hey, Quinn, want to play Sorry?"

Quinn pushed back her chair. "Sure, I haven't played that in a long time."

Blake's mom got up. "I'll get the game down for you kids. Frank, would you mind bringing in the lasagna pan? We'll clean up and watch a movie."

Frank's expression brightened, and he followed with the rest of the lasagna. Blake loved seeing his mom light up around Frank Ellis. It seemed the feeling was mutual.

Blake watched Quinn go inside too. "Quinn is being kind with the boys. You raised her right, Abby."

Abby leaned her elbows on the table. "She loves kids. She's already asking when she can babysit, and I told her I was twelve when I had my first babysitting gig. You'd have thought I told her she couldn't have candy for two years." Abby glanced around the circle of people. "Something is up. I can smell it under the scent of lasagna."

Paradise chuckled. "You always were perceptive. There's something we want to show you. Blake?" She took out her phone. "I want to see what I can find out about the governor's background." She tapped out a query.

He reached under the table and grabbed the folder leaning against his chair, then slid it to Abby, who was sitting next to Drew. "It looks like your dad was blackmailing people. It's a long shot since Ben isn't mentioned in the file, but I wondered if you might have seen him or any of his family at the ranch, meeting with your dad."

"Not that I know of. And we were just at the birthday party with the whole family. It's odd they didn't know me." She stopped and shook her head. "No, wait. Drew introduced me as McClellan, not Dillard. If they'd ever been there when I was a kid, they wouldn't recognize me now anyway." She scowled at Drew. "You thought I was keeping something from you?"

He took her hand. "Of course not. You're the same age as Paradise. I wouldn't expect you to have thought anything about it when you were nine, but I wondered if we jogged your memory, something might swim to the surface. I have a picture of him on my phone." He released her and grabbed his phone, then turned it around to show her the photo of Ben Collins.

Blake stared at it. He hadn't seen a picture of the man. His daughter, Taylor, had his blond hair and fair skin. In the picture he stood beside a yellow muscle car with the convertible top down. "That's the Hemi Barracuda Fletch mentioned. It was missing from the garage and has never been found."

The irritation ebbed from Abby's face, and she leaned forward to stare at the picture. "He doesn't look familiar, but the car does. My dad and I were supposed to go to town to pick up feed, and this yellow car pulled up. The engine was super loud, and my dad slapped the guy on the back like they were old friends. They stood and talked so long we never got to the store. I asked him who he was when he left, and Dad said he was the brother of an old friend."

"So Roger knew Bear?" Drew asked.

"He didn't mention his friend's name that I recall, but it's possible."

"It might be a way to get Bear to talk to us again." Drew tapped on his phone. "I asked Taylor if her uncle is still in town." A message sounded, and he glanced at the screen. "She said he's in town for another week. I think I'd better have a chat with him."

Blake drummed his fingers on the tabletop. "How did a car like that vanish without a trace? If someone took it because it was valuable, why didn't they sell it? It's puzzling."

"Let's ask how Ben acquired it," Paradise said. "Getting its history might be helpful. Didn't Fletch say it was a 1970? Maybe it was his dad's first vehicle." She sighed and dropped her phone to her lap. "Nothing problematic about the governor. Raised in a political family, she's never been involved in any controversy that I can see."

Blake stared at the picture on Drew's phone again. "Fletch said Ben collected classic cars. He might have bought it because he liked it."

Drew turned the phone around to examine the car more closely. "I'd like to find out if they searched for the car. I'd think its VIN number would be listed as stolen so it would pop up if someone tried to register it to drive on the road." He tapped on his phone again. "Wow, those things sell for a million bucks and more."

Drew frowned as he read through the article. "Only fourteen of these E-bodies were made so they're very rare, which is why they cost the earth when they get to auction. I wish it was still around. I'd like to see it."

Drew put his phone away. "Enough about work. I need to rest my brain." He rose and held out his hand to Abby. "Want to take a walk by the pond in the moonlight?"

"It's not dark yet," she pointed out, smiling as she stood.

"We'll take our time." He waggled his brows at Blake as the two of them walked away.

Paradise's soft chuckle expanded Blake's grin. "Your brother is on the hunt."

"I'd love to see him happy, and it would be incredible to have Abby as a sister." Paradise hopped out of her chair and took his hand. "Let me gather the plates, and we'll take a walk ourselves. In the opposite direction."

Just what Blake had hoped for.

CHAPTER 33

BEA'S VIEWING WOULD DRAW much of Pelican Harbor, so Paradise had come with the family as soon as the doors opened. Even so, ten people lined up ahead of them. Isaac clung to her hand while Blake corralled Levi.

Abby had come with Quinn, and Drew stood in the line with them. Quinn's eyes glistened with tears. She'd had Bea as a teacher at church for years. She was only a year older than Paradise had been when she lost her parents, and she well remembered that state between childhood and her teen years when she'd struggled with grief on her own. Quinn had her mother though, and she'd be fine.

Paradise caught sight of Abby's red-rimmed eyes. Maybe there was more to Quinn's grief besides the death of a beloved teacher. Paradise passed Isaac's hand to Jenna and mouthed that she needed to move back for a minute, then made her way to Abby. "You okay?"

Tears escaped and rolled down Abby's face. She took Paradise's hand and drew her to a quiet corner out of the line. "I told Quinn about her dad's remarriage. She was devastated and thinks she won't get to see him much. The bad thing is, I think she's right. She's not even invited to the wedding. They're flying to Jamaica and getting married there without any guests. Not even his daughter. He's such a slimeball."

Paradise squeezed her hand. "I'm so sorry, Abbs."

She waved off Paradise's sympathy. "I'm fine. I'm glad to be rid of his cheating, contemptuous behavior, but it's hard to watch Quinn's pain. It makes me wonder if I should break off whatever is happening with Drew. I don't want to go through anything like this ever again."

"Drew isn't like Jason. He was cheated on once too. You can trust him."

Abby gulped back a sob. "He was? He said he'd been hurt, but I haven't heard the details."

"I'm sure he'll tell you about it. I think being a detective has made him even more perceptive and empathetic. He's seen the worst of human behavior and yet he still fights for justice. My brother is a pretty awesome person."

"So's his sister." Abby hugged her. "We'd better get back in line."

They rejoined their group, and Paradise nudged her when she spotted Drew with his arm around Quinn talking to her. Quinn had her gaze fixed on his face, and her tears had stopped.

"Told you," Paradise whispered.

Blake took her hand. "I think that's Bea's daughter at the casket."

"She has two. The other one might be talking with other visitors." They stepped to the casket and took Bea's daughter's hand. "You look so much like your mother. She was a wonderful woman."

The woman's gaze lingered on Paradise's hair. "You're the new vet, the one investigating my dad."

"Well, not really. Your dad had nothing to do with the murders. At least we were able to assure your mom of his innocence."

Tears welled in the woman's eyes. "I can't believe she's gone. The police have no leads as to who did it or why. Do you know?"

"I'm sorry, but I don't. Your mom hadn't told us anything that would make someone come after her."

The woman swiped at her eyes. "Our attorney, Scott Foster, has something for you. He told me to have you call."

"I—I don't understand."

"Neither do I, but he said if you came by that I should tell you Mom left something for you." Her attention went over Paradise's shoulder to Jenna, and she smiled. Dismissed, Paradise and Blake moved past, taking a moment to linger over pictures of Bea's family.

"I think Bea's daughter didn't want to talk to us," Blake said.

"I can't blame her. Someone shot her mother, and it could be related to our investigation. She could have been holding something back that she isn't telling us."

They walked outside into the drowsy hum of bees hovering over the flowers flanking the path from the street to the church. "We could take a walk while we're waiting for everyone." Blake pointed out a line of storefronts. "There's an architect in that office. I think he has samples of his work in the windows."

They walked across the street to the building painted hunter green. Rogers and Shaw Architects. She lingered over the pictures of homes the firm had designed. In the center of the big pane of glass was the home of her dreams. A single story so similar to what she'd found that she caught her breath.

"See something you like?" Blake's breath stirred her hair, and he pressed a kiss on her temple.

"Doesn't this look like that one I found online?" She traced the floor plan with her finger. "Even the rooms are the same."

"I think you're right." He glanced at the hours. "They're closed now, but we can make an appointment and come back. I've heard good things about this firm. People say they work with your budget and guide you on ways to build most economically while getting the house you really want. They work with good contractors."

It seemed impossible that just a few months after she came back to Nova Cambridge she'd be hand in hand with the man she'd always loved. She had a beautiful engagement ring on her left hand and the promise of a life together with a larger family than she'd ever hoped for. And probably more to come.

If they could track down the shadowy figures who still threatened their happiness, they could make real plans for the future.

The Gator jolted over the ruts in the back field. After they'd gone to Bea's funeral today, the promise of new starts had lured them out for a walk. The late-afternoon air held the fragrance of newly mown hay from the Dillard Ranch field to the right and the rich aroma of upturned dirt in the planted field on the other side.

Blake pointed out the trees ahead. "There's our promised land. It's really pretty from this direction too."

Paradise turned a delighted smile his way. "I love calling it that!"

They both fell silent as the sun dipped to just over the treetops and washed the area with golden light. Blake could see them sitting on a back deck or patio watching the animals move across their land in the distance while the sun painted colors in the sky. "We'll be able to sit out here and smell God's green earth in the evenings. It's pretty perfect, babe."

At the back edge of the property, they got out of the Gator. "This area back here is beautiful too, but I still think the top of the knoll will give us a great view all around. Let's walk up that way and see what we think."

Paradise reached back to the Gator's floor. "What's this?"

He turned back toward her voice to see her holding up a mini tablet in a navy case. "Open it and see if it comes on. Maybe it belongs to one of the employees."

She flipped open the cover and the screen to the small iPad came on asking for a password. "There's a picture of the governor and Angela as the background. I told her she could use the Gator to get back to the parking lot when they were here. She must have forgotten it."

"We have to go to Pelican Harbor tomorrow to see the attorney. We could drop it off if we knew where she lives."

"An address is on the back." She held it up for him to see. "Wait, this has Governor George's address on it. Maybe it's hers and Angela had picked it up for her. This must be a second residence. Maybe we can catch her at home tomorrow. I think there's something hinky about the governor's relationship with Ben. I'm not sure if Governor George should be on our radar as a suspect, but I can't rule it out either. It's strange she warned us off Bear and Percy. Angela did too when I chatted with her alone."

He glanced at the tablet. "The address is in Fairhope. Our appointment with Foster isn't until one. There's time to do both." He slipped his arm around her waist. "We could go alone first thing in the morning and swing past the Dillard Ranch to get Drew on the way to Pelican Harbor. I love your brother, but I wouldn't mind three hours alone with you."

"I think he was planning to return the evidence kit."

"Perfect. We can reconvene here at the house for lunch before heading to the attorney's office."

The vegetation was higher back here and he went first, tramping it down for her so the weeds didn't scratch those gorgeous legs, bare from mid-thigh down, in the shorts she wore. "There are wild azaleas back here too." He pointed out the pink bushes on the slope. "Whoa, Paradise, there's a well here." He gestured to the pipes sticking out of the ground. "If it's still in working order, that will save us some money."

He stomped the weeds down a bit. "There are remnants of an old building here, maybe a cabin."

Paradise threw her arms around him. "I love this property so much, Blake. Almost as much as I love you."

His pulse rocketed and he pulled her close. Her lips were soft and inviting, and his surroundings vanished as he kissed her. He pulled back and palmed her cheek. "I'm a lucky man. How long do we have to wait for the wedding?"

Her amber eyes were alight with amusement. "Six weeks. Not that I'm counting or anything."

He groaned. "An eternity. But you're worth the wait." He stepped back and turned her around to see the view back toward The Sanctuary from their vantage point. "We'll have the best view in the state."

She took in the landscape silently, and he glanced over to see tears slipping down her cheeks. "Babe, what's wrong?"

"I never thought I'd have this, Blake. You, your family, my brother, and now this perfect spot for a home that we get to design together. I can see Isaac and Levi playing in a tree house you build right there." She pointed out a massive oak with the perfect Y-shape to anchor a platform. "Our kids will grow up here, their roots going deep into the land we all love so much. Someday our grandkids will come to spend the night and experience the same connection to God through this place that we've found. I can see us all piling in the van for church and gathering here for Sunday dinners. It's a dream come true, Blake."

She turned toward him again and laid her head against his chest. He buried his nose in the sweet scent of her hair and held her close, too overcome to speak. The future she saw rolled out in images in his head, and thankfulness to God overcame him. "God always knew the plans he had for us, but we sure couldn't see them in the rough times."

Blake pulled her away from his chest so he could see her face. "There will be more tough times, babe. Our whole lives those times will come. But let's hold on to this certainty that God has us, that his plan will work for our good because we love him and want his will."

"I'm going to do that."

He turned back to the expansive fields and rolling hills in his view. The Sanctuary was a bucolic scene out of a postcard from here, and they were privileged to care for what had been entrusted to them.

He exhaled. "I guess we'd better be getting back. It's nearly six, and Mom was going to have pizza delivered about then."

They walked back down the slope to the Gator. The ride back was just as bumpy, and he took his time, enjoying these last few minutes with her shoulder brushing his and her loving smiles directed his way. They got too little time together, but in six weeks she'd be in his arms at night, and they'd begin building that new life together.

CHAPTER 34

THE FAMILY SAT ON the back deck, and Frank crossed the yard toward them with a stack of pizza boxes. They converged at the steps, and Blake let Paradise go first. She leaned down to hug the boys when they ran to throw themselves at her legs. Sometimes their enthusiasm was so great they nearly knocked her down, but she loved it. They smelled of little-boy sweat and grass, and she didn't think there was any better fragrance in the world.

Frank's blond hair looked newly trimmed. "You're back just in time." He set the pizza boxes on the table.

"I'm starving," Paradise said. "Blake called Scott Foster and we have an appointment tomorrow afternoon to see what Bea left for us. It's very intriguing. Any guesses?" She directed her question to Drew, who sat beside Abby.

"Not a clue. I hope it's something that solves the case." He rubbed his forehead. "There's no clear direction."

"I think we should look at Bear. Too many people are trying to protect him."

Her brother pursed his lips. "You might have something there. I did a background check on him. He and Ben got into a physical fight that broke Ben's jaw. He spent six weeks with his jaw wired."

Paradise couldn't fathom fighting like that with a sibling. "Angela told me yesterday that she couldn't imagine him ever hurting anyone. Surely she knew about that incident. She claims to have known the family a long time."

"I want to see if Bear knows who I am," Abby said. "When we talk to him again, I want to watch his expression when I mention Ben driving the 'Cuda. We should ask the governor and Angela about that too. If Ben knew my dad, maybe they did too. They don't know my maiden name either."

Those conversations could be bombshells. "We took the Gator out to the property. It's so beautiful, Jenna. I can't thank you enough."

Frank cleared his throat. "About that. As a developer I have access to the best tradespeople in the area. I'm going to make a crazy suggestion—let me be your contractor. I'll take the house you love and contact subcontractors for the various pieces of what needs to be done: foundation, electrical, plumbing, drywall, everything you need. It will save you 30 to 40 percent on the cost of the house."

Unable to wrap her head around the offer for a moment, Paradise gaped at him. "Frank, are you serious?"

He grinned. "As a heart attack. I can pull strings to get it built quickly, too, probably in three months."

Blake put his arm around Paradise. "I—I can't even tell you how grateful we are. Paradise found a floor plan she loved. Go get the printout, babe, and we'll let Frank take it."

"It's on the kitchen table." She darted into the house and snatched the printout. She stepped back outside and handed it to Frank. "It's pretty perfect. We can finish renovating as we have money."

"We also found something interesting at the property: an old well. That will save some money if we can get it up and running."

Frank began to study the house plan. "Many of those old wells are fine and just need a new pump and pressure tank. I'll send someone out to take a look." He waved the paper in the air. "This is a good plan. The plumbing is all grouped together and the open spaces will make it feel spacious. Great outdoor space, too, with the big porch and back deck. Let me pull some numbers for you, but I think we can get this done reasonably. If you ever want to sell it, you'll have built-in equity."

Jenna finished handing out paper plates of pizza before coming to stand beside Frank. "I've kept track of the past year's checks you never cashed, Son. I deposited that money directly in your account this morning. It was eighty thousand dollars."

"What? No, you don't need to do that." Blake shook his head.

"I do. You've been the best son a mother could ask for. Always pitching in and helping with the park and with your brothers. I know you did it out of love, but it's time you take what's due you. We can afford it. And I'm giving you a raise."

"You just gave me one."

"You're getting another one." Jenna switched her attention to Paradise. "And I signed over Pawsome Pets to you free and clear this morning. No more payments, and I'm raising your salary here too. You can make your own decision about whether you want to sell the vet clinic or continue to work both places part time. Whatever you want we can make it work."

Paradise didn't know whether to laugh or cry. "All I want is right here." She swept her arm around the deck at all the people she loved.

Jenna drew her into a fierce hug. "You've had us since the day you walked in that door. We didn't know at the time how vital you were to The Sanctuary, but I had my suspicions. And I was right—none of this could have happened without you, Paradise. Thank you."

"I—I don't know what to say. Thank you for everything, Jenna." Paradise forced the words out in a wobbly voice.

Jenna released her. "Your pizza is getting cold." She gave her a nudge toward the table.

Paradise found the one they'd ordered for her with black olives no one else liked. People who loved you paid attention to the little things.

Blake had called the governor's office and left a message about the iPad, but there'd been no response yet. "Let's head up there anyway. We can leave it in the mailbox if she's not there. I hate to wait in case she needs it."

Paradise grabbed her purse and slipped her phone inside. "I'd like to ask her a few more questions, but we can always request an appointment." She paused at the door to slip her bare feet into sandals.

"Have I ever told you that even your feet are cute?"

She chuckled. "That's a first." Paradise dug her knuckles into his side playfully. "I never see your bare feet."

"I don't like to be without my shoes. It's a holdover from being a Marine—I never know when I'll be called into action."

"I'm sure they're quite attractive."

He held the door open for her. "How'd we start talking about *my* feet?"

"You introduced the subject."

He pulled the door shut behind him. "Sheesh, a guy can't give a girl a compliment these days."

He loved the glow on her face from yesterday. They'd stayed up late talking about the wedding and the house, and his eyes felt gritty. He'd reclaimed his bed in the apartment over the garage while Drew was staying at the Dillard Ranch, but he had still tossed and turned.

Paradise climbed in the truck and laid the tablet on her lap as she buckled in. It fell to the floor when she twisted, and the top of the cover folded back enough for it to come to life. As he leaned over to grab it for her, he noticed something in the background of the picture that he hadn't seen yesterday.

He folded the cover back fully and stared. "Babe, look over their shoulders at the building. You can see a little bit of something yellow in the window of the garage."

She took it and tried to enlarge it with her fingers, but it didn't work. "I wish I could make it bigger. You might be right. You think it could be the 'Cuda?" She shook her head. "That makes no sense though. It's clearly a current picture of them, and that car has been missing for twenty years. Angela's white hair is in the same style, and she wore that suit the first time they came here. Governor George looks the same too."

"Yeah, you're right. Maybe the governor has a yellow car and I'm grasping at straws."

But he couldn't convince himself of that as he drove to Fairhope. His mind kept playing through all the what-ifs. If it *was* the 'Cuda, how could it have ended up belonging to the governor?

The address was up ahead, and very few houses were around. "Are we sure about that address?"

She checked her phone and compared it to the back of the iPad. "Yes, it's correct. Our turn is the next one to the right."

He nodded and turned into the gravel lane leading to the address on the back of the iPad. There were steep ditches on both sides of the driveway. He gripped the wheel and paid attention so he didn't drive off the edge. "It's really narrow. I would have expected it to be paved and manicured."

"Maybe the governor likes her privacy and wants a place out of the public eye." Paradise's phone dinged with a text, and she glanced at it. "It's Angela telling us the governor won't be home and not to bother with the iPad. But we're already here."

No part of him wanted to go back, not yet. Something about this place didn't pass the sniff test. "Don't tell her that. Let's see what's up ahead. I can't turn around here anyway."

He continued to drive until the lane turned between two large oaks. The road ended at a large garage that probably held four cars. "Open that cover again."

Paradise flipped it off the screen, and the picture appeared. "That's the same garage, Blake."

"I thought so." He parked the truck. "Stay here. I'm going to look around."

She shoved open her door. "Not without me, you're not. I'm as curious as you."

Birds sang overhead, and nothing about the setting felt dangerous, but every sense was on high alert and he didn't know why. Maybe it was the possibility that the governor had something she was hiding. Maybe it was that glimpse of yellow through the window. Even from here he saw it.

It felt like overkill, but he pulled his gun from its holster anyway. "Stay behind me."

"I think you're overreacting." But she sheltered behind him.

Weeds poked through the gravel, and the place had an unkempt air. The windows were dirty, and the grass around the building hadn't been mowed yet this summer. It felt like they were a million miles from civilization out here. "Do you have your phone?"

She nodded. "Yes."

"Get your camera ready. We might need pictures." He approached the first window and peered inside to see the yellow hulk of an aging tractor. "Shoot, I was sure . . ."

"There's a car covered in a cloth over here."

He turned to find that she had gone to the end of the building. The glass was smeared where she'd swiped it with her hand. She knelt to wipe the dirt on her hand onto the grass. "Let's see what's under it."

"The garage is probably locked." And it was private property. But he couldn't resist the urge to try. He yanked on the door, but it wouldn't budge. "Let me try the side door and the back one."

The yard on the side of the garage was even more overgrown than the front. He brushed through the vegetation instead of trying to knock it down. He didn't want to leave a trail. The doorknob twisted in his hand but got stuck. "I don't think it's locked." He put his shoulder into it and nearly fell into the interior.

The spotless interior of the garage contrasted with the decaying exterior.

Paradise darted in after him and grabbed the edge of the car cover. "It's a yellow car."

He joined her and helped her pull it back to see more of the vehicle. The missing Barracuda sat gleaming in the sunshine coming in the windows.

CHAPTER 35

AT THE KITCHEN TABLE Drew flipped through the pictures Paradise had taken of the missing car. "This is incredible, but it doesn't make any sense. I spoke with the Pascagoula police about it, and they still have it listed as stolen property, yet the governor has had it all this time. If Ben gave it to the governor or she bought it from him, surely she would have mentioned it in the aftermath of his death."

Paradise grabbed a chicken salad croissant Jenna passed to her on a plate. "Unless she didn't know it had been reported missing." The taste of the chicken salad exploded on her tongue with goodness. She needed to get Jenna's recipe. "And the governor has connections, so I think she would have to know it had been reported missing."

"Anyone up for a trip to Pascagoula tomorrow? Let's talk to the family again," Blake said. "I'd suggest going this afternoon, but we have that appointment with Scott."

Paradise reached for her glass of sweet tea. "Any ideas what it could mean? Why would the murderer, whoever he is, take a car he or she can't sell? No one is even enjoying it. The weird thing is, the building is climate controlled and the car is in pristine condition. The garage is huge too, but there's only the car and an old tractor inside. Plus a couple of framed prints hanging on the walls, photographs of scenery. No tools, nothing else." Something felt familiar about the pictures, but it was probably that they were like dozens of others she'd seen over her life—vignettes of a person's favorite places.

"Maybe it's evidence of some kind," Drew suggested. "Whoever killed Ben knew the car could lead back to them. Blood evidence, fibers, whatever."

"Possible," Blake said. "It's been twenty years though. They could probably remove the VIN number and replace it or part the car out and still get quite a bit of money for it. It would be a shame though. It's an iconic piece of history."

"It's crazy to hide it all these years," Drew said. "If it had evidence in it, why not destroy it? Drop it at the bottom of a swamp or burn it. Storing it where it could be discovered is a little dicey."

"The property is in the boonies down a long, overgrown lane. I'm not sure she's been there in a long time. It's like it was backed into that garage and abandoned forever," Blake said.

Evidence. Paradise tried to think of the kind of evidence that could be hidden in the car. "Maybe there's a family member she's covering for."

"Let me check." Jenna's computer was on the island, and she pulled it to her. "Amelia George has been married for thirty-five years and has two kids, both sons. Jackson is her only grandchild. One son lives in Alabama and one is an aide to Taylor Murphy. Think there's a connection?"

Drew frowned at Jenna. "The son is what, thirty-two or thirty-three, tops? Twenty years ago he would have just been hitting his teen years. It's unlikely the governor is covering for him. I usually look hard at coincidences like this, but this situation feels like a fluke of no importance."

Paradise took a sip of her tea and set it back down on the table. "Don't be so fast to make a snap judgment. Maybe he took that car out for a joyride. You know how kids can be. Maybe he was injured and his blood is in the car, or he was caddying for Ben and they got into a fight so he grabbed the golf club. We hear of kids that age committing crimes all the time. We can't rule it out."

"Good point." Drew rose to read the bio Jenna had pulled up.

Paradise couldn't get the sight of the car out of her head. Perfect condition yet sitting there for twenty years. She thought Drew had the best theory—it was kept for a reason. "I wish we could go over it better and look for evidence. We were trespassing so we hightailed it out of there."

She told them about the message from Angela telling her not to deliver the iPad. "Why would the governor have that address on her tablet? If she's hiding the car, why have its location on her iPad?"

Drew sipped his tea and set it back on the table. "Good point." He drummed his fingers on the tabletop. "Maybe it's a taunt, like she dares anyone to find her out."

Paradise liked Governor George, not just because she'd done so much for The Sanctuary, but because she seemed to be a genuinely kind person who cared about her state and her constituents. "Maybe, but I hope not."

Blake took the last bite of his croissant and carried his plate to the dishwasher. "We'd better get going to Scott Foster's office. Thanks for lunch, Mom."

Paradise rose and grabbed her brother's plate. "Where are the boys?"

Jenna chuckled. "Abby picked them up for riding lessons again. They were so excited that I'd gotten them boots. They went off proudly wearing them."

Paradise side-eyed her brother and saw a slow smile start across his face. He was a goner for Abby. She made a mental note to tell him to talk to Abby about his first marriage that ended so quickly.

Scott Foster's French Quarter building in Pelican Harbor was pale brick with elaborate wrought-iron balconies peering out under a mansard-style black roof. Blake had always admired it, and he liked the leather furniture in the office even more.

Scott greeted them at the door. "Have a seat." He was in his sixties and whip thin with a shock of reddish-brown hair that had probably been bright red in his earlier years. He was also Hez and Savannah's attorney, and they thought highly of him.

Paradise sat in the middle highback chair. "Thanks for seeing us on such short notice."

"Of course. Bea was specific about wanting this in your hands as quickly as possible."

He placed a square box on the desk, and she put it on her lap. It was about four inches wide and nearly buried in tape. The plan was to examine it privately after they left the office, but her gaze lingered on it, and Blake knew she wanted to tear that tape off and see what the box contained.

Blake leaned over and took it to hold for her. It was light, almost as if there was nothing inside. He wanted to give it a shake, but that would interrupt the discussion. Besides, it had been left to Paradise. It was hers to open and examine first.

Scott slid a paper across the table to her. "Sign here that you received the bequest."

She scribbled her name. "Did Bea talk to you about this bequest at all?"

"She did, and she gave me permission to tell you." He steepled his fingers on his desk. "She was afraid of someone. I suspect whoever killed her wanted the contents of the box."

"Did she tell you what's in here?"

He shook his head. "She didn't want me in danger."

Drew leaned forward. "When did the box come into your possession?"

"A week before she died. She insisted on meeting me at Mac's just before it closed for the night. She was waiting at a back table in the corner, away from any windows, and the place was empty. We ordered something to drink, and she slipped this little box to me. I palmed it to tuck inside my pocket. We chatted like it was only a social meeting and left."

Drew scowled. "So you don't know anything about who she feared?"

"I tried to get her to tell me, but she refused."

"Did the police talk to you?"

Scott shook his head. "I had nothing of value to offer other than she feared for her life, which wasn't a secret. Her children knew, too, though she didn't reveal to them who intended her harm."

"They might have wanted to examine the contents of that box."

"It's not theirs to take. It belongs to Paradise, and I'm sure if there's anything in it that reveals a crime, she'll contact the authorities."

Paradise rose and took the box from Blake, then dropped it

into her large purse. "Thanks so much. I know you were fitting us in and you have clients waiting."

They filed out of the building without comment. Paradise reached the sidewalk. "There's a park over there." She pointed to a grassy area with a picnic table at the end of the building. "Anyone have scissors?"

"I have a knife in the truck that will work," Blake said. "But maybe we should open the box in private so no one knows you received anything. The family knows, but Bea's bequests wouldn't be common knowledge."

Paradise's expression went thoughtful. "I suppose you're right. It's so small that I can't imagine what's inside and whether it could be helpful."

Drew put his hand on her forearm. "Chief Dixon's office is right here in town. We could go straight there and open it in a conference room. That way if there's anything that helps us find the killer, she and Nora are there to advise."

Blake took Paradise's hand. "That's a great idea. Let's just walk. It will appear we're out for a stroll and just stopped in to speak to Jane."

They walked past the charming Pelican Harbor storefronts to the police station. Seagulls dive-bombed Blake's hair, and he waved them off as Paradise ducked. The briny scent of Bon Secour Bay mingled with the sweet aroma of beignets from Petit Charms. They found Jane talking to an officer at the front desk.

Her hazel eyes widened when she saw them. "What a pleasant surprise. Come on back." She led them to her office. "I just made a fresh pot of coffee. Want some?"

"I wouldn't say no." Blake went to the coffee bar to pour a cup and brought mugs back for Drew and Paradise.

Jane moved to the chair behind her desk. "I can see tension all over you, Paradise. What's up?"

Paradise pulled the small box from her purse and placed it on Jane's desk. "Bea left this for me with Scott Foster. He didn't know what's in it and just delivered it to me."

Jane reached for scissors. "May I?"

"Please do. I'm dying to see what's in it. It's so light."

Jane struggled to get the scissors through the tape. "Someone didn't want anyone in this thing." The blade of the scissors finally slit along the opening edge of the box, and she got the tape free enough to open it. She handed the box back to Paradise. "I'll let you do the honors."

Paradise lifted the top and peered inside. "It's camera film. Does anyone in town develop prints?"

"I can have them done through the station if you'd like. The drugstore will take a week, and I should be able to get them back in a couple of days."

"That would be great, Jane. Thank you," Paradise said.

"I'm hopeful some of the pictures will help us solve Bea's murder too. Thank you for trusting me with this." Jane rose. "Let me get these to the lab."

CHAPTER 36

WARMTH SPREAD THROUGH PARADISE'S chest at being in Brady's restaurant again. She stared at the gorgeous emerald on her engagement ring and remembered the light in Blake's eyes when he'd asked her to marry him. This place would always be special to her when she thought about that day and the family dinner that followed right here at this table.

She buttered a dinner roll and watched the door. "You think Bear's avoiding us? He's five minutes late."

Drew lifted a brow. "Traffic?"

Abby chuckled. "I don't think so. He might be delaying the inevitable as long as possible. At least he agreed to meet up for dinner. Taylor too. I'm surprised your grandparents didn't accept the invitation."

"They gave no excuses either," Drew said. "Just a 'Sorry we can't make it.' Maybe they're trying to preserve the warm feelings. Though Bear was welcoming."

Paradise glanced at the door again. "There they are." She rose and waved.

Drew's uncle and half sister threaded their way through the

tables to this larger one toward the back of the restaurant. Paradise had hoped to meet Taylor's husband, Troy, but oil executives were often out of town. Or so they'd told them at the party. She had to wonder if they were living apart. They had no children either.

Drew rose to greet them. He touched his sister's shoulder and she stepped back before he could hug her. He shook Bear's hand. "Thanks for joining us."

"Glad to spend more time with you," Bear said. "I was pulled away so often at the party we hardly got to know you."

Conversation paused as the server took their drink orders. Paradise smiled at Taylor. "You look lovely in that color." Taylor's robin's-egg-blue dress brought out the shade of her eyes.

"Thank you. I love your hair. I never told you that the other day."

"Thank you. We have a common acquaintance. Governor George has been to the refuge several times and has been a great help with saving the animals."

Taylor smiled. "Her son Josh is a treasure."

"He's a good kid," Bear said. "Tell me about how you guys came to own a refuge like The Sanctuary."

Paradise let Blake take over, and she watched Bear's face as he heard about the original roadside zoo owned by the Steerforths. "I think I visited that place once. I'm a nut for big cats, especially leopards. Black panthers are my favorite. I'll have to come see your place before I go back to Texas. It's not that far."

"No, it's not," Blake said. "Let us know when you're coming, and we'll give you the grand tour."

"Maybe Saturday? What kinds of big cats do you have?"

"Tigers, lions, ligers, jaguars, leopards, and cougars. We had a cheetah, but she was old and passed away last year. Big cats are my favorite too. Our white tigers are very popular."

"I look forward to the tour." Bear took a sip of his tea.

Paradise chose her words carefully. They'd decided not to tell anyone about the car in the governor's garage just yet. "The governor said your families have been close for years."

Taylor reached for a roll. "I've known them my whole life. When Josh applied to be my aide, I jumped on it. He's a little younger than me, and he's worked for me for five years."

Drew shot Paradise a "my turn" glance. "We've been thinking about how peculiar it is that Ben's Barracuda was taken. Do you know how he got it?"

Taylor shook her head. "It was in the garage as far back as I can remember."

Bear put his dinner roll on the plate. "Ben was a nut for muscle cars from the time he was a kid. He talked Dad into taking us to car shows, and the big Mopars were his favorite. He could spend hours going over specs and peering at interiors. Not me. Bored me to death, but Dad thought it was a good bonding experience for us." Bear reached for his drink. "He never understood the two of us were oil and water."

So the brothers were at odds before Pamela came into the picture. Paradise couldn't understand it. She loved Drew dearly and only wanted his happiness.

"It happens with siblings. Look at Cain and Abel," Drew said.

"Well, I never thought to murder him if that's what you're implying." Bear's tone rose a notch.

"Not at all. I just meant siblings are sometimes very different. I never had the luxury of finding out firsthand until this year." Drew's smile settled on Paradise. "First Paradise and now Taylor, Gray, and Parker. It's an abundance of riches. So about the car?"

The fire in Bear's eyes dimmed a bit. "It was all Amelia's doing back when we were in college. We ran into her and her dad at one of the car shows. Her dad had a car there in the competition, and she told Ben he had to see it. He took one look at it and fell in love. It had to be his. Dad laughed and told him he'd have to earn the money to buy it. Even back then when it wasn't worth much, it was more than Ben could afford. After the show Amelia's father gave it to Ben."

"Wow, that was generous."

"Ben had to promise to work for him as an intern during his first summer of college. He learned a lot and his future in politics was set. Amelia's dad knew a lot of people, and he helped to launch Ben's first run for state congressman. He even found Ben his campaign manager, Angela Burns. You've probably met her, right?"

"Oh yes. She came to the park with the governor. She's a powerhouse."

"She's never lost an election for her bosses. When Ben died, she went to work for Amelia and has been with her ever since. She's the loyal sort."

"Yes, she is," Drew said. "Did Ben and Amelia ever date?"

"In college, but it was never serious. But then, Ben was rarely serious about anyone." Bear's voice turned acerbic. "Ben had a short attention span when it came to women. Cars were another matter. Most of the cars in the garage he'd had for years. The 'Cuda was his first and favorite."

"Do you have any idea why someone would take that car and only that car?"

"It was worth the most money." Bear shrugged and reached for his tea. "Or maybe someone had always wanted one and couldn't afford it. It would be worth several million dollars today. Of course, the killer couldn't sell it. It would immediately implicate him."

Paradise leaned forward. "What size shoe did Ben wear?"

Bear lifted a brow. "Strange question, but he wore a ten. So do I. That was the only way we were alike."

"Did he have a favorite brand of sneaker?"

"Nike," Bear said. "He was particularly fond of Air Jordan 4."

Paradise forced her expression to go blank. The same shoe that was found at her parents' murder scene. But Ben was dead by then. Had someone tried to frame him?

Blake walked along the sand of the Gulf with Paradise and Drew in the twilight. Their feet were bare, and the cool sand felt good against his soles. The whitecaps rolling to the shore in the dimming light could have been on a postcard. They'd stopped before leaving Pascagoula to talk about what they'd learned from Bear and Taylor, but they'd all been curiously quiet about starting the discussion.

Blake had seen it in combat. The intensity of battle could cause a need to retreat from reality in jokes, cards, and books. The past months for them had been intense, but he could sense the resolution was nearly ready to step out of the shadows. Closure was coming.

Paradise let go of Blake's hand and ran to dip her feet in the waves. The wind blew her tawny hair around her face in a halo. She kicked at the waves before twirling in a circle with her arms above her head, the picture of joy. He smiled as he watched. She had no idea how entrancing she was.

Drew watched too. "You're a lucky guy, Blake. You take good care of my sister. She's one of a kind."

"I plan to spend the next fifty or sixty years doing just that."

A smiling Paradise returned to his side. "That was refreshing." She headed for a grassy park area with benches ahead, and the men followed.

Blake was alert and ready to unpack what they'd learned. Paradise settled on a long bench. Drew sat on her left side and Blake on her right. "A rose between two thorns," he said.

Her laugh sounded forced. "We might as well talk about it. I'm not convinced Bear had nothing to do with the murders." She turned her attention to Drew. "He got hostile and defensive when you mentioned Cain and Abel."

"I noticed that too. While I'm not ready to throw cuffs on him, he looks good for it."

"When he comes on Saturday, let's be ready with more questions. He clearly hated Ben, and it probably had to do with Pamela."

"I think it's more than that," Blake said. "Bear said they were oil and water. I suspect there was a lot of jealousy going back to childhood."

Drew moved restlessly. "I found out something today. My former partner in Atlanta has a friend who works at the Pascagoula PD. She told him she'd get me in to take a look at Ben's murder files, and I'm going to do that as soon as I can, hopefully next week. But the most interesting piece is that the toxicology report showed Ben was as high as a kite on Vicodin."

"Did he have a prescription for pain?" Blake asked.

"Nope. It's something the police held back from the news and the family. Someone could have dosed him with it before attacking him with the golf club. Bludgeoning is a very up-close-and-personal type of murder. It indicates rage, and I'd say Bear has a lot of that pent up about his brother."

Paradise shuddered and hugged herself. "It's hard for me

to wrap my head around anyone wanting to hurt their own brother."

Drew nudged her with his shoulder. "You mean I don't have to watch everything you fix me to eat and drink? That's a relief. I've been awake a lot at night worrying about what you'll do next."

She chuckled and nudged him back. "You can never be too sure."

He hugged her. "I'm glad we found each other, kiddo. That's just like God to give you what you weren't quite sure you needed."

"Oh, I always knew I needed a brother." Her voice wobbled.

Blake loved watching them interact. His brothers brought such joy to his life, and Drew was helping provide that firm foundation for her. He waited until Paradise pulled away and stared out at the moon glimmering on the water. "What's our next move?"

"Jane should have the pictures developed by tomorrow." Drew's phone sounded and he stared at the screen. "It's Jane. Adams has been captured. He's not talking yet though."

"And Abby is safe," Paradise said. "You don't have to stay out there any longer."

Drew turned off his phone. "That too."

Blake knew the lack of elation in his voice was only about the thought of those evenings with Abby ending. "We're shorthanded in the morning so I have to work. We can get the pictures in the afternoon."

"I can get the pictures first thing tomorrow," Paradise said. "We can reconvene after lunch and see if they hold the key to what happened. I'm trying not to get my hopes up though. I'd like to think that Bea would have told us if it's clear proof of who killed our parents."

Paradise always kept her expectations low, and it hurt Blake's heart to know she had been taught to expect the second shoe to drop. Her life had been one of such turmoil that she might never get over that inclination. He hoped eventually she'd learn to rest on God's promises and begin to look for the silver lining.

CHAPTER 37

JANE SMILED WHEN PARADISE arrived at her office door. "That was fast. I only texted you fifteen minutes ago."

Paradise shut the door behind her and followed Jane to her desk. She spotted the envelope of pictures beside Jane's keyboard. "I was already on the way here. I thought I'd hang out until they were ready." She sniffed the aroma of Costa Rican coffee. "That smells fresh."

"It's still brewing. I texted you, then started a fresh pot." Jane stepped past Paradise and picked up the pictures. "I haven't examined them yet. I meant to have a peek first, but I got called to the interrogation room to try to shake information out of Adams. It was an interesting conversation."

"What was he looking for at the Dillard Ranch? Do we know if he and Roger played any role in the murders of my parents?"

"It was totally unrelated. Roger had a folder of people who owed him 'favors.'" Jane used air quotes on the last word. "Adams was desperate to get ahold of it and see if he could find someone to help him disappear by using the information in the folder."

"That's what he was looking for at the ranch?"

Jane nodded and gestured to the chair before she reached for the prints. "You can look these over and hand them to me as you finish."

"I hope there's something we can use."

The coffeepot beeped, and Jane turned toward the sound. "I'll get us coffee. Want anything in yours? I have all kinds of flavors and heavy whipping cream."

"You have peppermint mocha creamer?"

"I do." Jane stepped to the pot and poured them both steaming mugs. She handed one to Paradise, then settled in her chair. "The report said there were fifteen pictures."

A shiver of excitement settled along Paradise's spine. She opened the envelope's flap and slid out fifteen eight-by-ten glossies. "Thanks for getting them so large."

The first one was a close-up of the Barracuda. The cover was gone, and a bright overhead light illuminated the gleaming seats with the convertible top down. The car looked like new, and maybe it was. "No date or location on these?"

"No, the tech thinks they came from an older 35-millimeter camera. A time stamp was common in the eighties but not everyone replaced cameras all that often unless they were photographers."

Paradise studied the photo. The floor and seats were empty, and the close-up didn't reveal much about the surroundings other than the concrete floor. It could have been in the garage where they'd found it, but she couldn't be sure. She handed it to Jane and picked up the next picture. It was more distant and caught the car in all its glory plus the back wall. "It's at Governor George's garage. I recognize the picture hanging behind it."

And that picture in the background was what had nagged at her. She carried the photo to the window and wished she had a close-up of just that. It appeared to be a photograph of woods with buildings situated nearby. She squinted to try to see the structures. One looked suspiciously like an animal pen of some kind similar to the way The Sanctuary held big cats. The view wasn't good enough to say anything to Jane about it, because it could have been a fence that held in anything—cattle, sheep. The detail was blurry that far out.

Why did it draw her? It could be anywhere, but it felt so familiar. There were some woods around The Sanctuary. Could it be one of those areas? That might explain its familiarity, but she couldn't be sure.

The trees were loblolly pine so the location could be anywhere in the South from East Texas to Florida. There were no identifying markers. She passed the photo to Jane without comment and picked up the third picture. This one was someone's hand over the frame with very little detail around it. She tried to make out anything on the sides but could identify nothing. The rest of the pictures offered no better view of that photograph on the wall she wanted to see. Only the car from various angles.

She handed Jane the last picture. "This feels like a bust. Why would Bea leave these to me?"

"The car has to be a clue of some kind. I think I can get a search warrant since the car is stolen."

"Even with it in the *governor's* possession?"

Jane fell silent, then grimaced. "I'd have to at least give her a chance to explain how it came to be in her possession. I can't go in with guns blazing the way I'd like."

"That's what I thought." Paradise rose and gathered up the pictures, then put them back in the envelope. "Maybe the guys will see something we missed. Do you have copies of these?"

"I do." Jane walked her to the door. "I'll see if I can talk to the governor. I might start with the Collins family and see if they gave it to the governor and haven't told her the truth about it. It's an election year. I have to make sure we're not accused of trying to sway the election with false claims."

Paradise nodded and walked back to her car. The promise she'd felt last night ebbed, leaving her deflated. She stepped into the bright sunshine and felt her spirits surge with an idea. She could go out to the garage. It should still be unlocked. A quick jaunt in and out, and she could get a better view of the photograph on the wall.

She got in her car and headed back to Fairhope. Blake would be working for several hours yet, and Drew was going to be on a conference call with his partner back in Atlanta until after lunch. She turned her radio up and the thirty-minute drive went quickly.

There was no traffic on the rutted county road back to the dirt driveway. She put her foot on the brake and idled a minute as she evaluated whether anyone had been here since the first time she'd seen it. The weedy track didn't look like it had seen tires since Blake drove back here. She took her foot off the brake and drove back toward the garage over the massive potholes and close calls with branches and weeds.

It was as deserted as she'd expected. She parked and got out, then went back through the tall weeds to the side door. It was still unlocked, and she slipped inside, then went directly to the picture hanging on the wall. She took out her phone and snapped a picture before studying it closely.

And the memory she'd tried to pull out emerged full blown. It had been a few days before her parents died, and her mother wanted to go for a drive. They stopped at the bookstore, Paradise's favorite place, and she'd been allowed to buy a book before they drove into the countryside. The drive had taken them near the Dillard Ranch because Paradise had begged to stop and see Abby, but her mom said they didn't have time for a visit.

Her mother had stopped at a woods and had made her stay in the car while she got out to speak to a woman. They'd argued, and the woman had shoved her mom. Mom had fallen into the weeds, and when the woman turned, Paradise had seen her face.

"You shouldn't have come here."

Paradise whirled at the voice and turned to see the woman she'd finally remembered.

Paradise should have been back by now. It was after two o'clock and Drew was waiting with Blake on the back patio. The boys were out with Mom checking on the new beavers. Drew had been closemouthed about what he'd found out at the police department since he wanted to unpack it with Blake and Paradise together, and he paced the cedar boards.

Blake had tried calling her, and it had gone to voice mail. "I'll see when she left Jane's." Jane answered on the first ring. "Paradise isn't still with you, is she?"

"She left an hour and a half ago. I thought she was going home." Jane's volume went up with alarm. "You can't find her?"

"She's not answering her phone." She should have been back here in fifteen minutes, twenty if she had a lot of traffic. "Did she say if she had another stop?"

"No, I thought she was heading back to The Sanctuary. Paradise and I studied the photographs, and a picture on the wall of the governor's remote garage seemed to trigger a memory or alarm in her. She seemed eager to discuss it all with you and

Drew. Maybe the call isn't going through. I've been having trouble with calls today. There's been sunspot activity."

"I'll check the tracker app on her phone. If I run into trouble, I'll let you know." He ended the call and launched the app, then pinched the screen to figure out where she was by nearby roads. His pulse blipped when he located the crossroads. "She's near Fairhope at the senator's garage where we found the Barracuda."

"Maybe the call isn't going through," Drew said. "But just in case let's head that way."

"According to the app, she's been there nearly an hour." He handed his phone to Drew. "You keep an eye on her location. We're only about forty-five minutes away."

Drew carried his computer with him and launched the hot spot on his phone in the truck. Blake kept an eye on his screen from the corner of his eye as he headed toward Fairhope. "Do you think it's Bear?"

Drew glanced up. "Yeah, yeah, I do. The police have camera footage of him at a gas station meeting up with a known drug dealer three days before Ben died. While they can't prove he bought Vicodin, the drug could have been acquired then. The dealer ended up dead before they could talk to him. I think Bear is as dirty as they come. The police couldn't gather enough evidence to charge him, but the file is still open."

"Try Paradise again," Blake said.

Drew nodded and laid Blake's phone down to pull out his own. After a few moments, he shook his head and took the phone from his ear. "Still no answer. I got her voice mail."

"I don't like it."

"I'm trying to believe the call isn't going through, but I've got a knot in my stomach."

Drew's voice mail alert sounded, and he read the message.

"Huh, this is interesting. They got a hit on where the leopard collars were sold. They were dog collars that were bought by the park gift shop."

Blake frowned. "They were sold through The Sanctuary?"

"That's what Rod says. Maybe Warren had the leopard. We'll never know since he's dead, but it's worth checking out any property he owns. He was renting his house, but he could have owned land somewhere and kept animals out there. If he did, they could be in a bad way if they're not being fed and watered."

Blake hit the brakes at an accident ahead. There was no road to get around it, and they were stuck.

CHAPTER 38

PARADISE BACKED AWAY FROM the woman illuminated by the sunlight through the open door. "Angela? I—I can explain. I found the car when we came to return the iPad, and I wanted another look at it." Angela moved her hand, and the gun Paradise hadn't noticed glinted in the sun. "W-what's going on?"

Angela left the door open and advanced into the room. "I knew from the start you'd be the problem. You were an inquisitive child too. We should have taken care of you right from the start, but we were too softhearted." She smiled when Paradise gulped. "You thought it was Amelia, didn't you?" Her tone held self-satisfaction. "If you and your squad thought that, everyone else will too. With you gone we'll be able to put this behind us. We've laid a careful trail right to the governor's door."

"Why implicate her?"

Angela brushed her white hair out of her eyes. "She was another of Ben's conquests. She needs to be punished just like your mother. Like Pamela."

"You wanted Ben?"

"He wanted *me*, but floozies always focused on him. He had

no backbone. We were engaged once, but I asked no one to mention it once it was over, and even his family honored my request. He was mine first."

This was obsession on full display. Paradise gestured to the gun. "I wouldn't have known you were the murderer if you didn't have that."

"You saw me that day. You would have remembered."

"But I didn't see you at the house. A man killed my mother, though I didn't see his face."

"You would have told the police, and they would have figured it out. But you're going to suffer a tragic accident." She gestured with the gun toward the phone in Paradise's hand. "Give me your phone."

Paradise handed it over. It was still on, and she watched Angela launch the Notes app. "What are you doing?"

"Adding to your notes. I knew you'd have notes about your investigation. I'm going to add a clue that you're going to investigate a caged black panther. They won't know where to look until it's too late." Angela dropped the phone onto the floor and kicked it under the car. "That will take them a while to find." She stepped out of the path and gestured to the door. "Let's go."

Paradise saw no weapons handy, not even a piece of wood or a metal tool. She exited the garage and was about to dart for her car when another figure blocked her way.

Bear.

Paradise took a step back. "You killed your own brother?"

"Shut up," Angela snapped. "Took you long enough, Bear."

"How'd you know I was here?" Paradise asked.

He gave her a cold smile. "Cameras, of course. You don't think we'd leave a car this valuable out here with no security, do you?"

He grabbed her upper arm in a tight grip and pushed her toward a panel van parked behind her car. He opened the back. "Get in."

If she complied, she was as good as dead. She jerked her arm out of his grip and took two steps before a dart zinged into her thigh. She gasped and turned to see that Angela had grabbed a tranquilizer gun from the front passenger seat. Paradise tried to move, but her actions felt slow and awkward. Tranqs took a while to work. What had they given her?

"It's not a tranquilizer. It's a little stronger than that." Bear's smile held triumph. He grabbed her and shoved her into the back of the van.

Stay awake. Her mental order didn't stop her vision from blurring and her lids from drooping. When she opened her eyes again, she was face down on the dirty carpet of the old van smelling of big cat. "Blake?" she murmured. She was still groggy, but when she turned her head and saw her surroundings, she snapped awake.

She was in the back of the van. The outlines of two figures in the front seats moved across her blurry vision.

"We have to wait until the drug is out of her system," Angela said from the passenger seat.

They didn't know she was awake yet. Paradise closed her eyes and forced her breathing to slow while she thought about how to escape. They planned to hold her somewhere. The stench of big cat made her heart race as she tried to figure out why they would have a van with that kind of odor. Wait, they'd never discovered the owner of the leopard stalking her. Bear had said he loved big cats. Was this his vehicle?

The van bottomed out in a pothole and made a sharp turn that rolled her against the van's side wall. A cold metal item was at her hand, and she quickly tucked it into the pocket of her denim shorts without identifying it. Whatever it was might come in handy. The vehicle lurched down an unpaved track with looming trees that cast deep shadows outside. Paradise kept her eyes slitted enough to glance around for another weapon. There was a collar that might fit a golden retriever.

Or a big cat.

She took it and stuffed it in her other pocket, then pulled her long tee over her shorts just in time for the van to stop. She slammed her eyes shut again until she heard both doors open and close. Her plan was to jump to her feet and lock the doors so they couldn't get in, but her muscles didn't want to obey her, and by the time she had crawled two feet, Bear had the back open and was pulling her out by the ankles.

"Nice try," he said, lifting her out and setting her upright.

She swayed where she stood and her head spun. Angela prodded her with the gun, and Paradise staggered forward a few feet before falling to her hands and knees again. When Bear yanked her up again, she recognized the woods in the picture on the wall in the garage. How far had they gone? No one would know where to look for her, not with her phone left behind in the garage.

She heard the big cat hiss before she spotted the enclosure, and her gut clenched. Her guess had been correct. Bear or someone he'd hired had sent the leopard to The Sanctuary to warn her off, and he had another big cat here. She tried to run, but her legs still barely held her. Bear grabbed her in a fierce grip and marched her toward the gate Angela had opened. He shoved her inside and locked her in.

The biggest black jaguar she'd ever seen stalked the inner enclosure and bared his teeth at her. He couldn't get to her. Not yet.

Paradise's car was still parked outside, but she wasn't in the garage or anywhere on the property that Blake could see. He'd even checked the trunk of the Barracuda. Someone had taken her. It was the only answer, and he had no idea where to look.

He pulled out his phone. "Her phone pings here somewhere. I'm going to try calling her."

Drew nodded and went to the framed photograph on the wall. "Jane said she lingered over the picture of this print. Do you know where this is?"

"The vegetation is similar to this area, but it could be anywhere."

Blake's call went through, and music sounded from somewhere in the building. Blake tracked the sound to under the car. He dropped to his belly and reached under the 'Cuda to retrieve Paradise's phone.

The light was on, and he swiped it to answer his own call, then ended it. It immediately went to locked screen. What might her password be? He tried her birth date, but that didn't work. His password was the last six digits of his social security, but he didn't know hers. Mom would have it. He shot a quick text to his mother asking her to check Paradise's employment records.

While he waited for his mother to answer, he went to check the photograph on the wall. "It looks familiar, but I can't quite place it. I'm sending it to Mom."

Drew glanced up from his phone. "I'm having my former partner see if Bear owns any property nearby. It's somewhere to start."

"I'm glad you're here because I don't know where to look. I'm texting Jane and Rod." Blake shot off texts to them asking for help identifying the spot in the picture. His phone pinged with a message from his mother.

I looked up property near here on the county website. Warren has a plot of land close to here. I'm sending you the address.

Blake showed the text to Drew. "Jane said the collars were sold to the park. I think Bear might have been working with Warren." His phone sounded again. "Here's the address. We can head back toward the park since we know it's in the general neighborhood. Come on." He rushed for the door with Drew on his heels and climbed into the truck. He handed Drew Paradise's phone. "Mom is sending me Paradise's social security number. See if you can get her phone unlocked."

Drew took it and Blake stomped on the gas to get out to the main road. The truck tires slammed into potholes all the way out, but it was smooth sailing once they reached pavement.

His phone sounded with another text from his mom, and he had Blake try the last six digits, but it didn't work. "Try the first six."

"That's it, and I'm in! I'll check her emails and texts first." Drew fell silent before shaking his head. "Nothing pertaining to the investigation. I'll check her Notes app." After a minute he growled, a sound of frustration. "She says she saw a black leopard and is going to follow it. I don't like the sound of this, Blake."

"That makes no sense. Her car is still at the garage, and she wouldn't follow a black leopard on foot. She's terrified of them. She has no weapon or any way to capture it. Someone else put that in her phone. She's in trouble, Drew."

Think, think! It was hard to grab hold of his thoughts with fear clouding his mind.

"My text still isn't going through to Jane," Drew said. "I tried calling too, but it's dead air. Jane must be having trouble with her service."

"I'll call Mason." Blake placed a quick call to The Sanctuary's young volunteer. "Mason, can you put your drone up over the Dillard Ranch and any other land around the park? We're looking for Paradise."

"Sure, Blake. If it's too far, my dad can get me closer. Is she in trouble?"

"I think so, buddy. We need to find her as soon as possible. And keep an eye out for a black panther."

"Okay. I'm on it." The teenager ended the call.

Drew was tense and jumpy. Blake wanted to comfort him, but he didn't have the words when fear choked his own throat too. This was bad, very bad. Mason might be looking in the wrong place, but they had no better directions to send him.

CHAPTER 39

PARADISE KEPT ONE EYE on the jaguar and the other eye on her two captors. Her head still felt fuzzy with scattered thoughts from the drug they'd given her, but the cobwebs blew away the longer she was awake. The big cat sprayed urine her way, and the stench cleared her fog even more. She spotted more animals in another enclosure deeper in the trees. A couple of foxes and a wolverine.

Angela and Bear's plans for her were clear. They intended to let the jaguar in with her. Every time she thought of that gate opening, her breath came hard and fast. Her fear could be her undoing, and she had to master it. The animal would be able to tell and she wouldn't be able to assert dominance.

She moved closer to where they stood talking quietly. "The authorities will know you did this. You own the property, Bear. What will you gain by killing me?"

The gun was in Bear's possession now, stuffed in his belt. He stared back at Paradise impassively. "Neither of us own this property. You will have simply vanished."

"You paid Warren? Is this his property?"

"I told you she was too smart for her own good," Angela said.

"How did you even know him?"

Angela shrugged. "He mowed lawns for your parents when he was a teenager, and I paid him to keep an eye on Becky for years. He was useful when it was time to end it."

Paradise managed to swallow down the ball of terror forming. "Why kill my parents? They did nothing to you or Bear. They were innocent."

Angela's fists clenched and her face reddened. "Nothing? Your mother was just a whore. She was married yet she still got in Ben's head and confused him. Ben and I were finally going to be together like it should have been all along until *she* came back into his life."

Paradise saw it all in the woman's twisted mouth and angry eyes. That final rejection had snapped her sanity. "This was all you, wasn't it, Angela? He rejected you and if you couldn't have him, then no one could, right? You drugged him, then bludgeoned him with the golf club." She stared at Bear. "She couldn't kill both my parents alone. How did she talk you into doing her dirty work? And how did you even know Warren, Bear?"

He shrugged. "I thought a cable guy would seem innocent enough. I saw Warren a few streets over one day and offered him five grand if he'd do a couple of things for me. He thought the music box was a surprise birthday present for you, and I convinced him to leave the door unlocked for a surprise party. After the murders he was too scared to go to the police. I kept feeding him money through the years to keep him quiet."

She hated his arrogant expression. "There was missing evidence on the murders, but with your power, you could get it removed. Did you threaten Sheriff Davis and he felt he had no choice but to hide it? Was he your mole inside the department? And how did you know the music box was something I would want?"

He shrugged. "Ben had bought it for you before he died. He would know what you liked."

"Enough!" Angela took a step closer. "The drugs are out of her system, Bear. It's time to shut her up for good. Shoot her and let the panther have the remains."

His jaw flexed. "The murders were a long time ago, Ang. Why commit another one now and make it worse?"

"We'll be long gone before her remains are ever found. No one will know what happened to her. The investigation will die with her. She's the one driving it all."

Paradise gripped the fence with both hands. "You're wrong. Ben was Drew's father. He'll keep pushing for the truth. Taking him down will be a lot harder than killing me. He has the entire police force to help him."

Bear moved restlessly. "She might be right. I can't just shoot her. Let's hop on our plane and leave her here and get out of the country."

"And then what? She'll die without food or water anyway."

"If she's ever found, the police will think she got trapped in here and the panther got to her. You left the note about her following a lead on a black panther. She came in here to check out the cat and got trapped. I thought letting the cat kill her was the plan."

"You're being ridiculous. Shoot her and get it over with."

"I thought it was all behind us. The guilt has eaten at me." Bear's tone turned coaxing. "We'll be on the beach sipping piña coladas. We can spend the rest of our lives forgetting about what happened. I still can't believe after it was all over, we found each other."

Paradise had to know everything. How had Angela convinced Bear to help her? And how had Pamela died? She thought through the sequence of events. "You found out my mother was pregnant, didn't you? You finally realized Ben was never going to be with you, so you drugged him and killed him. Did Pamela figure out you killed him? Or did she think it was Bear?"

Bear and Angela exchanged a dismayed glance, and she knew she was right. "She accused Bear and he spilled the truth, didn't he?"

"I didn't touch her," Bear said.

"But Angela did. She went back to the house and took care of her since you couldn't do it, right? You're not a killer, Bear. Don't let her do this."

"Shut up!" Angela's face reddened. "Shoot her, Bear."

But he didn't raise the gun in his hand. "Let's go, Angela. A bullet will be proof we killed her. Let's be smart about it."

"Why did you help Angela kill my parents? What was in it for you?" Paradise had to ask the questions aloud to think through them on her own, and then it all clicked into place. "At least part of it was quid pro quo, wasn't it? You wanted his Senate seat. Ben had to die for his infidelity, and if she killed him, you'd kill my mother. Only Dad came home unexpectedly, and you had to kill them both."

Angela's agitation grew with every question. "Ben led me on, for years and years. He was always going to leave Pamela, and then when he finally told her he was leaving, it was for Becky. And she was having the baby that should have been *mine*."

Paradise took a step back. Obsession was an ugly thing, so hideous that it had led to the murders of four people.

Bear took a step closer to Paradise. "If you'd just let it go, we wouldn't be here. We tried to warn you off, but you just kept digging and digging."

"I wanted justice," Paradise said.

"Instead you get to be dead," Angela said in a monotone voice.

Bear took Angela's chin and turned her face toward him. "Let's just leave her here. It was twenty years ago, Ang. Let's not taint our future with a fresh murder. The others were bad enough. I don't want to do this."

Angela stared at him, then finally nodded. "All right, all right, Bear. Whatever you say. We'll drive straight to Pensacola and fly out. We can buy all new things when we get there."

Hand in hand they walked toward the van. Paradise eyed the fence and kicked off her shoes to try to climb it, then she caught Angela's expression as she gazed back. She was smiling and her expression was triumphant.

This wasn't over.

The lush green turf of the property spread as far as Blake could see. Though the map had shown the land was farmed, he'd held out hope there would be some barn or other structure where he'd find Paradise imprisoned, but there was only a small, empty garage. He slammed the steering wheel with his palms but managed not to scream out his frustration.

Drew pointed out the truck window to his left. "The land ends at that fence and the one on the other side. The line of scrubby brush is the back property line. Nothing here."

The dejection in his voice matched how Blake felt. Jane and Rod were looking too, but they were stymied. What if he talked to the governor himself?

"I'm calling the governor." Blake turned off the radio, then yanked out his phone and called up her number. When the receptionist answered, he gave his name and said he was worried about his fiancée. "If you tell the governor my name, I think she'll speak to me."

"Hold, please."

After what seemed an eternity with music playing in his ear, Governor George was on the line. "Blake, what's going on?"

He plunged into the story about the car and Paradise's disappearance. As he spooled it out, he realized how crazy it sounded that he'd called the governor. They'd trespassed on her land. And what if she was behind Paradise's disappearance? But no, she was in Montgomery at her office. That was the number he'd called.

"Whoa, whoa, back up. You're saying this land and garage with the car is in *my* name? I don't have any land in Baldwin County. This is very puzzling. And Ben's stolen car is there?"

"Yes, ma'am. Drew checked the VIN number, and it's the missing car." He flipped his phone speaker on. "I have you on speakerphone, Governor. Drew is here too."

"That's fine. Maybe the three of us can get to the bottom of what's happened. Of course you thought I had something to do with Ben's murder. That would make sense. I'm surprised you called me if you thought I was complicit."

"I ran through what I know about you and thought maybe you were given the car quietly and the Collins family didn't want anyone to know. I believe you're a woman of integrity, Governor."

"Thank you for that vote of confidence, but this is all news to me. You're sure it's the same car that my father gave to Ben?"

"Yes, ma'am."

The governor cleared her throat. "I've been concerned about, um, about Angela's behavior lately. She's been short with me and the staff and was missing a lot of work. She tendered her resignation last week, and I've tried to call her several times, but she hasn't answered. The car is all mixed up in it too. Her father bought it for her originally. She gave it to my dad and was upset when he gave it away. She said if he was going to give it away, he should have given it to her. Dad tried to find another one like it to make things right with Angela, but they're very rare."

"That's what we found out when we were researching it. Is it possible she took it because she felt it belonged to her?" Blake glanced across the truck at Drew, who was busy on his phone with something, and Blake hoped it had to do with Paradise's whereabouts.

"It's possible."

Drew muttered something, then held up his phone. "Governor, this is Drew. I did a search on our database about when the property transferred to your name. It was six months ago. It was originally in Angela's name. She's owned it for twenty years."

"Since the murders," Blake said. "We suspected Bear, but Angela might be the one behind everything."

"It's hard to think she could be a murderer. She's been my friend and confidant for many years. She dated Ben for a while. Maybe you didn't know that. Angela dated him for a year and they were engaged, though he never gave her a ring. She was crazy about him and thought she could change his philandering ways. He broke up with her when he met Pamela."

Blake pointed to Drew's phone. "Drew, can you check and see if Angela owns any other property around? Maybe she's taken Paradise."

"Sis is fierce. A woman would have trouble forcing her to go with her."

"She could have knocked her out. And if Angela committed the murders, she's no slouch."

"Angela is stronger than she looks. She's been a gym rat the entire time I've known her," the governor said. "And maybe she's not working alone. She's been seeing Bear Collins for about two years. They've been talking about marriage."

"We suspected Bear after talking to him. He held a lot of animosity toward his brother. But there isn't enough evidence to put out an APB on either of them. It's all speculation. One other thing—have either of them mentioned having a black panther in captivity? Or any kind of leopard, really?"

"What an odd question. Bear loves big cats, but he's not around enough to keep one." Taps on a keyboard sounded in the background. "I might have something. I'll call you back."

Where could they look? Who might Bear have connected with around here?

CHAPTER 40

ALMOST THERE. **PARADISE GRIPPED** her bare toes into the ten-foot-high fence and, wincing at the metal biting into her bare skin, inched her way to the top. Her sandals awaited her on the other side—if she made it. The panther roared and hissed behind the higher fence separating them. Her right hand slapped the fence's top rail, but the muscles in her arms burned from hanging on.

She forced herself to climb a little more until her left hand gripped the top as well. She gathered her strength for the final push, but her right hand slipped. She grabbed at the fence again and missed.

The frantic movement dislodged her from her perch, and she plummeted to the ground. The force of the fall left her gasping for air on the red dirt, and the jaguar leaped at the other side of the fence to try to grab her.

She sat up and brushed the dirt from her face and hair. "You're a beautiful boy, aren't you?" If she talked to it in a soothing voice, maybe the big cat would calm down. The sun on the cat's fur picked out the detail of the spots showing through the black.

The collar.

She pulled the collar from her back pocket and held it toward the fence for him to smell. Instead of soothing him, it enraged him. He snarled and leaped at the fence again, and she scuttled back in the dirt.

The panther wasn't paying attention to her though. Its striking blue eyes watched something behind her. She turned but saw nothing. Then the sound of an engine reverberated through the treetops and tires popped on gravel. Was Angela back to finish the job? Paradise stood and faced the vehicle, but it wasn't the van that had brought her here.

The white truck wasn't familiar, but the driver was. Creed Greene. Had he followed her while investigating?

"Creed! I've never been so glad to see anyone in my life." She went to the gate. "Do you have a key?"

"Looks like Abyss would like to meet you. Or eat you."

He laughed at his joke, but something in his eyes made her pulse skip. "Creed? How did you know I was here?"

"Bear called me to tidy up his mess. Typical of him."

"You know him?"

"My bank account knows him well. He paid well for terrorizing you with the rattlesnake and everything else. Warren's an old friend from our teen years, and he enlisted my help. For a good price too. I've been the face behind everything—the texts, all the efforts to stop you. I can't remember when I enjoyed something more than terrorizing you, but the best is yet to come."

He came close enough for her to catch a whiff of his cologne. "Abyss likes to work for his food. We won't make it easy for him."

He intends to kill me.

"You don't want to be dragged into a murder case, do you? Angela and Bear killed my parents, and Drew's father."

"You think that's news to me? Bear enlisted my help when you first came back. We'd hoped you all would stay busy with the problems at the park and your obsession with digging into a twenty-year-old murder would evaporate, but you're the persistent sort, aren't you? Just remember, you brought this on yourself. We tried everything to convince you to let it alone."

"Even training a leopard to track people?"

His smile didn't reach his eyes. "I share Bear's passion for big cats. We had great fun training the two, but our jaguar is especially proficient at tracking prey. You're about to find out just how good Abyss is."

She suppressed a shudder. "You haven't killed anyone yet, Creed. There's no need to make yourself the focus of a murder now. Let me go and I won't implicate you in anything. You'll be the man who saved me, a hero in everyone's eyes."

"You think I'm stupid?" He slammed his palm against the fence, and it shuddered and clanged enough that the panther sprang away with a snarl. "I'm in too deep after I had to take care of Bea and remove evidence from the sheriff's department. No loose ends. All the evidence is gone."

He'd killed Bea. "You killed her for money?"

"What else? It's her own fault. Bea thought Gerald was having an affair with Becky, so Bea had been watching the house. She saw the murders and decided to blackmail Angela. Bear finally had me put an end to the blackmail—and Bea."

Paradise struggled for something to say, some way to convince Creed to let her go, but the words wouldn't come. He'd been involved right from the beginning.

The indecision vanished from his face, and his eyes went hard. He didn't speak but went along to the side fence and approached the big cat. The jaguar came close and made a chuffing noise of happiness at seeing him. "You're hungry, aren't you? Just a little longer, and you can have fresh meat."

Creed disappeared inside the small shed beside the main enclosure. Paradise heard a creaking sound and the gate began to open between her and Abyss. Not enough for him to get through, but the panther sprang at it and thrust his paw through the opening. She backed away.

Creed reappeared and came around to where she stood with her back pressed against the outside fence. "It will take him a while to shred through that, but make no mistake, those claws will be plenty sharp enough when he reaches you. Abyss is a terrific hunter. You can spend your last few minutes alive remembering all the ways you could have acted differently and saved yourself." He strode toward his truck and didn't look back.

Paradise watched the jaguar worry the gate, pulling at the metal with his scalpel-like two-inch claws until the gate began to bend back toward the inside. How long did she have? Her muscles found new strength, and she leaped at the fence and began to climb again. Her feet hurt and bled as she climbed and fought her way to the top. With both hands on the rail, she spared a glance toward the panther again. His head was nearly through.

With a final scrambling of her feet, she heaved her left leg over the top and dropped onto the other side of the perimeter. Her hands couldn't hold on any longer, and she fell to the ground as Abyss charged through the bent and mangled gate.

Snarling, the jaguar paced the fence, but he couldn't get to her. In the next instant the big cat leaped onto the fence and began to climb. The inner fence was angled inward to keep in the predators, but the other fence had no such safety feature.

Paradise barely took time to shove her feet into her sandals. She ran down the dirt track to where it split into a Y. Which way should she go to get to the road? If the panther succeeded in climbing the fence, tracking her would be easy.

She felt her back pocket for the item she'd picked up in the truck. The screwdriver wouldn't be much of a weapon, but it was all she had.

Stymied. Blake vibrated with the need to *do something*, but he and Drew sat paralyzed in the truck waiting for direction. He didn't dare head for a location in case he was in the exact wrong spot to save Paradise.

The seconds ticked by like hours as he considered what to do. Blake's phone rang, and he grabbed it. "It's the governor."

"Blake, I pulled some strings and did a trace on Angela's bank account for the past year. And Bear's. He's been paying a Creed Greene ten thousand dollars every two months for the past six months. He appears to work in the sheriff's department in Baldwin County, so I suspect some involvement with whatever Angela and Bear are doing."

It all slammed into place with a sickening thud in Blake's core. "Since Paradise came back and started poking into her parents' murders, Creed's had it in for her. It makes sense. It has to be Creed. And he's had a few wild animals. Did you happen to look up any property he owns? I know of one piece of land where he's kept wolverines." But no big cats that they could see.

"He has three properties in Baldwin County." The governor rattled off the first two locations.

"I know about those."

"The last one is along Nolte Creek, and it's an odd shape that winds back to another area. Did you search all of it?"

Blake headed for the truck with Drew running beside him. "We'll head there now."

"I'm getting in touch with the state police since the sheriff's department is compromised. I'll have them send out some officers."

"Thanks again." Blake ended the call and held out the address to Drew. "Get me directions and send this to Mason."

Before Drew could contact him, Blake's phone sounded with a call from Mason. "Hey, buddy, you find anything?"

"I just spotted a black panther!"

Mason's voice was nearly a scream in Blake's ear and he held the phone out an inch. "Where?"

"Off Nolte Creek. I'm out with Dad and we're driving around and flying the drone. I almost didn't see it in the shadows, but then it looked up. It's got blue eyes, Blake. I've never seen that before. And it's a big cat. Huge. I'll bet it's three hundred pounds and over six feet long not counting the tail."

"That's close to us. We're only five miles from there." Blake headed for the truck and motioned for Drew to get in too. "Keep the cat in sight and watch for Paradise. We're on our way. Call Drew with updates because I'll be driving."

Blake started the truck and pulled away from the property with a plume of dust behind him. At least they were close. He prayed for Paradise's safety and for her to know help was coming.

Drew buckled his seat belt when the alarm began to ding. "That Mason is a good kid. He's streaming the video from his drone straight to my phone. I see the panther, and it's on a mission. I'm afraid it might be tracking something. And the kid is right—it's huge."

Blake accelerated. It had to be tracking Paradise, but they were only a mile away from the property. A white truck passed, going the opposite direction. "That was Creed Greene!" Blake slammed on his brakes, then shook his head and resumed driving. "I'm not going after him. He'd only lie anyway. Does the drone see her at all?"

"No. Oh, wait, there she is. She's only a few yards ahead of the cat. She's stopping and facing it with something in her hands. Maybe a screwdriver? She's holding it like a knife, but I don't think it's going to stop that panther."

Drew gestured. "Turn right here at the next little drive. I think it's all dirt."

Blake gripped the steering wheel. "Get your gun ready." The truck fishtailed as he made the right turn without slowing. "Any idea how far?"

"I can't tell for sure. Not far though."

The track was tight with vegetation brushing both sides of his pickup. The hump in the middle of the path meant that the truck tried to head for the ditch every chance it got, and he didn't dare go as fast as he'd like around the curves in case he came out of one and hit Paradise.

"That kid deserves a medal! He's got the drone dive-bombing the cat. The panther looks like it's hissing and spitting at the thing, and it's not watching Paradise. I hope she takes the opportunity to run while the cat is distracted. It might gain enough time for us to get there."

Where was she? Blake tried to peer through the shadows cast by the big trees on both sides of the truck. Was this even the right drive? He still hadn't spotted anything that might hold big cats.

CHAPTER 41

BLESS MASON. HE HAD to have been the one to send the drone down to distract Abyss.

Paradise took off as fast as she could while the jaguar was occupied with leaping at the drone. She spotted a big branch. It might be a better weapon than the screwdriver if the jaguar came after her. And she would lay money that he would. She tucked the screwdriver away and grabbed the branch. It was about the width and length of a baseball bat.

Her lungs burned but adrenaline fueled her limbs. She set her jaw with determination and ran for all she was worth. If she survived this, she'd take up jogging so she was ready next time. Something nudged her to look behind her, and when she did, her heart faltered in her chest. The panther was behind her and closing in fast.

Never turn your back on a jaguar.

She whirled with the stick in front of her and jabbed at the panther with it. "Get back! I'll break your beautiful back with this if I have to, but I don't want to hurt you."

The panther stared at her with uncanny blue eyes, but she

avoided eye contact, which the big cat would take as a challenge. The jaguar bit at the leaves she shook in his face. His teeth made her shudder. Jaguars were dwarfed only by lions and tigers, but a jaguar's bite was worse. It could crack a croc's head like an egg.

The thought of those teeth in her neck nearly paralyzed her, but her attack seemed to be having an effect. The jaguar seemed unsure how to deal with all the shaking and noise. The terror that had gripped her eased, and she realized Abyss was a beautiful and powerful animal. Creed and Bear had trained the panther to hunt, and while the cat's natural instinct was to track down his food, he wouldn't have considered humans as prey without the men's influence. That didn't make the danger to her any less dire, but she felt sorry for the panther instead of terrified.

She shook the stick again. "Get out of here, Abyss. Find a squirrel or something. I'm not your dinner."

The panther bared his teeth and snapped at the leaves again. Huge muscles coiled in his back legs, and she knew the cat had gotten over his fear. She nearly froze in place to wait for the clamp of those mighty jaws on her neck.

"I won't go down without a fight, Abyss." She jabbed at the panther's chest with the hard edge of the branch. "Go on, git!"

A dark shape dove toward them again, and Abyss turned and snarled at the drone. A surge of hope lifted Paradise's chin and she raised her fist in exultation. "Yes! Thank you, Mason!" The boy hadn't abandoned her. She wasn't alone to face this.

She jabbed outward with the branch again and backed away so she didn't attract the cat's attention. Her breath was loud in her ears. Once she couldn't see the jaguar any longer, she began to run. Her vision narrowed to the dirt road in front of her. If she could make it out of the woods, the cat might give up the chase.

Dust plumes billowed from behind a truck heading her way,

and she recognized Blake's determined face behind the wheel. The truck skidded to a stop, and with the engine still running, Blake spilled from one side of the pickup and her brother from the other. Tears blurred her vision, and she started toward them.

Drew's gun was in his hand. He motioned to her right. "Get out of the way!" He was aiming over her shoulder and to the left.

Paradise turned to see the jaguar charging at full speed, and she leaped into the ditch. Her belly hit the vegetation, and leaves and grass were in her mouth and hair. She scrambled to her hands and knees to regain her feet, but she expected to feel teeth in the back of her neck.

The black shadow of the jaguar was still coming. The big cat changed directions, but Drew's gun barked, and the animal leaped in the air as a bullet nicked his foot. The big cat growled and bit at the injury, then lay down and licked the wound.

Blake ran to her and pulled her out of the ditch. He turned her away from the big cat. "Get in the truck. I'll tranq it." He brought up a pistol and fired a dart at the cat. It lodged in the jaguar's back flank, but Abyss didn't seem to notice with the blood still oozing from his foot.

Now that she was safe, the strength vanished from Paradise's legs, and she wobbled as she headed for the pickup. She opened the passenger door and nearly collapsed onto the seat. She couldn't stop shaking, and even her teeth chattered. *Shock.*

Both men watched the jaguar put his head on his paws. It would be a few minutes before it was safe to approach the animal, and that was fine with her.

She reached for the bottle of water on Blake's side of the console and downed what was left in one gulp. She was still thirsty, but the shaking ebbed. Tears felt dangerously close. *Thank you, God.* It was a bona fide miracle that the men she loved had found her in time. Five minutes later and parts of her would have been in the panther's belly, and the rest would have been up a tree waiting for Abyss's next meal.

Paradise rested and tried to gather her thoughts on their next steps, but the only thing she wanted right this minute was Blake's arms around her. Only then would she be sure she had survived this ordeal.

He jogged back to the truck and opened the door to lean in. "The cat's asleep. We'll load him in a few minutes. Are you hurt?"

She sank into the love in his blue eyes and cupped his face in her hands. "Just hold me a minute until I stop shaking. I thought I'd never see you again."

He leaned into the truck and gathered her close. "Take all the time you need. I wasn't sure I'd even find you."

She closed her eyes and inhaled his masculine scent. *Home.* This was where she belonged. Even the sound of sirens heading their way wasn't as much comfort as Blake's arms.

Blake and Drew sat with Paradise in the ER exam room while the doctor cleaned and bandaged her poor feet from the brutal climb out of the jaguar enclosure. Her cheeks held more color, and her amber eyes glowed with contentment. After all these months of trauma and fear, it was over. She had answers and he rejoiced with her.

"Did you text your mom?" she asked when the doctor left.

"I did. She's been praying constantly during the search, the boys too. They're all waiting to welcome you home."

Her smile widened. "It's over, Blake. I can't believe it."

He turned at a tap on the door, and Jane poked her head in.

"I was told our patient is doing well and ready for discharge. I thought you'd like to know Bear and Angela were picked up at the Pensacola airport."

He exhaled. "That's great news. What about Creed?"

"Rod chased him into Louisiana, and in the capture, Creed's truck went airborne and ended up on its roof. He's dead."

"I feel bad about the Collins family," Paradise said softly. "They've had so much loss already."

"Do you feel up to telling me the story? I'm still murky on all of the details."

Blake wondered the same. All he knew was that Bear and Angela had taken her from the garage, but he didn't know who had committed the murders and why.

Paradise sat up on the exam table and dangled her feet over the side. There were twigs in her hair and dirt on all her exposed skin. She brushed at the mud on her knees. "I sure need a shower. Do I need to come down to the station so you can record it all?"

Jane held up her phone. "This is fine for now. You've been through a terrible ordeal."

"I'll take the reprieve." Paradise took a deep breath, then dove in. "There was something about a photo on the wall of the garage that nagged at me, and I decided to examine it again. I went out to the garage by myself and realized there was fencing in the picture that could have been to contain a big cat. I thought it might lead me to whoever had released that leopard onto our property, the one we found with a collar. While I was there, Bear and Angela came in."

Blake could see the scene in his head. They'd walked in to her trespassing, and it had escalated into so much more. "How'd they take you?"

"I'll get to that. Angela snapped when she found out Ben was leaving Pamela for my mom. The pregnancy was the final straw. She said the baby should have been hers. After all these years, he owed her. She drugged him and bludgeoned him with the golf club. Pamela figured it out and confronted Bear, who confessed. Angela heard and killed her too."

"And your parents?" Jane asked.

"I think that was simple hatred and revenge. She called my mother a whore. Bear killed them for her. He wanted Ben's Senate seat, but that didn't happen. I'm not sure why."

"I can answer that," Drew said. "While we were waiting for the nurse to let us come back to see you, I did some research on Bear. The Mississippi governor called for a special election to replace Ben, and Bear ran. He lost. I'm sure he thought sympathy for the loss of his brother would carry the day, but he still didn't connect with the voters."

"So he never got what he wanted," Blake said. "That's a bit of justice right there."

"Wow, it's a testament to what obsession will do," Jane said. "How did the muscle car play into it all?"

"I don't know. We didn't talk about that."

Blake held up his hand. "I can answer that. I called the governor. She said the car had originally belonged to Angela's father. He'd sold it to the governor's father for a song, and then when Ben wanted it so badly, her dad gave it to Ben. We think with him dead, Angela wanted it back. I think she wanted her whole life back—all the time she'd wasted waiting on Ben to 'do the right thing' and marry her."

Paradise nodded. "And Bear convinced her to leave with him, assuming I could climb out. But she smiled triumphantly at me as they left, and I knew it wasn't over. They'd been gone about half an hour when Creed showed up to finish the job. I'd been trying and failing to climb the fence. Creed opened the gate between the perimeters enough for the jaguar to begin to claw his way through and left me there. That's when I took another stab at climbing the fence. I got out and started to run. The jaguar was climbing the fence when I looked back last, and I'd hoped once I was out of view, it would give up. But Creed and Bear had trained Abyss to track and kill prey."

"God had to have protected you," Blake said.

She took his hand. "Absolutely, and I'm so thankful."

"This will be a trial that will grip the entire nation," Jane said. "Jealousy, obsession, and even a black jaguar. What about Bea?"

Paradise glanced at Blake and Drew. "She had been trying to catch Sheriff Davis with my mom. She saw Angela the night of the murders and covered it up. For a price. Angela got tired of paying the blackmail money."

Jane's hazel eyes narrowed. "So much pain and death over money and obsession. I don't see them wiggling out of this." She turned toward the door. "Get a shower, hold some happy boys, and we'll get your statement tomorrow. I'm glad you survived, Paradise."

"Not as glad as me," Blake murmured as he kissed Paradise.

Drew unwound from the chair and followed Jane. "I'm going to get coffee. Any takers?"

"I'll have some," Blake said.

Paradise chimed in with a request as well. "And chocolate-covered peanuts."

Drew smiled. "You got it."

When the door shut behind her brother, Paradise patted the exam table beside her. "I'd like you a little closer."

Blake would like nothing better himself. He perched on the edge of the table. "I don't think they're going to keep you overnight. I'll take you home to the boys as soon as they let you loose. Do your feet hurt?"

She took his hand. "I'm too happy to feel any pain. Justice feels good, Blake. It was something I wasn't sure would happen. It won't bring my parents back, but their killer isn't still out there somewhere living their life without punishment. I won't be spending the rest of my life staring into people's faces and wondering if they killed my parents. I'm free of that compulsion. I feel like I could float away on a breeze."

"We can stop and get some chocolate-peanut-butter ice cream to help weigh you down."

She poked him in the ribs with her index finger. "I'd settle for chocolate-covered peanuts and some of your mom's brownies."

Her joy radiated to him, and he pulled her closer. "It's over, babe. Our next chapter is right in front of us."

EPILOGUE

IT WAS ALL PARADISE could do to keep a straight face. This surprise would blow Blake's mind. Hez and Savannah were primed and ready for picture taking. Paradise sneaked a glance across the truck at the strong planes and angles of Blake's face and the way his cowlick, just like Levi's, stood up at his crown. Being married to him was the best.

The past four months of marriage had been, well, bliss. After all they'd been through, she knew him well, and he accepted all her quirks without complaint—except for the way she left her hair ties strewn around the small apartment above Pawsome Pets.

The cats played with them and left them in strange places—like his shoes. She was working on trying to remember to put them in the bathroom drawer. The new primary bath had drawers with little compartments for everything. It had been the perfect workaround—if she remembered. She'd had to adjust to how early he got up even when he didn't have to work. She was becoming just like him—up at five with her Bible on her lap. It wasn't a bad thing.

Blake pulled into the newly blacktopped driveway and parked

in front of the garage. "It's all ours, per Frank. The last paint touch-ups are even finished. Ready, babe?"

"More than ready." They'd been waiting for this moment since the wedding, and the best part was, they'd be able to have Christmas in their new place.

They walked hand in hand to the front door, and she admired the lines of the home and the metal roof. "It's so perfect, Blake."

"You're perfect." He punched in the lock code, then pushed the door open wide.

Before she could react he swept her into his arms and carried her into the house. The scent of recently installed floors and fresh paint swirled around them. She clung to his neck and her eyes burned with thankful tears as she stared into his blue eyes. This moment was the culmination of all their dreams.

They were in their new home, planned from the ground up, but even more than that, she had something important to tell him.

He kissed her, and she clung to him a long moment before he set her on her feet. She held his hand and gazed at the high ceilings and the tasteful greige wall color. Abby had helped her pick out the furniture, and light oak floors contrasted beautifully with the area rug. And though it was everything she'd dreamed, Paradise would live with Blake in a barn at The Sanctuary.

They walked through the house, exclaiming over all the touches. The kitchen with its gray cabinets and mostly white granite counters was even more beautiful than she'd hoped. They'd sleep here tonight for the first time, but there was one room she couldn't wait to show him.

"We haven't seen the guest rooms. I want to see if they feel as large and comfortable with furniture in them as I'd hoped."

He came along agreeably, and she strained to hear past the shut door ahead. Was that a giggle? The sound stopped, and she quickly started pointing out the beautiful woodwork and numerous outlets.

Her heart raced when she touched the doorknob to the smallest of the bedrooms. "Let's start here." She swung open the door to a room filled with family and friends—Jenna and Frank, the boys, Drew, Clark, Abby, Hez and Savannah, Simon, and Mason with his father. Hez was busy snapping pictures by the baby bed that Abby and Drew had erected for the surprise. The two of them were still together and talking marriage, and Frank had already proposed and been accepted by Jenna. Paradise's heart was full with all the family and extended family.

Drew was settled into his new job at the Bon Secour sheriff's substation, and he'd quickly found out his father's side of his family tree wasn't much interested in a relationship beyond a distant one. His sister and brothers, as well as his grandparents, blamed him for Bear's prison sentence. Drew didn't seem to care. He had Abby and Quinn now, and contentment oozed off him.

Plus one more.

Isaac sprang forward and launched himself against Blake's legs. "Blake, you're going to be a daddy!"

Blake gasped and stared at Paradise. "W-what? Are you . . . are we—?"

She motioned to Levi, who ran to give Blake a positive pregnancy test. Blake lost his color before it came surging back. He whooped and scooped her up to swing her around. "A baby! We're having a baby!"

Tears spilled onto her cheeks even as she laughed so hard her stomach hurt. "We're due really close to our first anniversary."

He set her down and stared around at all the ones who loved them so much. He walked over and touched the baby bed with a reverent hand. "The oak will work for a boy or a girl."

"It's a girl," Isaac announced. "I already know."

Blake touched his brother on the head. "I hope so, buddy."

"I want a nephew," Levi said. "I can teach him how to climb trees."

"I'll teach him," Isaac said. "I can climb better than you."

"But we aren't changing diapers," Levi said.

Isaac nodded vigorously. "Uncles don't do that."

Paradise picked him up. "You're going to be the best uncles in the world."

"Okay, well, *maybe* I'll change the diapers." Isaac buried his face in her hair and ran his fingers through the long locks. "Will you still love us when you have your own baby?"

"Even more," she promised. She set him down and linked arms with Blake. "I think we pulled off the best surprise in the world."

He took her in his arms. "The very best. And let me say I didn't know I could love you any more, but I think I do." Blake pulled back and tenderly cradled her belly. "And our baby."

Love nearly exploded her chest. She'd look back at this moment when things got hard as they always did in life. Everything had been worth it.

A NOTE FROM THE AUTHOR

DEAR READER,

I can't believe we've made it to the end of the series. I've loved every minute spent with Paradise and Blake, and I hope you have too! My grandsons provided much of the inspiration for Levi and Isaac, and I smiled during every scene I wrote with those little guys.

I spent a lot of time deciding on how the engagement and final scenes would go, and it seemed especially important to Paradise to include family. Family is as important to her and Blake as it is to me, and I loved having the whole clan be a part of everything.

I am sad to say goodbye to them as well as Hez, Savannah, and Simon for now. They've become close friends, and it's been fun weaving three series—Pelican Harbor, Tupelo Grove, and The Sanctuary—together. It was challenging to keep everything straight, but I hope you've enjoyed catching up with old friends. 😊

I love hearing from you, so drop me a note at colleen@colleencoble.com or chime in on the conversation over at https://www.facebook.com/colleencoblebooks.

Love you all,

Colleen

ACKNOWLEDGMENTS

My HarperCollins family is the best! Always supportive, always encouraging, they make the writing journey so wonderful. I'm especially grateful to publisher, editor, and friend Amanda Bostic, who has been such a huge cheerleader in my life.

A special thanks to my freelance editor Julee Schwarzburg, whose touch on my manuscript always makes it so much better. Thank you, Julee!

I have the best critique partner in Denise Hunter! We have critiqued each other's work for twenty-six years. Amazing! She knows what's missing before I do and offers the best support and help. Thank you, Denise!

My husband, Dave, and our kids, Dave and Kara, have always been the best support team at home for me, and my grandkids, Alexa, Elijah, and Silas, make the journey even sweeter. Thank you all!

DISCUSSION QUESTIONS

1. Have you ever feared something like Paradise fears big cats? Have you attempted to overcome your fear? If so, what has worked?

2. Have you ever visited a true wildlife park like The Sanctuary? My favorite place is Out of Africa Wildlife Park in Arizona. Do you have a favorite?

3. Blake wasn't sure Paradise was ready for marriage yet, but he got up the courage to ask anyway. Have you ever had to face a relationship fear like that, and if so, did it turn out well or not the way you'd hoped?

4. What was your favorite animal in this series?

5. Have you ever moved closer to family like Drew did? This past year we moved to Arizona to be able to see our grandsons more often.

6. Did you ever receive a gift that belonged to one of your grandparents? What did it mean to you?

7. Jealousy among family members can be so hurtful. Have you ever had to deal with it, and if so, how did you handle it?

8. Paradise wanted justice for her parents. Why does justice feel so important to most of us?

ABOUT THE AUTHOR

Photo by EAH Creative

COLLEEN COBLE is the *USA TODAY* bestselling author of more than seventy-five books and is best known for her coastal romantic suspense novels.

Connect with her online at colleencoble.com
Instagram: @colleencoble
Facebook: @colleencoblebooks
X: @colleencoble

DON'T MISS THE TUPELO GROVE SERIES FROM **COLLEEN COBLE** AND **RICK ACKER**

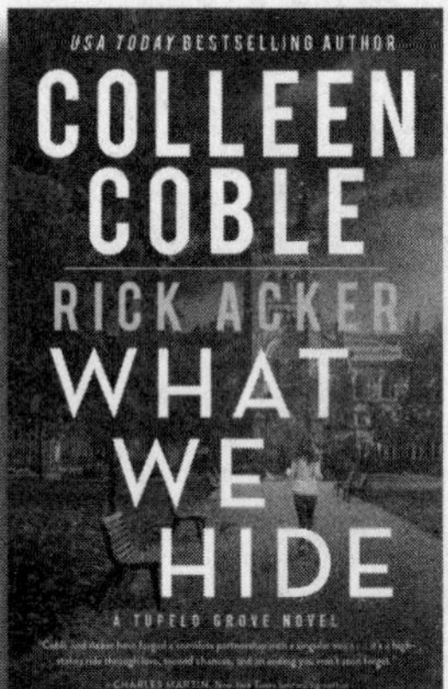

AVAILABLE IN PRINT, E-BOOK, AND AUDIO